A LESSON IN THERAPY AND MURDER

DAVID UNGER, PHD

Copyright 2020 by David Unger, PhD. All rights reserved

Artwork by Damonza

ISBN: 978-1-7323395-0-7

alessonintherapyandmurder.com

THE LESSON SERIES

A Lesson in Sex and Murder
A Lesson in Music and Murder
A Lesson in Therapy and Murder
A Lesson in Mystery and Murder
A Lesson in Baseball and Murder
A Lesson in Cowboys and Murder

Coming soon
A Lesson in Comedy and Murder

THE RELATIONSHIP TRAINING MANUALS

The Relationship Training Manual for Men
The Relationship Training Manual for Men* Women's Edition
Parenting Your Teen: A Relationship Training Manual

"Love and work... work and love, that's all there is."

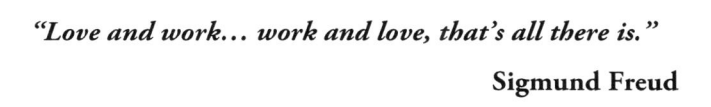

Sigmund Freud

PROLOGUE

"The best I ever had? That's tough."

"Come on. I'm sure you've had plenty."

"Well, I've certainly had more than my share. But picking the best, that's not easy."

"Okay, how about you pick the best 'aha' moment? You know, a time when the light went on and the world lined up just right."

"I haven't had many of those, but there's one that stands out."

"Come on. Let's hear it."

"I was sitting naked in one of the hot tubs at Esalen, looking out at the Pacific Ocean after a blissful massage, and suddenly realized my life was crap."

"What? That was a peak moment?"

"Well, not in a kumbaya way. But, right then I knew I needed to feel more like I did in that moment. My life, which looked good enough on the outside, wasn't going the way I'd hoped it would."

"Yeah. I know that feeling."

"So what about you? What's the best therapy–kumbaya–'aha' moment you've ever had?"

I was kind of curious to hear it for myself. Eavesdropping on these women while they stood in the reception line, I hadn't been surprised by what the first had said. We can all relate in some way. Maybe not in the naked-Esalen-tub way, but in the way of our lives not being all we'd like them to be. Sometimes it becomes abundantly clear that if we don't do something, nothing is going to change. That realization is terrifying, liberating, empowering, and life-altering all at once.

So, yeah, I was curious what her friend had to say.

"I'm gonna go another way. I can relate to the realization that your life needs some upgrading, but the moment I'm thinking about is when I was lost in bliss."

"How's that?"

"You know that moment right after you have a really good climax and all the tension leaves your body and you feel light and carefree?"

"Boy, do I. I wouldn't mind some more of that this week."

"I'm with you on that."

Me too.

"I was in the midst of one of those glorious moments. I had nothing to do but languish in it. It was serene. I was lost in space, just floating aimlessly with no cares, when I heard my husband yell out from downstairs, 'Where the hell is dinner?'"

"What? No, you're kidding."

"Bless the man. I knew right then and there I couldn't live with him another day. That was one of the best days of my life, right there."

I don't know if it was one of her husband's best days, but maybe. If that relationship wasn't right for her, it wasn't right for him. But that's easy for me to say as I didn't have to go through that upheaval.

I was enjoying listening to these women swap stories about impactful moments in their lives. I suppose this was as good a place as any to be having those discussions. We were checking in to the American Association of Humanistic Psychology's 1983 annual conference in Santa Barbara, California. Most of the attendees were therapists, graduate students, or educators, here for a ten-day conference dedicated to learning and experiencing the latest theories and practices.

It wasn't long ago that I'd been to the Annual Conference of Sex Therapists and Surrogates and got caught up in a murder mystery. I'd stood in that reception line and overheard a couple of women talking about the best sex of their lives. Soon thereafter, the keynote speaker had been kidnapped, then murdered. I got swept up in the action—it was a sex conference, after all—and ended up solving the mystery. Here I was, back in the reception line of another annual conference, overhearing two women talk about peak therapeutic experiences.

Go figure.

CHAPTER ONE
And So It Begins

July 27th, 1983

I HAVE TWO jobs. As a licensed therapist I'm required by the state licensing bureau to obtain thirty-six hours of continuing education every two years. As a professor, I don't have to keep brushing up on my skills. Colleges assume you'll keep on learning as you go. As a therapist, I have to log in that learning. One way of obtaining those hours is to go to a conference, attend some workshops and learn a thing or two that will theoretically help you improve your therapeutic endeavors.

I pay lip service to mandatory continuing education because we all can learn more about how to work and live better. I whine about having to attend conferences because they require my time and money, and I don't always feel like I get full value in return. Of course, you could say you get out what you put in, and you wouldn't be wrong. It's just that I sometimes prefer to talk the talk than walk the walk.

Still, here I was in my hotel room, unpacking and wondering where to eat. The opening session didn't begin till seven, so I had a couple of hours to kill.

I hadn't been to Santa Barbara before. Less than two hours north of Los Angeles, it was an easy drive, but one I'd never made. If I had to give up ten days of my life, why not spend it on the American Riviera and learn a thing or two?

The first thing I needed to learn was where to eat and how to get there.

The Miramar had its own restaurant. I figured I'd be spending plenty of time there, so I decided to go see some of the town. A bright-eyed college-aged receptionist recommended La Super-Rica for some "authentic" Mexican cuisine. Sounded good to me.

The Miramar stood at the western edge of Montecito, the upscale part of town with more estates than homes. The property was on a prime piece of oceanfront real estate, but with flaws that made it affordable. I don't know which came first—the hotel, the train, or the freeway. Either way, there was this quaint hotel by the ocean that had a freeway on one side, the ocean on the other, and a train track running in between.

I drove over the freeway and onto a frontage road that passed a golf course; that, too, was cursed by the freeway. Milpas Street had car-repair shops, a Winchell's Donuts, appliance stores, and a faded turquoise wooden shack—the home of La Super-Rica Taqueria. The menu was written on a chalkboard on the wall and didn't look like it changed often. I ordered Tacos de Bistec and a Corona and sat in a covered porch area with tables.

I'm mostly comfortable eating by myself, though I like a book for companionship. I was reading *The Last Good Kiss* by James Crumley and appreciating what one reviewer called his "curled-lip repartee."

"Excuse me, may I join you?"

"Sure, sugar," is what Crumley might have written, but I opted for, "Why not?"

"Thanks. I'm having an issue and I thought, well, hoped, you could be of assistance."

"What's going on?" I said as I closed the book.

"I know you may not know anything, but I have to think you know something."

"That's kind of you."

"You're welcome. Is it all right with you if I have a bite of your taco? I haven't eaten since I can't remember when, and my order won't be ready for a while. You can have some of mine when I get it."

I gestured toward my plate at about the same time as she scooped up a steak taco; chewed vigorously, and quickly finished it off. I have to admit, I was impressed. Partly that she'd eaten the whole thing—which went against my sharing creed—but mainly that she did so quickly without getting any sauce on her face, hands, or clothes.

When she was done, she leaned forward to take some of my beer, then thought better of it. Instead, she got up and went over to a shelf where the utensils, napkins and drinking water were housed. I got a better look at her as she stood there and drank a full glass of water. She caught me looking at her and gave me a "I needed that" look. Which from all appearances, she did.

She was a good-looking woman. Brown shoulder-length hair, blue eyes, warm countenance and a pleasing figure. But there was no sense of her being at peace with the world. She was clearly agitated. Though she had her assertion skills down pat.

"Here's the story," she began as she sat down. "I saw you in the reception line at the hotel so I figured you're a shrink or a teacher or have some acquaintance with the healing profession. Right?"

"I'd say you got three out of three on that."

"Good. See, I told you I thought you knew something. You chose to come to this conference. That tells me something about you. You could have gone to the American Psychological Association's annual conference but I'm betting that group is too tight-assed for you."

"Your batting average is holding."

"So, given those qualifications, I thought you could help me out."

"Well, you have my attention. Not sure if I can bat as well as you, but I'm happy to come up to the plate. Waddaya got?"

"That's part of the problem. I can't tell you. I need your help and right now I really can't tell you why."

"You want me to help you out but you can't tell me why, is that right?"

"Yes. Later, I can tell you, but now I can't."

"Okay. How about telling me what you want me to do?"

"Well, I can't really tell you that either." She shrugged as if to suggest that it was no big deal. "You're just going to have to trust me."

"All right, let me see if I get this. You want me to help you. You're not going to tell me why, or what you want me to do. Is that it?"

"See? You're a good listener. I knew you'd be able to help."

"Thank you for the gracious words and for trying to butter me up. Can you give me any more information? Like a little of what you want me to do aside from sit with you and share my tacos?"

"Certainly. It's really quite simple. When we finish our tacos, I want you to leave with me. When we get around the corner I'm going to blindfold you, take you to my car, and drive you somewhere. Once we get there I can explain more."

"That's it? That's all you want?"

"Yeah."

"The opening session at the conference begins at seven. It's almost six now. If we do this can I get back in time?"

"That's not going to happen."

"There's the problem. Otherwise it sounds like a promising evening."

"Don't worry about the opening session. It'll just be some welcome speeches."

"That would be true at the American Association, but not at the Humanistic Association. At this conference they'll do something experiential to get us involved. Plus, I need to get four hours of Continuing Credit signed off."

"You'll have other opportunities to get the hours, but this moment is about something else."

"I'm on a tight schedule with those hours. I've sort of charted out what I need to do and when I can take off. I was counting on getting those four."

"It's only the beginning. Lighten up. Now come on, eat up and let's go."

She got up and collected her order. When she came back she said, "Besides, they'll probably call off the evening because somebody will get kidnapped or something."

"Yeah, that'll happen."

"You never know."

"I have to admit, I'm intrigued. But we need to have a little talk first."

"Go on," she said as she ate her taco without offering me any.

"I'm not really into domination. If you're going to tie me up and have me do things I'd rather not do, I'm going to the conference."

"No no no. This is nothing like that. I need to take you someplace and you can't know where it is. Once we're there, I'll take the blindfold off."

"That's comforting. Can you give me some idea about what's going to happen when we get there? Do I need to be concerned about bodily harm?"

"That's where the trust comes in. I need you to trust me."

CHAPTER TWO
Blindfolded

SOME PEOPLE WOULDN'T trust her, and some would. What I've learned is that trust is less about trusting the other person and more about trusting that regardless of what happens you'll be okay. I needed that kind of trust, but I wasn't feeling reassured. Maybe A– or B+. In the therapy world, that's close enough to take the chance. Of course, that's what the therapists talk, not always what they walk.

I can't say I liked walking down the street blindfolded, but if I was here to have a week of experiential learning this certainly qualified. Just not with the licensing board. I've done trust walks a few times—both as participant and leader—but those were always in a more controlled environment. Once, I'd had my eyes covered and my partner told me she was leading me onto an open field. When we got there, she let go of my hand and told me we were going to run side-by-side at full tilt without touching. She assured me we wouldn't run into anything. Tentatively—very tentatively—I got up to full speed. As I sprinted into the darkness, I felt freer, more powerful and exhilarated with each stride. That was one of my aha–kumbaya moments.

I wasn't sure if this trust walk would be empowering and exhilarating but without my vision I became keenly aware of the lack of noise on the street. There wasn't much traffic. We were making our way down a residential street at supper time in the summer. I couldn't smell anyone barbequing. I didn't hear anyone talking in their yard or walking the dog. When I'd parked earlier, I'd seen a couple of people gardening in their yards. I didn't know if they were still there and observing me now. If they were, they weren't saying anything about it to me.

She helped me into the back seat of a large vehicle. When she started it up it sounded like a muscle car. She told me to lie down and I did. Soon I felt us moving up into the foothills on a curving road.

"I want to thank you for trusting me. This means a lot to me."

"I'm not quite sure what it means to me, but I'm glad it feels good to you. I don't mind saying, there's a part of me that thinks I've taken myself too far out of my comfort zone."

"If it's any consolation, I've been out of mine all day."

"Not sure if that's consoling. But it might explain why you're reaching out for some help."

"Believe me, I'd much rather be somewhere else doing something else."

"I might go along with that. But I suspect you're thinking you're stuck in the moment and I could be a way out."

"You or the police."

The car wound its way up the hillside, then down and through a valley, and back up another hill. It was unfamiliarly quiet. Her window was open but there was no smell of exhaust, no honk of horns or other familiar signs of city life. After ten minutes, I felt her turn off the road. Things got a little bumpier, but soon she stopped and parked.

"Come on," she said as she opened the door. "Watch your head."

I got out. There was gravel under my feet and I could smell jasmine in a slight breeze that cooled the evening. She came, took my elbow, and led me down a path. We went about a hundred feet and she stopped. I felt her body shift, and there was the sound of an opening door. She took us through an entrance and into a house. I heard her close the door behind us.

Then, as promised, she took off my blindfold.

It was an hour before sunset but the light was starting to change. We were standing in a small house that could have been in the Alps. I half-expected to hear someone yodeling in the distance. There were multiple levels and a lot of dark wood that made the place a little dreary even with the evening's sunlight shining through a large window that overlooked the hills. If the view wasn't enough, there were paintings of mountains with wildflowers on the wall, but no Alpine snow.

I looked around, and then at her. "Would it be all right if I asked your name?"

"We sort of skipped that stage. I'm Rachel Madison. I'd prefer it if you didn't call me Rae, but if you want you can call me Rach."

"Hi, Rachel. I'm David Unger. I would say it's good to meet you but I'm not sure yet."

"Well, when you see what I'm going to show you, you'll be less sure."

She led me up some steps to what would usually have been a living room but looked more like a study. There was a stuffed bookshelf on one wall, a Rolling Stones American Tour poster on another, and a lot of windows. There were a couple of comfortable-looking chairs and a large desk that had been a dining table at one stage. The desk was strewn with books, papers, folders, a phone, some pictures, a couple of snow globes, what looked like an autographed Babe Ruth baseball, an ashtray with a partially smoked joint, and a typewriter with a piece of paper in it.

"Read it," she said.

I did.

Someone is going to kill me. I have done a terrible thing and deserve to die. If you read this before you hear of my death, do not contact the police. They'll only make things worse. The only thing that can help me is me.

I am truly sorry for my actions as I know I have seriously hurt people. To those people and their families, I do not seek forgiveness but understanding. I did what I did because at the time I saw no other path. Now I do, but I fear it is too late. I have begun to make amends, but there is more to do. I am going to try to do that, but may not have enough time. I will

That's where it ended. I looked up.

"My stepfather wrote that," she said, then started crying. She slumped in one of the chairs by the desk. I sat in the other and watched her. She was full throttle and wasn't going to stop any time soon. I took a closer look at the surroundings.

The books on the wall and desk were mostly psychology books, with some Philip Roth, Norman Mailer and Salinger thrown in. Most I knew. Some I didn't. The handwriting on the papers on the desk was worse than mine. There were piles of papers and folders by the typewriter. The place seemed casually organized. One of the pictures on the desk showed a girl who looked like Rachel at maybe eight or nine, standing on a beach as the sun set behind her. Another was of a good-looking, stylishly dressed woman in her forties; she was standing in a hotel lobby. A third showed three men holding fishing poles on what looked like a camping trip.

I was arranging the pictures in my head and making up a story—Rachel, person of interest, camping buddies—when she took me out of my reverie.

"I'm sorry. It's been a rough day."

"I can see. Want to tell me about it?"

"This is my stepfather Cliff's house. I wanted to surprise him this morning, so I came by. And found this note. I've been scrambling all day, trying to find him. Unfortunately, I don't know him well as we've just begun rebuilding our relationship. He married my mother when I was about four and left us five years later. He broke my mother's heart. Mine too. She never forgave him. Nor did I until a few months ago when he reached out to me."

She made some eye contact but was basically in her own world.

"I was hesitant at first, but I wrote him back and we've seen each other a half-dozen times since then. It's been challenging, but we've been getting closer slowly. I'm a psych grad student at UCLA and came up for the conference. I wanted to surprise him. I was going to wait until this evening as I knew he'd be at the conference, but thought it would be fun to come here…"

That caused her to cry some more. It's hard enough losing someone you love, but to lose them, find them, and maybe lose them again causes yet another level of pain.

None of us really knows anyone else. We like to think we do—that there's nothing they could do that would really surprise us. Reading that note must have caught Rachel off guard in a few different ways, thus impeding their rapprochement.

I had lots of questions I knew she couldn't answer. Why had he stopped writing mid-sentence? What horrible thing had he done? Where was he? And why had she needed to blindfold me? It wasn't the time to ask, but that didn't stop me posing them to myself.

When she'd composed herself enough to continue, she got up and found some Kleenex. Now more settled, she continued. "I don't know much about him so I don't know who his friends or other relatives are… who to call, where to look. I'd ask my mom, but she's no longer alive. I've talked to neighbors, driven around town, checked at the conference, tried to discover what happened to him… and what he did that made him think he deserved to die."

"Yeah. I guess you'd usually call the police, but his note was pretty clear on that account."

"That's why I found you. I need someone to help me figure my way through this. You looked promising. There must be something I can do and I'm hoping you can help me."

"Glad I look promising and I do have some problem-solving skills, but I'm not sure I can come up with anything more than you have."

"If nothing else, maybe you can help calm me down. Though, truthfully, I don't want to calm down. I want to find him."

"All right. Let's see what we can do. But I have a question. Why the blindfold?"

"I didn't know if you'd help and I didn't want you to know where he lived if you backed out. If you hadn't agreed to help I'd have driven you back to the restaurant and you wouldn't have been able to tell the police where you'd been taken."

"Okay. That makes sense. But now that I've offered to help, want to tell me where we are?"

"Not really. We're in his home in the foothills. That's enough for now."

"Alright. So there are three pictures. One looks to be you when you were a kid, and he was married to your mother so is that a picture of her?"

"No. I don't know who that is."

"What about the camping picture? I'm assuming one of the men is your stepfather. Do you know those other guys?"

"No, I don't."

"So much for an easy next step. Have you looked through his papers and these files on the desk?"

"Some, but it would be good to do it with another pair of eyes."

CHAPTER THREE

Around the House

I was looking at a baseball hall of fame snow globe when the phone rang.

Rachel looked at me as if to ask, What do you think? My expression held the same question.

While this experience was new to me, it did evoke a certain familiarity.

Those of you who've read my other books know I'm a bit of an out-of-the-box therapist. While I see clients in my office for the standard fifty minutes, I also do extended hours. I've gone to people's homes and facilitated family meetings. I've accompanied a client at her work and observed how she handled the day and made comments/suggestions along the way. I've gone on plane rides, first dates, and once to a music festival.

While Rachel hadn't exactly asked me to be her therapist, and I hadn't exactly consented to be, she'd asked me for help and I'd offered to do what I could. What I could do in this moment was defer to her. That would show her I trusted her judgment.

"Hello?" she said.

She listened. I was sitting almost close enough to discern what the man said, but not quite.

"Yes, Cliff, my dad, isn't here now."

The caller said something akin to *Never mind. I'll call back.*

"Before you go, I have a question. I don't know you, Michael, but can you tell me how you know my dad?"

She kept him on the phone a good ten minutes.

Without telling him what was happening she got him to agree to come over right away—he also lived in Santa Barbara. Evidently, her ability to lure me in worked with others. After she'd hung up, she pointed at the photo of the three men. "That's Michael on the left. My dad's in the middle. The other guy is Alan. They met in grad school."

"That's good information."

"When he comes over we can fill him in and hopefully he can help us."

"Great. Things are moving right along."

"Let's look through his papers," she said. She grabbed a stack and started sorting through them. I did the same. I wasn't sure what I was looking for, but figured I'd know it when I saw it.

There was a folder with a July/August calendar on which a few dates had been marked with notes. July 27: *AHP 7 p.m.* August 12: *MS BD.* August 21: *Peter Tosh Bowl.* There was a stack of pictures and articles about places to go that had been torn out of a magazine or newspaper.

I opened a folder with pictures drawn by a child. "Hey," I said, holding up some of the pictures. "Are these yours?"

"I don't know. They could be."

"They may be from when you lived with him. It's sweet of him to have kept them."

"I suppose so. But they could also be someone else's drawings."

"There's that too."

"There's a folder of buildings, houses, landscapes and articles about places to go. Do you think he was planning on moving?"

"Could be. I don't know."

"Well, they're a starting point. He's got good taste, I'll say that," I said, then realized that might not have been the most tactful of responses. In situations like that, when I open my mouth and don't like what comes out, I usually keep talking. "Some of the places are out of town. Maybe he's planning on leaving and the note was a way of him saying he's going."

"You think he staged the whole thing?" she said with some irritation.

"I'm thinking about the note. On the one hand, he could have been interrupted while he was writing it and been taken away by the person who's going to kill him. Or he could have written it as a kind of cliffhanger. It's hard to say."

"I don't like either of those scenarios."

Nor did I, and I could see I wasn't helping any.

"Is it okay if I take a stroll around the place and see what I can see?"

"Sure. Michael will be here in about twenty minutes."

Off the living room area was a guest bathroom that also had a view of the mountains. There was another staircase to a lower area. I walked down, saw the bedroom, and presumed he'd spent many happy hours there. The living room had a large window, but the bedroom was something else—half the wall space was glass. I felt like I was in a treehouse. The king-size bed had a tapestry cover and several sumptuous pillows. Under different circumstances I wouldn't have minded house-sitting for the weekend.

I looked in his closet and found a few business suits and button-down shirts. Next to them were Hawaiian shirts, jeans and shelves of T-shirts. No women's clothing.

The bathroom also had a treehouse feel. The shower was glass-walled. If anybody built a house on the adjoining acres, they'd ruin his view and get a good look into his private life.

By the bed was a stack of books. Irvin Yalom's *Existential*

Psychotherapy, Alice Miller's *The Drama of the Gifted Child*, Erik Erikson's *The Life Cycle Completed* and John Irving's *The Hotel New Hampshire*. I try to keep my professional books out of the bedroom, but to each their own. Next to the bed was a digital alarm clock with a radio. I had one not too different in my bedroom. There was a lamp, a box of Kleenex, and an ashtray with a few partially smoked joints in it. In the drawer I found a good supply of condoms and lubricant. It certainly looked like he enjoyed his time here, although the professional books could tone it down a bit.

I heard the doorbell ring and hurried back up the steps to the study area. Rachel met Michael at the entry. He looked a lot like his picture. He was six foot, sturdily built, had a full head of wavy brown hair and a beard he'd been working on for a few years. He came in and gave Rachel a big hug. I could see she needed it and wondered why I hadn't offered.

He made his way up to the living room and extended his hand. "Hi, I'm Michael. A good friend of Cliff's. And you?"

"Hi, Michael. I'm David. I'm here to help out Rachel."

"Good to meet you both. What's going on? Why did you need me to come over right away?"

"As I told you on the phone, I came here this morning to surprise my dad. When I arrived he wasn't here, which isn't a big deal. But this was here," Rachel said, pointing at the note on the typewriter.

Michael read it.

"I was afraid of that," Michael said with concern. "I told him to be careful. Very careful. And he was. Until it looks like he wasn't."

"I'm sorry?" Rachel said. "Can you start at the beginning and tell me what's going on? Why can't we call the police? What did my dad do? What's happened to him?"

"It's not that long a story. But it's a complicated one."

"Tell us."

"Your dad and I have been close friends for years. We've partied together, been single, been married, been single again. Been through it all. But recently something shifted. It's not that we aren't close anymore… we are. It's just that he's become more closed off. He's been working on something and didn't want to get into it with me. This from a guy who's broken down his sex life in detail to me. But, this, he wanted to keep a secret."

"We all have secrets, but what are close friends for if not for sharing the truths of our lives?" I said, sounding more like a therapist than I'd intended. "That's too bad he felt the need to keep part of his life private."

"Well, it wasn't a big deal at first. I figured sooner or later he'd tell me. At first there really wasn't much different about him, but the few times he talked to me about it I could tell it was taking up more and more of his life. That wasn't necessarily a bad thing, but it meant we didn't get together as much, and when we did he wasn't fully present."

"Was he addicted to something?" Rachel asked.

"This wasn't a drug thing per se. But it was a thing. It was taking over his life. I knew it wasn't a new woman because even if she were married to a mob boss he'd have told me about it. This was something else."

"And that's all you know about this other thing?" I asked.

"No. I know more. I know what this letter is about. I know who he thinks will kill him and why he deserves it."

CHAPTER FOUR

Another Letter

WE WERE DRIVING in Michael's dated Fiat through the evening light. We could have been on any number of country roads that weaved through the foothills and valleys with houses spaced far apart. I grew up on the east coast so I'm used to a more verdant landscape than the one Southern California has to offer, but as with most things it had its own beauty.

I wasn't sure where we were going as it was all unfamiliar to me, but I could tell we were getting nearer to town as the houses were getting closer together. Not city-close but close enough so you'd hear your neighbor's teenage drummer or a drink-fueled argument. I've lived next to those people.

I'd yet to see a commercial building when we turned into a driveway called Riviera Park. We drove a short distance to a set of large white Spanish Colonial stucco buildings with terracotta roof tiles. Michael told us that they had been built in the 1920s and there'd once been a school on the site. Evidently, students hadn't liked being up in the foothills and having to trek into town, so now the space was mostly offices.

We walked into a courtyard that was home to a long rectangular pool with a small fountain and bench where you could idle away some time. We went past an iron gate, stepped inside the building and down a hallway with terracotta floor tiles. Halfway down, Michael stopped, took out a key, and opened a door.

He turned on the light. It was a pleasant office with a window overlooking the covered walkway that surrounded the building. On the walls there were some posters of the coastline and an autographed picture of Ernie Banks. There was a small bookcase holding many therapy books that I knew well and some assorted baseball memorabilia, a small desk, a sofa and a few chairs.

"This is my office," Michael said.

"Good move," I said.

"Thanks. It's a great space, but I didn't bring you here to show off. I brought you here, Rachel, to show you something that your dad gave me last week."

He gestured for us to sit, went behind his desk, and took out an envelope. He handed it to Rachel. She read the envelope out loud: *Do not open unless you don't hear from me.*

She sighed and opened it up.

Michael,

I know you're worried about me. Heck, I'm worried about me too. If you're reading this, it means you're really worried about me. And maybe you should be. But maybe you shouldn't. Don't mean to should on you, pal. What I am trying to say is, I have a plan. I don't know if it's a good one, but if everything goes the way I want, all will be good. And if it doesn't, well, you might kill me. Joking. I don't think you'd kill me, but for a moment or two you might want to. But if I don't come out of this alive, I hope you'll be able to figure out who did me in.

Since I don't know how long it will take before you start actively worrying, you can relax until August 1. If you don't hear from me by then, start looking.

I love you,

Cliff

"That's somewhat good news," I said. "Today's the twenty-seventh."

"That's right," said Michael. He looked at Rachel. "Maybe we can relax a little. Whatever's going on is going on. Your dad's a smart cookie. A secretive, risky one at times, but if he tells me not to worry until the first, I'll go back to my usual worries. We need to trust him."

"I agree," I said. "I know there's a level of concern, especially with his note just trailing off, but it does sound like your dad knows what he's doing and has a plan to make things right."

"I know you're both trying to make me feel better and I'm somewhat relieved. This has been a harrowing day so at least I don't have to panic yet. But I'm still really worried."

"Of course you are," Michael said. "This doesn't make everything better, but it does give us an explanation and allows us to take a breath. Maybe not a deep one, but one nonetheless."

Michael had therapeutic skills. What he said was both empathetic and understandable.

He drove us back to Cliff's house and Rachel returned me to the restaurant. She told me that being a grad student meant she couldn't afford to stay at the Miramar. Instead, she was at the Hotel Santa Barbara six blocks from the beach on State Street, the main street in town.

We agreed to meet the next day.

CHAPTER FIVE

Shrinks

July 28, 1983

EITHER I'D SLEPT really well or the trains hadn't been running during the night. I got up and looked out the window toward the ocean. I couldn't see it, but I could hear it and smell it. Maybe later I'd actually get to go in it.

I sat in the restaurant as a train passed some forty yards away. It was strange yet somehow settling. I was enjoying the juxtaposition when Michael came into the dining area. He spotted me and gestured whether it was okay to join me. I waved him over.

"Hi," I said. "I didn't know you were staying here."

"I'm not. I've lived in town for a little over a year, but Alan, Cliff, and I usually have breakfast together before we go to the workshops."

"I guess we're all here to get those continuing-ed credits. So the three of you met in grad school. Are you all therapists?"

"Yup. Guilty as charged. Cliff also writes. I teach and Alan gambles."

"Do you all live in town?"

"No, Alan lives in Tahoe. He's more the outdoor type."

"So this was supposed to be a bit of a reunion?"

"Kind of. We've been doing these conferences every year to catch up and take care of those credits."

"Have your eye on any workshop this morning?"

"I haven't made up my mind. What about you?"

Before I could answer the server came, poured coffee, and took our orders. Michael went for a bagel and lox. I had the granola.

"I'm partial to 'Making Your Dreams Come True.' I figure that ought to be worth the time."

"So, David, what dreams do you want to come true?"

"It's funny. I want to go to the workshop but haven't really thought about what I want from it. The fame-and-fortune dreams I used to have are sort of receding into the background."

"Why's that?"

"Someone once asked me whether I'd choose fame or fortune, and at that time I wanted fame. Now, I'm more interested in fortune. And even that's toned down. I'd settle for financial security."

"Why the shift?"

Leave it to a shrink to keep probing.

"I like my privacy too much to want the fame. While I certainly wouldn't mind the recognition, I do like being able to go out where I want, when I want. And, within limits, do pretty much what I want."

"What would you like the recognition for?"

"I will answer that, but I want to ask you something first, since you've been to these conferences before. I'm a little leery of being surrounded by therapists all week. Are we going to get to talk about sex, drugs and rock and roll sometime?"

"Right after you tell me what you'd like to be recognized for."

"Well, Doc, I suppose I'd like the world to acknowledge how wise and witty I am, and what a pleasure it is to be with me."

"Your parents didn't give you enough of that?"

"I guess not."

"Ain't that the way it always goes. We crave what we didn't get."

I was rescued from what passed for conversation between therapists by the arrival of someone who looked like the more outdoor person. He was average height with jet-black hair tied in a ponytail, and wearing wire-rimmed glasses, jeans, a flannel shirt... and a distraught look.

"Did you hear the news?" he asked Michael when he was close enough to be heard.

"What news?"

"I just checked my messages and Cliff's in the ER at Cottage Hospital. His body was found by the courthouse. He had my number in his wallet and they called me. I'm going over there now."

Michael gasped. "That's horrible. I'll go with you."

"Okay."

He started to get up, then said, "Wait, I just ordered. From the sound of it, there isn't going to be an update any time soon. Why not join us and then we can go over?"

"I'm not sure about that."

"It'll be okay. We can worry here just as well as we can worry there."

The other guy hesitated, then sat down.

Michael made the introductions. It was indeed Alan.

"Do you think Rachel knows?" I asked.

"Who's Rachel?" Alan said.

"I'm going to the lobby to call her. Michael can explain. I'll be right back."

I asked the receptionist to dial the Santa Barbara Hotel. She did and handed me the phone. The front desk answered and forwarded me to Rachel's room. There was no answer. I called back and asked for the desk, then dictated a short message asking Rachel to call me about her dad and to meet me at the hospital.

When I got back to the table, Michael was finishing up his breakfast, Alan was drinking coffee, and my granola was waiting.

"As soon as Alan's finished we're going over to the hospital,"

Michael told me. "It would be a good idea for you to stay here in case Rachel tries to reach you. I'll leave you a message here once we know more."

CHAPTER SIX

Making Dreams Come True

THE GOOD NEWS was that Rachel didn't need to worry any longer about finding her father. Now she could focus on worrying about his mending. It was unclear what kind of condition he was in but being in the ER didn't bode well.

Had he resolved his difficulties? Were his wounds the result of his coming out on the losing or the winning end? We wouldn't know until he could tell us. In the meantime, I thought I'd try to figure out what dreams I wanted to have come true.

The conference registration desk was attended by two eager-to-help-you women and one overly anxious man.

I gave them my name and they gave me a name tag. They asked me which workshop I was attending and told me it would earn me four hours of credit, which they marked down next to my name. I asked them to remind me how many credits the previous evening's event had garnered and was also told four.

At home I'd sat down with the program and charted out which activities I wanted to attend. Thirty-six hours of credit was a stretch; I couldn't afford to lose four. If I didn't get those credits it meant four other hours doing something I'd prefer not to. I already was feeling a little of that; I didn't want more.

Now, of course, we all do things we don't want to do. Like you, I'm used to that. But, when I'm spending money, I prefer to do things I want to do. I wanted to spend some time in Santa Barbara as a tourist. I wanted to play hooky, go to the beach, see a matinee, take a nature walk, read a book, have a nap, and enjoy my time away from home. Maybe even have a conference romance. That sounded like a pretty good dream to have come true.

Being at the conference was like being back at school where I had to attend classes to get a diploma. I had to devote a lot of time and energy to things I'd much rather have avoided. Aside from the diploma, I never felt I got a good return on my investment, such as it was.

If you haven't guessed by now, I wasn't the best student. I have a bit of a "this is a waste of time" attitude. I did well enough to get through, but it wasn't because I loved it. I wanted the diploma so I could go out in the world and try to make it better with some letters after my name that implied I knew more than I did.

I don't want you to get the wrong impression of me. Yes, I do sometimes have a bad attitude and can be a wiseass. I have a harsh opinion of my profession and colleagues. And, while I'm at it, I'm not always be the most sensitive and considerate person. Plus, I'm not very good at foreplay in its many forms. But I don't make a habit of lying. I endeavor to be as truthful as I can. And when I do lie, it's to the authorities. Even the humanistic ones.

"I'm sorry," I said, offering my most charming smile. "Last night I neglected to sign in for the activity. Is it too late to do that now?"

"I told you," one said to the other.

"That's why we made the announcement at the end for everyone who hadn't signed in, so they wouldn't lose the credits."

"Yeah. I heard that, and I was on my way to do just that when—and pardon me for saying this—I had a personal emergency. I hope it's not too late now." I gave them the look I gave my mom when I really wanted something.

"Okay, but make sure to sign in for all the rest."

"You bet. Thanks," I said, and went to learn how to make the rest of my dreams come true for four more credits.

We all use our skills in whatever ways we can. If getting them to feel sorry for me would get me four hours, well, as you can see, I wasn't afraid to do it. I'm courageous that way.

Since the title of this book has the word "therapy" in it, I told myself when I began writing I would be honest and not try to present things so you'd think I'm a better person than I really am. It wouldn't be therapeutic of me to do that. I like to think I have redeeming qualities, but I also know some of my qualities could use some redeeming.

I rationalized my lying by telling myself I'd done a good deed the night before. I'd helped someone out and had certainly been involved in experiential learning.

If you're not clear on what experiential learning means, remember back when you were in school and someone explained something to you. That isn't experiential learning. The only thing you're experiencing is listening, daydreaming and a sore butt. If that class had been more experientially oriented, they'd have had you doing something that would have offered hands-on experience of the material.

Still, my justification was bullshit. I'd lied and gotten away with it, which would only make me more likely to do it again.

A middle-aged woman and man were on welcoming duty. They introduced themselves to me but I quickly forgot their names. They gave me a poster-sized piece of paper and some crayons, then told me to go draw/write/create the dream I wanted to come true—they were already working the experiential angle.

There were twenty to thirty people, all intently focused on their paper. Nobody I knew was there. I sat at a round table with four other participants. No one in the group looked like they could make any of my dreams about a conference romance come true.

I looked at what people were doing. All of them had significantly better drawing skills than me, which isn't saying much. There were colorful pictures of people, places, things and words. My artistic skills peaked at the stick-figure stage.

They seem like basic enough questions, don't they? What are your dreams? What do you want? What would make your life more to your liking?

As I'd told Michael, at one point I would have said fame and fortune. In my twenties I'd have opted for more excitement and adventure. Now in my late thirties, I liked my adventures in less exciting ways.

I could illustrate my poster with a dream to create world peace. Or to end poverty and sickness. While I would never fully achieve those things, I could dedicate more of my life to those endeavors, and could reap greater peace of mind and a sense of fulfillment few people achieve. I could go on a peace march, join some groups that work to prevent poverty, heal the suffering, promote social justice. That would certainly help make my life richer at a deeper level.

I knew those weren't really walk-the-walk dreams for me but I could talk them if we ended up having a group discussion and I was called upon to share… although I'd like to think I'd share the lofty dreams as well as the less lofty ones, whatever they were.

What dream did I want to come true, right now, in this moment? Not a big pie-in-the-sky one, but something real I could actually put some effort into, make happen and draw on the paper. Freud said it was all about work and love. Maybe I could…

"I need you to come with me," Rachel said as she tapped me on the shoulder.

CHAPTER SEVEN
The Clerk

We were back in Rachel's car. This time, I was in the front seat and could see.

"Are we going to the hospital?" I asked.

"Been there, done that. He got beat up pretty badly. We won't know anything for a few hours. I could have stayed there and driven myself crazy but I decided to find you and drive you crazy."

"That's very thoughtful of you. Any particular crazy you're planning on driving me?"

"Just the usual. But before I forget, thanks for the heads-up."

"You're welcome. I met Alan, the other guy in the picture, and he told Michael and me about your dad. Did you see them at the hospital?"

"No, I must have missed them. We need to find out what happened to my dad. I know it won't make any difference to whether he pulls through, but it will give me something constructive to do."

"Makes sense."

"But some things don't."

"Such as?"

"Such as why my dad was found at the courthouse. From what I've gathered, he does his best to stay away from legal types."

"Do you think he got beat up at the courthouse or do you think someone dropped him off there? If they dropped him there on purpose, we might be able to figure out the connection."

"That's where we're headed."

I guess it's no surprise that in many cities the most impressive structures are the places of worship and the spaces where justice prevails, or at least tries to. The courthouse had been built by people who cared what things looked like and had the money to make it happen. We usually call those people lawyers and politicians. The courthouse took up a city block and had been built in the early 1900s around a vast courtyard. The Spanish influence extended to the tile floors, archways, iron gates and murals… a beautiful place where not-always-beautiful things happened.

There was an information kiosk and Rachel went up and asked a question that probably wasn't asked there every day.

"Can you tell me where my dad got beat up?"

They seemed to know which dad she meant and soon we were out of the building and on our way to a corner office. There were some steps leading up to it. That's where they'd found her father.

I looked up at the sign: *County Clerk and Recorder.*

There wasn't a lot to glean standing there.

"What do you say you go in there and see if you can get them to tell you if your dad had any recent business with them?"

"I can try, but they have people coming in here all day to get marriage licenses, passports and whatever else it is that clerks record. I'm not sure they'll let me see anything."

"Tell them your dad just got dumped on their doorstep and you really need their help to find the connection. I don't know what is and isn't a public record. Go and talk with the person who looks most sympathetic."

I followed her in. The corner space had intricate wood paneling and was designed for people who could come to work and be glad they were lucky enough to be there. I don't know what bureaucratic offices you've been in lately, but comfortable, cozy and mostly empty may not be what you encountered. There were two people in a line.

You can take a bureaucrat out of their nondescript office, but you can't take them out of their prescribed role. As easy as it had been for Rachel to get me and Michael to do her bidding, she wasn't doing so well with Ellen Withers. I decided to try my hand.

"Hi," I said in my most pleasant voice. "Rachel, why don't you show this helpful person a picture of your father and she can let you know if he's been in here recently. I bet if she recognized your dad she'd tell you. And maybe she'll remember what kind of business it was that brought him here." I followed that up with a big smile.

Rachel opened her purse. Luckily, she had a plastic pack of pictures that included one of her and her dad.

"Here he is," she said. "Of course, this picture is from when I was younger, but aside from his hair turning gray he looks about the same."

Ellen looked at the picture.

"I was afraid of that," she said. "It was horrible what happened to Dr. Anderson. I can't believe anyone would beat him up and leave him here. My heart goes out to you."

"Thank you. That's very kind of you."

"Sounds like you know Dr. Anderson," I said.

"It's a small town and he's been in here a lot lately."

"Really? Can you tell us why?" said Rachel.

"Not really. You may know about the marriage. That was a bit of a snafu, but it's all straightened out now."

"I missed the snafu part," I said. "I was out of town. Can you share a little of it so I don't say the wrong thing to someone?"

"You know. It's on. It's off. Then they got the name wrong and had to redo all the paperwork. We're used to it, but on top of the other stuff it was just a lot."

"I bet. But when it comes to managing all that, I bet you really know your stuff."

I can kiss ass with the best of them.

"I sure do. But you can't go changing titles and names willy-nilly. I kept telling them to find a name they liked and stick with it. Quit changing your mind every day."

"I hear you. One day it's this, the next day it's that. What did he finally end up with?"

"To tell you the truth, he may have ended up back where he started. I'm not sure."

"You've been very helpful," Rachel told her. "There's one more thing I hope you can do for us. I certainly don't think that anyone in this office would have beaten up my father, but was there someone here who he got into an argument with?"

"The only one he was arguing with was his fiancée."

CHAPTER EIGHT

At the Hospital

When we left the courthouse Rachel said she wanted to go to the hospital and since I was along for the ride I went with her. Though I'm very grateful they exist, I'm not a big hospital guy—they're full of sick and worried people.

We joined the worriers.

Michael and Alan were in the ER waiting room. I introduced Alan to Rachel.

"How is he? Any news?" she asked.

"He's stable but still in critical condition. They should know more soon."

"How's everyone holding up?" I asked. We were all therapists after all (well, technically Rachel was a therapist-in-training) so how-are-you questions tend to garner more than the usual I'm-fine-how-are-you response.

"We're okay," Michael said. "We've actually been able to do some catching up so that's good. It's just too bad Cliff can't be with us right now."

I turned to Rachel. "How about asking the guys some follow-on questions from our morning excursion?"

"I was just about to do that."

If you've read my other books you'll know I tend to cut to the chase. I know I'd be better served if I tiptoed into things, and sometimes I manage to do just that. Other times, I step into the batter's box, hit the first pitch, and run straight to second base.

Maybe if I'd waited a moment, she'd have asked on her own and that would have been more empowering for her. She hadn't hired me to empower her, but when you ask me for help empowerment is usually part of the package. She hadn't demonstrated any lack of ability in that department and I suspected her asking me for help hadn't come easy. Now she wanted to prove—to herself and to me—that she was quite capable of handling things.

"We went to the courthouse and talked to a person who works in the recorder's office. She told us a few things about dad I suppose you already know. Let's start with marriage. Anything you can tell me about that?"

I had to hand it to her. Her question hadn't revealed much of what she knew, but it told them she knew something.

"Yes. That's a dubious story," said Alan.

"I don't know how much you know about your dad," said Michael. "I know it's only recently that you've rekindled your relationship and you're just beginning to rediscover each other. Your dad's love life has been robust in some ways and shallow in others. He's always been with beautiful, mostly smart and sexy women, so his relationships have been a pleasure for Alan and me in the main. Yet, all the women have had flaws… something sufficiently off-kilter to make the relationships untenable."

"Truly not viable," said Alan.

"The result is, he's had a series of one-, two-, three-year relationships that were fine but left him despondent. No, that's too strong a word. Discouraged would be better. Not outwardly. But inwardly. When we get real and aren't just talking about guy stuff, that emptiness comes out."

"But Margot is different," said Alan.

"Different and yet the same," said Michael. "Margot has the requisite beauty, brains and poise. Plus, she's loaded. But she comes with baggage."

"As do we all."

"Certainly, and yet her baggage causes drama. Not a tsunami-load, but more than Cliff's used to confronting."

"Excessive would capture it," added Alan.

"That's it," agreed Michael. "It is, and yet it isn't an excessive amount."

"It would have been excessive in other times."

"Truthfully, your dad wants to settle down, and Margot is big bucks. Her family is old Santa Barbara money. They have a big cattle ranch up the coast and own a bunch of downtown properties. She'd take away any financial concerns and replace them with *Which country should we visit today?*"

"Hasn't everyone's parent said at some point, 'It's just as easy to love a rich person as a poor one'?" I said. When that bombed, I added. "So what was the drama about? Money?"

"It's not that simple," said Alan.

"That's right. Some of it's about the money. She wanted a pre-nup. He didn't. She relented. She didn't. She did. Then she didn't. But it's not just about money. She wants him to quit working and to travel more and live abroad for part of the year. He wants to stay home more and work. He has his own dreams. They argue about it a lot."

"Yeah. The perpetual problem," said Alan.

"Right.," I said wanting them to know I knew about that. "Couples argue about the same topic over and over."

"But it's part what they fight about and part how."

"Somebody not playing by the rule book?" I asked.

"Yeah, and one of her rules is that when she gets fed up she storms out and won't talk with him for days," Michael said empathically. "He has to come to her, when she should be coming to him. It's not cool to slam the door on the conversation."

"I don't like that play either," I said. "If you've had enough, say so and take a time-out. Then arrange for when you'll pick up the discussion again. At least, that's the rule I try to follow."

"Spoken like a true systems therapist."

"I don't consider myself one, but yeah, couples benefit from having a few ground rules to help them out when the going gets rough."

"So, therapists, can I get us back on track?" Rachel said. "What's the status of their relationship? Are they getting married?"

"It's a go," said Michael. "We were expecting to get an update when we were all together."

"So, if it's a go, where is she?" I asked.

"The last time I spoke to Cliff he mentioned Europe. I think she left yesterday. I'm not sure how to reach her."

"Did she leave because they argued and she was shutting him out?"

"Could be," said Alan.

A doctor approached us. Michael made the introductions.

"Hi, Dr. Novatt. This is Cliff's daughter, Rachel, and her friend, David."

"Good to meet you. I'm sorry for the circumstances. Your father got beaten very badly and it's too early to say what the outcome will be. We're transferring him to the critical-care ward. I'm sorry, but for the next twenty-four hours he can't have any visitors."

"Is he going to be okay?" Michael asked.

"We hope so. I know this isn't the news you want to hear. His body's been pretty badly broken, but let's hope his spirit hasn't. Your father remains unconscious. He's stable. We'll know more tomorrow. Why don't you come back at eleven and ask someone to get me? I'll give you an update. And if anything changes we'll let you know. Just leave your numbers with the nurse at the station."

I wasn't sure about the doctor's bedside manner. He wasn't big on details, which may have been for the better. Still, the news was that there was no news.

The four of us stepped outside into the seventy-degree ocean-cleansed air.

"I suppose we could meet back here tomorrow," Michael said.

"Let's have dinner together," Rachel said, and we arranged to meet them at a restaurant on the pier.

Once again, she'd lured them in.

CHAPTER NINE

Creative Visualization

IT WAS BACK to the conference for me. Rachel told me she'd pick me up later for dinner, but in the meantime, I had credits to obtain. Eight down, twenty-eight to go.

I had lunch and debated how to follow up the dreams workshop. I hadn't exactly left with a clear vision of my dream or how to make it come true.

The afternoon presented its own challenges. There were a bunch of workshops on offer but, for me, the options boiled down to "Creative Visualization" or "Feeling Good."

Nine times out of ten, I'd opt for "Feeling Good." Let's face it, the bottom line often is: if it makes you feel good, do it. You want to be able to get into bed at the end of the day, close your eyes, recall the day's highlights and gratefully fall asleep. It sure would be helpful to know how to do that more.

My curiosity being what it is though, I wanted to help Rachel work out what her dad was up to and brushing up on my visualization skills could help. I hadn't been asked to solve a mystery—maybe there wasn't even one—but somebody had done a good job of beating up Cliff, and he wasn't telling us who, what, when and why. If

I could work out whodunit I'd get to go to bed feeling good about my day.

What's going on? Why am I doing this? Am I attracted to the damsel in distress? Is solving mysteries what makes me feel good?
 I tend to ask myself more questions than I care to answer. But I knew the answers to those questions. Yes and yes, though with a caveat. I was attracted to Rachel, but not in a sexual way. Sure, I wouldn't have minded having sex with her, but I usually look for more than just not minding. Maybe more would happen, but my first reactions to people tend to be reliable. I was attracted to Rachel because she had an assertive spunkiness. I was more interested in her as a friend than as a lover. A friend who needed some help.

Too many impression-making stories based on *King Arthur and His Knights of the Round Table* taught me that the hero saves the damsel in distress. Heroes don't balance the budget, cook the food, or fix the leaky sink—or at least, they didn't in the books I read. I grew up wanting to be a hero but not having any vision of how to make that happen.

Heroism was not a major when I went to college. I eventually found my way to Psychology. Turns out I like to help people— that's the truth of it. It makes me feel good... for them and for me. I'm drawn to solving the mysteries in people's lives, be it through therapy or some other means. Perhaps my dream was to have a good mystery to solve, and to write a book about it so that I could be the hero.

I signed up for "Creative Visualization" and upped my credits total to twelve. I entered a room filled with fifteen visualizers. There seemed to be a common denominator to the workshops. Drawing. Once again, I was given a big piece of paper with instructions: *Draw something you visualize. Anything.*

I sat down at a table with two men and a woman. One of the

men must have gotten there early as his picture of a bike had a lot of detail. The other guy smirked at me; his paper was as full as mine. The woman was doing an awfully good job of portraying a Craftsman house.

I'm a lousy drawer. If I'd drawn that house all the proportions would have been out of proportion. I needed to keep my visualizations simple.

I closed my eyes and scanned my mind. Everything I saw would be a challenge to recreate. A car, a guitar, maybe a chocolate bar. Then I saw a straight line run across the horizon. I figured I could draw a mostly-straight line. But then I thought, *This is creative visualization.* Use your imagination. I could change that straight line in my mind to a crooked one. Images of wiggly lines danced across my brain.

I opened my eyes. Another man had slipped in silently while I was lost in my imaginings. My radar pinged as soon as I saw him. There are some people who just look scary and he was one of them.

His presence threw me a bit, but I'd been daydreaming and wanted to talk about it. As a therapist, I'm not big on dream interpretation but someone at the table could be. If I was dreaming of wiggly lines, could that have been triggered by recent events? Was that what my subconscious was telling me?

"Hey," I said. "I was wondering if any of you work with dreams. I have one I'd like to talk about if anyone's interested."

"I'm a Jungian," said the early guy. "We live in dreams."

"That could be a bit too heavy for me, but let me share it and you all can take a shot, okay?"

There was sufficient encouragement. They were therapists, after all. Used to listening and encouraging. Except the one guy, who didn't do anything but look at me in a way that made me look away.

"I had this dream about two minutes ago. I know I'm not supposed to talk this way about myself, but this is the way I talk: I'm a lousy drawer. I was looking at your two drawings," I said, pointing to the bike and the house, "and the talent you have. I got a little self-conscious about sharing one of my lesser skill sets, so I thought about drawing a straight line. That I could mostly do. But I couldn't do it perfectly. I know I said perfectly—you can come back to that later if you want—but, in my thoughts, I was able to accept that I could draw a good enough straight line. But then, just as I was okay about doing a good enough job drawing the line, I realized I was in a creative-visualization workshop. I could take artistic license with my line and make it as curvy as I wanted. Then I saw all sorts of wiggly lines. That's when I stopped and asked you all what you thought. Any thoughts?"

"That's a very telling dream," Early said.

"I knew you'd have something to say. But before we talk about my mother I want to add another piece of information."

"It's the Freudian who'd say it was about your mother. He's a Jungian. What's the other piece of information?" said the other guy.

"That's it!" I said, realization dawning. "I want to thank you for this. It was very helpful. I have to go now but I hope to see you again."

As I got up to leave the room, I saw the off-guy's eyes on me. There was definitely something about him.

CHAPTER TEN

Home Visit

I WENT TO the lobby and called Rachel's hotel. This time she answered.

"Hi, it's David. What are you doing? Well, you don't have to answer that if you don't want to. More importantly, we need to talk. There are some things we could figure out. You did a pretty nifty job of getting information out of that clerk. We could see if there are other places we can put that skill to work."

She told me she'd meet me out front in thirty minutes.

It probably would have been helpful to hear what other people thought of my dream—my perfectionism, my mother, and anything else they'd thrown at me. Instead, I sat outside in the sun and looked at the ocean, taking advantage of what the moment presented. I'd been here almost a day and hadn't been to the beach or the pool. At least I could see the Pacific on the other side of the train tracks and visualize myself swimming in it.

Being on the anal side of dealing with time, I was attentively waiting for Rachel after twenty-five minutes. She arrived a few minutes later, which was well within my narrow window of acceptability. I have an issue with people not showing up when they say they'll show up. If they say thirty and come in forty-five, I'd have preferred they say thirty to forty-five. Preferred is too nice a word.

I'd be annoyed with them and want to talk about it. Rachel saved us that conversation.

"Waddaya got, Doc," she asked as soon as I got into her car.

"You able to drive and talk?"

"I'm a California native."

"Very well. Please drive anywhere so I can see what I'm missing and we can talk."

I like sightseeing. It's a preferred activity for therapists. We're professional voyeurs, used to living our lives helping others live theirs. Sightseeing allows you to pass by people, places, and things and observe. You don't have to do anything. You have no real connection to the place but it's yours to watch in the moment.

She drove us down a road that shouldered the beach. Palms trees lined a walkway and the beach stretched out a hundred yards to the Pacific Ocean. Some people were playing volleyball, others were tossing Frisbees, talking walks, sunbathing, bodysurfing. It looked awfully inviting.

"We need to find out how to get in touch with Margot. Your dad must have an emergency phone number for her. We can look in his address book. We also need to find out more about the other paperwork he was doing at the county clerk's office. We have no idea why he got beat up and what he was into, but I'm guessing it had something to do with either love or money. Maybe both."

"I agree," said Rachel. "We need to talk with Margot. She might be able to answer a lot and would certainly want to be here. We didn't really search his place. Let's do another sweep."

With that she took a right turn and drove away from the beach toward the mountains and her dad's house. I knew because I wasn't blindfolded. But was I seeing a straight or crooked line?

We divvied up the tasks. I'd look through everything on the desk; she'd search for places where things were stored or possibly hidden and then check his mailbox. We'd both look for his address book.

I picked up the picture of the woman, who I now assumed was Margot. There was no phone number on the back or inscription on the photograph. Looking more closely, I could see that she was in an expensive hotel lobby and that her clothes were appropriately tasteful. She had a very cultured look, not cold, but not one you could cozy up to right away.

If she were my fiancée where would I keep her address, phone number and dress size? I'd either put it in my address book or jot it down somewhere and leave it on my desk. Of course, that was just my way but it was as good a way as any.

I couldn't find an address book so I leafed through the pile of papers and folders. Cliff liked to doodle. He was a better drawer than I was, but still stuck to basics. He had colored in some of his letters. He'd write a name and number down and then trace it over and over so that everything became thicker and bolder. Some pages included phone numbers but no name. I copied them. I could always call them up later and see what I got.

Evidently Cliff didn't throw out much. The pile next to his typewriter was a good eight inches high. The more recent additions were on top. There were a lot of articles clipped from magazines and newspapers; some had numbers and notes written in the margins. There were messages to call Margot, the plumber, Michael, and other names—some with a number, some without.

Toward the bottom of the pile were more references to Margot, and I found a page with her name doodled on it numerous times. It reminded me of when I first started dating girls and would call them. While I chatted, I'd write their name over and over.

Her full name had been overwritten numerous times. Margot Spalding.

I found the phone book.

The Spaldings were well represented in town. They might as well have been Smiths or Joneses. Many of the entries were corporate names: Spalding Enterprises, Spalding Equestrian Center, Spalding

Plaza, Spalding Camp, Spalding Foundation. I ripped out the page and went to find Rachel.

She was sitting outside on a porch, crying. I wanted to leave her alone, but she'd heard me approaching and said, "It's all right. I'm just having a moment."

"I can come back later."

"No, don't worry. The tears will come back. I got overwhelmed looking through his stuff. He's my stepdad, but I don't really know him. Rifling through his belongings like this, well, it makes me feel like he's already dead."

"I get that. It's weird going through someone else's private life, especially if you don't really know the person."

"I felt very close to him when I was a child. But then nothing. He left my mom and me and never contacted us again. She re-married. Two times. But I never got close to either of them. Nor did my mom, actually. And then out of the blue I get a letter. I don't know how he tracked me down. I was in LA, which is where we lived when he married my mom. His letter threw me for a loop."

"I'm sure."

"Yeah, it took me some time to respond. He'd already hurt me once. I didn't want him to do it again. But he wrote that he'd always missed me, wondered what had become of me, and welcomed the opportunity to get to know me again."

"That sounds promising."

"It was. It is. So I wrote back and we arranged to meet. He drove down to LA and we had lunch and shared life stories. I had a lot of built-up anger and resistance to liking him, but I liked him. It felt good to be with him. But I needed to go slow. He agreed. And so we set up another time to meet, and gradually over the last few months we've been building something new."

"That sounds good."

"Then he leaves me again. Did he know this would happen? I can't help but think that when he reached out to me he did."

Rachel needed to talk. Therefore, I needed to listen. It isn't always easy to put other people first. I get paid to do it, so at least I know how to do it. But on my own time, I can talk when it would be wise to listen. Listening gets you into a lot less trouble.

Still, I was excited. I could be the hero. I'd found Margot's last name. We could track her down. I wanted to show off. Get some praise and appreciation.

Since this is the therapy book I ought to acknowledge I have leftover issues from my youth about not getting enough recognition. I don't know where the line is between enough and not enough, but I fell below it.

I'm guessing most of us wouldn't mind—maybe even hunger for—more recognition and appreciation. But the moment was hers, so I kept quiet and tried to look like I was engaged even though I wasn't fully listening. I wanted to talk about finding Margot and moving things along, but she needed to speak her truth. Maybe I could manage my own needs and not impose them on her, but there was a limit.

"He wanted to know me because he sensed his days might be numbered. But he also wanted me to care about him… enough to want to find out what happened if he got into trouble."

"That makes sense."

"I got that we really have a special bond, and even though he screwed it up we could mend it. He knew that. He wanted me to come to the rescue just like he would for me. I feel that. It's kind of wonderful and invigorating. I could be reading way more into it than is there, but until proven wrong that's the line I'm taking."

"You're becoming your parent's parent and him his child's child."

"I read that in one of my textbooks."

"Yeah. It has the ring of truth to it and it sounds good. Can I ask what textbook? You said you were a psych grad student but not what you're studying. I assumed it was clinical psych, but you know what they say about assumptions. We've yet to have the 'Hi, how are you? What do you do?' conversation."

"I'm Rachel. Not so fine. The textbook was for my Human Development class. I'm getting my doctorate in clinical psychology."

"Congratulations. Join the family. It seems everyone here's a shrink. I can't remember when I've been surrounded by so many therapist types."

"Are you one too?"

"Yeah. I have a private practice and I'm a professor."

"Good to meet you."

"Good to meet you too. Now, I don't want to change the subject per se but I have some breaking news I'd like to share if you're up for it."

"Let's have it."

"I have Margot's last name. Spalding. I looked her up in the phone book. She's in there along with umpteen Spalding business/philanthropy-type things. By the looks of it, they are definitely big money."

"Let's call her and see what happens."

Nothing happened. The phone rang and rang so we hung up.

"Let's call some of these other numbers and see if we can find a family member," Rachel said.

We started with E Spalding. No answer. John. No answer. Then Larry. He answered but didn't know Margot. Nancy didn't answer.

"What do you say we go on over to Spalding Enterprises and see if we can get some help there? There's a local address."

CHAPTER ELEVEN

John

I WAS RAISED in New York where tall buildings reach a hundred floors. In Santa Barbara tall is fewer than ten. The directory sent us up to the top floor. The elevator opened to a large waiting area that had black-and-white pictures of Santa Barbara in an age when there hadn't been much to the city. An attractive woman sat behind a large desk and gave us a welcoming smile.

"Hello," Rachel said. "We're hoping you or someone can help us. We know Margot Spalding is in Europe but there's been an emergency and we need to get a hold of her."

"That's terrible but I'm afraid I can't give out personal information."

"Nor should you," I said. "We have her phone number so it's not really a matter of needing her personal information. Perhaps there's someone here we could speak with to help us out."

"Let me see if John is available," she said. She dialed a number. "Hi, John. I'm sorry to bother you, but I have a couple of people here who say there's been an emergency and they need to get a hold of Margot." She listened, then thanked him. "He'll be right out."

"Thank you," we said in unison. Rachel sat down and I went and looked at the pictures up close. Some were of the beach and downtown area. Others featured men on horseback who looked like they were on a cattle drive, or they were lined up, riding in a parade.

A stocky, six-foot forty-something man came into the lobby and strode right up to us. He was wearing cowboy boots. Maybe he wasn't quite as tall after all.

"Hi," he said. "I'm John Spalding. Margot's brother. What's going on?"

It wasn't what he said, but how he said it. Perhaps he was used to Margot causing trouble or emergencies because his tone had a *What now?* ring to it.

"Hi," said Rachel. "I'm Cliff Anderson's daughter, Rachel, and this is David Unger."

"Oh," he said. "I didn't know Cliff had a daughter."

"Actually, I'm his stepdaughter."

"Oh, yes. He did mention you to me. It's good to meet you both."

I nodded, and Rachel said, "You, as well. Is it all right with you if we go to your office to talk?"

"Sure. Come on in."

We followed him down a hallway with more pictures of horses and ranch life. There were also some vintage posters of the Old Spanish Days Fiesta that featured the mission, dancers, and a rodeo.

We went into the corner office. It was hard not to look past the desk and through the window at the harbor. It was the kind of view that would have made me turn my chair around for a good part of the day. John's near-empty desk indicated his attention might be drawn that way as well.

We sat and Rachel said, "I don't know if you heard but Cliff is in the hospital. He got beat up pretty badly and is in intensive care. We wanted to let Margot know."

"That's horrible. I hadn't heard anything. I'm sure Margot will want to know although she could be hard to track down."

"We heard she was traveling in Europe."

"Yup. Sounds about right. I have some numbers. I can try to

get a hold of her but it's sometimes difficult when she goes off on these jaunts."

"If it would help, we'd be glad to reach out to her," I said.

"That's very considerate, but it's not a problem. I'll leave some messages at the usual places. She usually checks in now and then."

"We hope you can reach her as I'm sure she'd want to be here," said Rachel.

"Yes, I'm sure she would…"

And then Margot came into the office.

She looked much like her picture except instead of a dress she was wearing jeans and a white blouse. She'd cut her hair but still looked quite stylish.

"Oh, hi, Elizabeth."

Elizabeth? Something was off. I looked at Rachel, who gave me a *what-the hell* look while John and Elizabeth hugged.

"Let me introduce you to Cliff's stepdaughter, Rachel, and her friend David."

"Hello," we said.

"They just told me Cliff's been beaten up and is in the critical-care unit at the hospital."

"What? When did that happen? Is he all right? Does Margot know?"

"No, she doesn't. That's why they came—to try to get some help locating her. I'm sure she'd want to be here."

"Certainly. Did you try calling Françoise?"

"Not yet. They just got here. I'll get her number. I'm sure dad has it. I'll go ask. Excuse me, I'll be right back."

CHAPTER TWELVE
Elizabeth

"Pardon me for asking—most likely you've been asked this too many times already—but I've never met Margot. I've just seen a picture. But you could be her."

"We're identical twins. I'm older by a few minutes. What happened to Cliff? How is he?"

"He's stable," Rachel said, "but in critical condition. They won't let us see him for another day. He was beat up pretty badly."

"That's dreadful. Do you know how this happened? Did they catch the people who did it?"

"You know almost as much as we do," Rachel replied. "He was found by the courthouse. We're not sure if he was beat up there or dumped there afterwards, but from what the doctor told us he took a lot of punishment."

"How awful. I hope he'll be all right."

"Can I ask you something?" I said, unsure of why I kept asking permission to do something I'm going to do anyway. "What could have happened? People usually don't get beat up like that without there being some reason. I don't know if he had his wallet with him or not. Maybe someone robbed him. But how badly do you have to get beaten up before you say, 'Go ahead. Take the thirty-five bucks'?"

"It does seem excessive. Plus, Cliff is not the type to put up much of a fight. If someone stuck him up he'd just hand over the money and hope he could keep his license and pictures."

"Could he have been involved in something that upset anyone?" Rachel asked.

"I wouldn't know about that. Perhaps. Maybe it was a gang thing. There's been some of that happening recently."

John came back into the room. "Françoise would like to speak with you, Rachel."

They left. Before I could open my mouth, Elizabeth said, "Do you live in Santa Barbara?"

"No, actually this is my first time here. But I wouldn't mind living here. Aside from the natural beauty of the place, it has a lot of architectural integrity. From what I've seen so far, the city is reminiscent of another place and time."

"They call it Spanish Derivative. It's a bit incongruous because the mission, which was built in the 1700s, is Greco-Roman."

"Honestly, I wouldn't know the difference, but I'm looking forward to seeing it."

"While there are certain differences, the Greco-Roman and Spanish Baroque are more similar than different as they evolved about the same time. So even though the architecture isn't really pure, it's lovely and coalesces well."

"I noticed all the pictures and posters on the walls. Can you tell me something about them?"

"By all means. We're an old ranching family. We've been here since the 1860s."

"Wow. That's hard to fathom. My grandparents were in Europe, my parents in New York, and I'm here. Well, LA, which I guess isn't really here."

"Not really."

"I don't know either Cliff or your sister but I gather they were going to get married."

"Maybe."

"Maybe?"

"Theirs isn't the easiest of relationships."

"I heard the marriage was on, off and back on."

"For now."

"So did a jealous ex-lover beat him up?"

"Hardly."

"Who then?"

"I'm sure I have no idea."

"No idea about what?" John asked as he came back in the room with Rachel.

"No idea who did this to Cliff."

"Any luck with Françoise?" I asked.

"Yes and no," John said.

"We were able to speak with her," Rachel said. "But Margot wasn't with her. She thinks she can find her and told us she'd call back as soon as she knows more."

"That's promising," I said, and Elizabeth nodded.

"Unfortunately, we have to go," John announced. Then added, "We'll see you this evening."

"Thanks again for helping out," said Rachel.

"Of course," John replied. "You're almost family."

Rachel had arranged for "us" to see them later for cocktails at the Biltmore.

"And another one bites the dust," I said.

"What?"

"You have a unique talent. You're able to lure people—no, let me correct that—you're able to encourage people to do things for you. You got me to help you out. Michael and Alan are having dinner with us, and now John has invited us to join the family for cocktails. You're a force to be reckoned with."

"Thanks. I want to know more about the family my dad is going to marry into. There's something off there. Did you sense anything when you spoke with Elizabeth?"

"They both are very polished, polite. They have that old-money ease about them. They aren't very open, but they appear to be very nice. Is that what you meant?"

"Kind of. They know more than they're letting on. They seemed evasive to me. Not obviously, but when it came to the bottom line they didn't really tell us anything."

"Well, John did have you speak to Françoise."

"Maybe. But how do I know Françoise isn't some French-accented secretary who'd been told what to tell me?"

I was thinking maybe Rachel believed in conspiracy theories.

"Anything's possible. Do have anything in mind for us to do now?"

"We're meeting the family for cocktails and then Michael and Alan for dinner, so our evening is pretty full. We can go our separate ways this afternoon… unless there's something else we could be doing?"

"I have a couple of thoughts, but I do kind of need to check in to the conference. I have to go to a workshop this afternoon otherwise I'm going to end up playing even more catch-up."

"Let's hear the ideas."

"We could go to the local library and do a little research into Spalding Enterprises."

"Great minds think alike."

"You had the same idea?"

"No, I didn't. I'm not so sure we're both great minds either."

"Nice."

"Just joking. It's a good idea. Why don't I do that this afternoon while you go learn a thing or two. I'll let you know what I found out when I come by the hotel and pick you up."

CHAPTER THIRTEEN
The Empty Chair

I HADN'T OPTIMIZED my learning opportunities at the conference but hoped the afternoon session would take care of some of that. Or at least give me four more credits.

The workshop was titled "The Empty Chair." I'd heard that this Gestalt Therapy technique could be very powerful and wanted to learn more about it. There were about twenty of us in a circle. In the middle of the room was an empty chair.

The facilitator was a serious-looking woman who talked about Laura and Fritz Perls, the originators of Gestalt Therapy. She shared a quote from Fritz that had resonated with her, and I guess with me as I still remember it—"Lose your mind and come to your senses." For someone who can think too much, that seemed like good advice.

The facilitator gave an overview of the theory—which I'll spare you—then announced that she wanted to demonstrate the technique. Thankfully there are always people who volunteer for things. I'm not one of them. I watched as the facilitator asked the volunteer about her life and the people who most affected her. If you guessed her parents, you wouldn't be wrong, but there were others too. The facilitator asked her to choose one with whom she had unfinished business. Not surprisingly, she chose mom.

I suppose coincidences happen all the time that we barely notice. When the odd guy from the visualization workshop showed up late, I noticed him right away. He didn't do anything unusual other than look ominous. If people choose therapists because of how they look this guy probably didn't get a lot of takers. He wasn't tall and he had a bit of gut, but there was something threatening in his face. It could have been the large scar below his eye or the lack of facial expression. Whatever it was, looking at him made me uncomfortable.

I tried to ignore him as the therapist had the volunteer picture her mother in the empty chair and talk with her as if she were in the room.

"Whatever you say, your mother won't hear. So, please tell your mom the uncensored version of what you want to say."

The volunteer was uncomfortable and hesitant at first, but then got into it. The facilitator asked her periodically if there was more she wanted to say or if she could explain something further. There were a lot of four-letter words, tears, and recriminations. When the volunteer said she didn't have anything further to add, the facilitator asked her to sit in the empty chair and respond as if she were her mother.

There was another round of four-letter words, tears, and raised voices. When she felt finished she went back to her seat and spoke to her mother as herself. Things went back and forth until we all were exhausted. The facilitator checked in with the volunteer, who said she felt drained but also rejuvenated. The facilitator then asked the rest of us how we were doing. A heated conversation ensued, which I'll also spare you.

What became clear to me is there are lots of people, places, and things in our lives that we're neither able nor willing to directly address. Lifting a restriction on speaking freely can unfetter us. I had a momentary lightbulb of awareness as I realized that my clients the following week would be taking a turn with the empty chair.

And if I wanted to, I could have a talk with any of the significant people, places or things in my life. Maybe I could even talk to Cliff.

As I left, I looked behind me. It would have been better if I hadn't because the moment I did, Scarface bent down to pick up something that wasn't there.

CHAPTER FOURTEEN

The Family

THE BILTMORE WAS the fanciest hotel in town. Built in the 1920s, the architecture, according to a brochure in the lobby, was a mix of Mediterranean Revival, Spanish Colonial and Moorish Revival. Resting by the ocean, it was both sumptuous and refined as the evening light bounced off it.

The Miramar—a half mile away and where the conference was located—was more than adequate and affordable but the Biltmore spoke to a different crowd. I felt like I should have worn a tux or a polo outfit.

A well-tailored man stood behind the reception desk. His name tag read Ray Friend. I wanted to comment on his name but knew he'd prefer if I didn't. He directed us to the bar.

A group stood by the fireplace. Elizabeth and John were among them, along with another man and woman about their age and an older couple I assumed were the parents. They all had that healthy wealthy look. Everything good on the outside but who knew what on the inside.

Introductions were made. The other middle-aged couple were the respective spouses of Elizabeth and John. Elizabeth looked like she'd found an outsider. While he certainly would have cut a dashing figure in a polo outfit, he wasn't quite as Stepford-looking as the others.

John looked like he'd bought himself a Playmate. If she hadn't actually been one, she certainly could have been, and still had the looks and fashion sense to show for it.

Mom and pop looked like they had known happiness together a long time ago but were now committed to having as little to do with each other as possible. He looked like he'd been quite a catch when he was younger, and a player on the people-with-money singles circuit. His big money and swagger had landed him something he'd never have: class. She was the royalty of the group. A Lauren Bacall-type sixty-something woman who looked out of place and possibly had married him for security or some misbegotten deed.

I make a lot of assumptions based on how things look, which I know better than to do, but still do anyway.

Given that the reason for the gathering was for Rachel to meet her prospective family, I glommed on to the outsider. Elizabeth's husband was more casually dressed than everyone else and didn't look overjoyed to be there.

"Hi. I'm David. Since I'm an outsider here and it looks like you are as well, I thought I'd come over and talk with you."

"I guess it takes one to know one. I'm Brendon. Are you and Rachel an item?"

"We're not a romantic item. I thought about it, still consider it, but I'm not sure about it. And, of course, she would have something to say about it as well. We're more of a Nick and Nora Charles kind of team, but without the dog. Although I do like dogs."

"You're detectives?"

"No, that was a bit of an exaggeration on my part. I'm a therapist and a professor. I'm in town for a conference and we just met. It seems like weeks ago, but it was actually yesterday."

"So why Nick and Nora?"

"It's actually the reason we're all here. Rachel's stepfather, Cliff, is Margot's fiancé."

"Oh, a meet-the-family thing?"

"Exactly, but with a twist."

"I'll bite."

"You may have heard Rachel's dad was found quite badly beaten up this morning. So it's been an emotionally charged day. He's stable but critical and she can't see him until tomorrow so there are pins and needles involved."

"I imagine so."

"Rachel wanted to let Margot know but a friend of Cliff's told us she's in Europe. We went and found John and he's trying to find Margot. And in the meantime, it's meet the family."

"That's quite a day you're having."

"It hasn't been boring. How about you? How's your day going?"

"My days exist in a rut. A pleasant enough rut, but still constraining."

"Ruts can do that to you. What's keeping you in it?"

"Ah, I neglected to consider that I'm speaking with a therapist. Take a look around you. This is my rut. There are many worse. But it's a hard rut to break out of. Not a lot of incentive. Just a lot of ennui."

"Ruts are weary-making. It's not easy making peace with them. There's a word I know, but I don't personally experience often enough. It's contentment. That's a place I'd like to hang out in more. I'm guessing you can relate to that."

"Brother, can I."

"So, brother, let me ask you a non-therapy question. Who beat up Cliff and why?"

"Nick Charles, you dog, you. Getting right to the heart of the matter."

"What do you think?"

"People don't just get beat up for nothing here. We take our beatings more verbally," he said with a wave of his hand. "My guess is Cliff was messing where he shouldn't mess."

"That's kind of what I was thinking. From the looks of it, there may be some people here who've crossed over the line a time or two. I expect there's a certain acceptance, just as long as it's done the 'proper way.' I'm also guessing Cliff stepped outside those parameters."

"You have yourself a mystery."

"So help me. Who did it?"

"When you live in a rut, Dave, you learn the proper way to answer that question: I have no idea."

Rachel and I debriefed on the drive to meet Michael and Alan for dinner.

She gave me a rundown on the family.

John—due to be the primary inheritor. He spent a lot of money on partying and women before getting married recently. According to his father, who kept a close rein on him, he was helping to run the business and not doing a very good job of it.

Kimberly, the would-be Playmate—spent a lot of money and had John tied around her finger… one that housed a diamond megaplex.

Elizabeth—the smartest of the bunch. Could have been living some other place doing some other thing. Supported Brendon, who seemingly had a hold on her.

Mom, Eleanor—out of place and not interested. Carried herself with an air of being better than the rest. Suffered her lot for unknown reasons.

Dad, Vic—like his son, he hadn't lived up to his father's expectations. Living with that inheritance he now did whatever he wanted whenever he wanted because who would dare mess with the patriarch and holder of the purse strings?

Rachel was putting her clinical assessment skills to good use. She could get a swift read on people as well as being able to get them to open up and do what she asked of them.

I told her the crew appeared distant with each other, like they all had secrets, and that it was understood—we all look the other way.

I said that Brendon had thought it possible that her dad had been messing where he ought not to have been. But he wouldn't tell me where because it was against the code and jeopardize the rut he'd so comfortably uncomfortably found himself in.

"Figures. I just hope I see Dad tomorrow and he gives us a satisfactory explanation. Then we can stop suspecting everyone of anything."

CHAPTER FIFTEEN

The Friends

I LIKE PIERS. They extend your boundaries and provide an unfamiliar vantage. We drove slowly down the wooden planks that extended a good distance out into the ocean, and parked at the end. It was beautiful. There was a harbor to the north with all manner of boats moored in its haven. To the south, the coast extended to a haze in the distance that I guessed was LA. To the east was Santa Barbara and the mountains behind it. To the west was the ocean and the horizon. The air was salty, the atmosphere casual, and the restaurant basic. Experience has taught me that the better the view the more I need to make sure I enjoy it.

Michael and Alan were standing outside the Harbor restaurant along with two friendly-looking women. Another round of introductions ensued. Michael's wife, Beth, was a gentle-faced woman with an engaging smile. Paula was Alan's long-standing girlfriend. She had a bit of a know-it-all attitude about her. They all appeared to be in their early fifties and had that California-healthy appearance.

I'm not great at striking up friendships. It's that foreplay thing. I don't want to have to go through all the niceties. Actually, that's not true. I don't mind talking about where I'm from and what I do and hearing their equivalent. What I don't like is the time it takes me to feel comfortable enough just to be myself and not on my best behavior, which at times isn't always the best. When I meet people, I have to monitor what I say and do more than usual, which results in my feeling inhibited.

When we'd finished ordering and there was a moment, I said, "You're all close to Cliff and know him as well as anybody. Will somebody please take a guess at what's gone on here? Hopefully we'll see Cliff in the morning and he'll tell us, and it will be an unfortunate twist of fate. He'll be better and healing and ready to move on. But, in the meantime, what do you think happened?"

"I'll tell you," said Michael. "It's not wise to speculate. It could be anything. Let's just focus on getting to know one another."

"Let me tell you what happened," said Paula. "Cliff pushed things to the limit one time too many. He often takes things to extremes that the rest of us don't, well, not anymore. Well, maybe once a year. Twice. Here and there."

"To get beaten like that, someone has to be real pissed off," said Alan.

"Michael and Alan, I know you're therapists. Are you ladies?"

"I am," said Beth.

"I'm a realtor," said Paula.

"Here's my psychology question, though I'm sure we can all have a theory about it. Why would someone beat you to within an inch of your life instead of killing you? I'm guessing the person had that option but chose not to take it. Why didn't they go all the way?"

"There could be two reasons," said Michael. "One, they wanted him to suffer and keep suffering. Two, they had some injunction against killing him. They wanted to, but for some reason couldn't."

"I wouldn't rule out love," said Paula. "This could be a love/hate thing. We don't know how he was beaten and what exactly happened. Maybe he was beaten with the heel of a shoe. That would be quite different than if fists had been used."

"Money," said Alan.

"Money and love," Beth said.

CHAPTER SIXTEEN
Horribilizing

July 29, 1983

I WAS HAVING breakfast at the hotel and reading the *LA Times* and the *Santa Barbara News-Press*. I'm always surprised by how much front pages differ. Of the half-dozen or so front page stories, only two were the same. I guess what's newsworthy in your town is different in mine.

The *LA Times* covered the national scene, entertainment scene, sports scene and pretty much every other scene in greater detail. Plus, they had an article about the two-year anniversary of Prince Charles and Lady Diana's wedding. Reading through the paper, I felt I had an overview on what was happening in the world. Reading the *Santa Barbara News-Press* gave me insight into what was happening locally. I hadn't found out from the *Times* that Ellen Withers from the county clerk's office had been killed.

There weren't a lot of details. Her body had been found near her Chevrolet Caprice by the courthouse parking lot. She'd been shot in the heart and had slight bruises. She was dead when her body was discovered by the late-night cleaning crew.

Ellen hadn't initially been forthcoming but had opened up the more we talked to her. I wondered if she'd opened up to someone else too, and paid dearly for it.

I called Rachel but there was no answer. She, Michael, Alan and I had plans to meet at the hospital at eleven. That would give me enough time to stop by the county clerk's office and pay my respects.

But first I'd attend the "Managing Your Stress" workshop—three credits, moving me up to a total of nineteen. If I walked the beach for the same amount of time I'd manage my stress equally well, but it wouldn't get me any credits, and that would stress me out.

The facilitator had one idea that I found intriguing. He had us rank the top things in our lives that were causing us stress right now. Then he had us list the worst possible thing that could happen with the top one.

My worst worry had me ending up being unemployed, homeless or at death's door.

Another worry was Scarface.

I want to say it disturbed me to call him Scarface as I don't like name-calling. But it didn't. I talk things better than I walk them.

He came late into the workshop and gave the room a once-over. When he saw me there, he decided to stay, or so it seemed. Was he late because he'd checked for me in the other workshops? If so, why was he following me? What had I done to deserve that? My stress level was definitely rising.

The presenter told us that worry progresses from the present moment to future moments. We take our current worry and—either consciously or unconsciously— anticipate what might happen next. Then, fear by fear, we add to our worry and spiral down from there.

"What are the odds of that worst thing happening?" the facilitator asked us.

He pointed out that the odds of it happening in the foreseeable future were small. So, why put a lot of time and energy into worrying about something that was highly unlikely to happen? Why not worry about something where the odds were more likely to come into play? Worry about more realistic things, he encouraged us.

Hmm. What was more my immediate realistic worry?

That Scarface would follow me after the workshop and, if I was lucky, put me in a bed next to Cliff instead of the morgue next to Ellen.

Maybe I was getting carried away.

Breathe, David, I told myself. *The guy could just be one of those people who always shows up late.* I'd dated people like that.

The presenter had a word for worst-case futuristic worry. He called it horribilizing, and suggested we consider knocking it off.

That didn't stop me from horribilizing about Scarface, but it did give me a name to call it. As I left the room and made my way to the restaurant for a late breakfast, I made sure I was surrounded by a group of people.

CHAPTER SEVENTEEN

News

I drove over to the courthouse and parked in the parking lot. As far as I could tell, Scarface hadn't followed me. Police tape blocked off an area. I got out of the car and did a couple of three-sixties to reassure myself, though maybe Ellen had done the same thing.

The recorder's office looked pretty much the same as the last time I'd been there, minus one person. I wasn't sure what or who to ask, but got in line and figured something would come to me when the time came.

"Good morning," I said to an efficient-looking man. "I remember you from the last time I was here. Such a tragedy that Ellen died. And so violently."

"Yes, we were all shocked. How can I help you?"

"I'm sure you were. What do you think happened?"

"I really have no idea. Now, how can I help you?"

"Well, I'm not sure. You know Cliff Anderson, the man who was found beat up on your doorstep?"

"Yes, that was also distressing."

"Indeed. Here's my problem. Cliff is in intensive care and we're not sure he's going to pull through. In recent weeks he's been in here doing some paperwork that I'm involved with, but with him not being able to communicate I'm not exactly sure where he left things off. Is there some way you could check his filings and make sure everything's set to go forward? Or do we need some more signatures? Could you check under his name and Margot Spalding's?"

"Let me see."

He went into a backroom while I congratulated myself on having broken through a wall. When he came back he said, "I looked at the register. Everything filed recently is in order."

"Ah, that's great to hear. I was really worried. I know there were difficulties with the names. Does it look like that got straightened out?"

"I don't know about that.."

"One more thing. Can you check the dates? I know there was some confusion about that as well. I just want to make sure we got that nailed down."

He went back through the closed door and returned quickly.

"The marriage license was signed last week, July twenty-second. So was the business license, will and property deed. The names are duly listed."

"That's very comforting. Thank you."

Some answers make for more questions. The marriage license had been signed last Friday, which meant that Margot had been in town until at least the twenty-second. Had she also signed the property deed, will and business license? Was this all part of the pre-nuptial agreement or something else?

All my questions could come to naught depending what happened at the hospital.

Rachel, Michael and Alan were already there when I arrived. We shared pleasantries and settled in.

"Anyone know anything about any legal matters Cliff was involved in?"

Blank stares.

"For what it's worth, Cliff and Margot signed their marriage license last week along with some other documents. I know there were some issues about a pre-nup. Anyone know the latest status on that?"

Shrugs.

We waited. I guess that's what waiting rooms are for, but it wasn't like we were enjoying the fact it was living up to its name. Close to noon, Dr. Novatt came down the hall. I couldn't tell much from his gait. He couldn't tell us much from what he knew. Cliff remained stable. He hadn't gained consciousness. His vital signs were good. The doctor didn't seem concerned that he remained unconscious and said he'd contact Rachel when he knew more. In the meantime, he'd be happy to meet us again the following morning.

Rachel asked if she could see Cliff and the doctor escorted her into the room but told her not to touch him. When she returned a short time later she was both consoled and disturbed. Leave it to three therapists to do their best to empathetically hear her out until she said she wanted to move on.

That was that. It wasn't bad news. It wasn't good news. Just news. You could read into it whatever you wanted. Michael and Alan were going to catch an afternoon workshop at the conference, and again we agreed to meet at eleven the next day.

Rachel and I had lunch at the hospital cafeteria—one of the worst places to eat. Hardly anyone is happy to be there. Horribilizing is the main item on the menu. We each had a salad that left a good deal to be desired, but it didn't seem to matter.

"How you holding up?" I asked.

"I don't know if it was a good idea or not to see him. He's all bandaged up and there are tubes and monitors everywhere."

"I'm sure it wasn't easy seeing him that way, but he's alive and being taken care of so hopefully things will be well."

"I wanted things to be better today and maybe they are. I don't like not knowing. It's like being in limbo. I don't want him to be a vegetable or die, but I want what's going to happen to happen already. I go from being hopeful to despondent."

"I'm sure. Not knowing is almost worse than knowing things went south. If he does die or become impaired, you'll be hurting but you'll deal with it. Not knowing leaves you open to imagining all sorts of things, which, I just learned, is called horribilizing."

"At least something good is coming of this. I have a new word in my vocabulary. Now let's do something so I don't have to horribilize anymore.

"I have a couple of ideas."

"Let's hear 'em."

"Margot signed those papers last week and now she's lost in Europe. I take it you haven't heard anything."

"I was going to call John after I heard about Dad. I ought to do that soon."

"That's a good idea. While you're at it, why not ask when Margot left? I'm curious about why she'd sign the papers, then leave right after. Maybe they had their first almost-married fight and she took off.. We could explore that."

"Okay. We can do that.. Next?"

"Did you read the local paper today?"

"There's a local paper?"

"Yeah. Every town with more than a hundred people has a newspaper. This one had some news you'll find interesting. Do you remember Ellen from the county clerk's office?"

"Sure."

"She got herself killed yesterday evening… by her car next to the courthouse."

"What?"

"Yeah, you heard me. Suspicious, yes?"

"Very. That's awful. What happened?"

"You know everything I know. I went over there this morning. You remember the rather rigid guy who was in the background?"

"Kind of."

"He was standing in for her. I tried to get some details out of him but, as you know, that place isn't exactly a wellspring of information. Basically, a marriage license, a will, a property deed, and a business license were all filed on the twenty-second."

"That's great. Good snooping. What does it all mean?"

"Yeah, that's the question. What does it mean, and did Ellen met her demise because of it?"

"Someone threatened my dad but needed to shut up Ellen. Threatening wouldn't do for her."

"The conspiracy angle, of course. If that's the case, we're talking some serious badness. It's one thing to beat someone up, but killing ups the ante."

"Not that much given the kind of beating Dad got, but I know what you mean. I feel so sorry for her and her family. She didn't do anything wrong."

"That we know of. We don't know if she's an innocent victim or part of the conspiracy. All we know is, someone upped the ante."

"You're right—she could be innocent or guilty. She might have been killed because someone thought she'd say something that would get the killer in trouble. Or maybe she did something to the files. You said the guy found them."

"No, I didn't say that. I said he looked at a register and saw when they were filed and under what names. I don't think he ever actually pulled the paperwork."

"You thinking what I'm thinking?"

"Someone got Ellen to get those files out of there? Is that what you're thinking?"

"How do we get the guy to look for them?"

"You've got that skill set covered. Do your thing."

"'This is very unusual' is what he told me," Rachel said. "I got him to go look for the actual files. When he came back he had a look of consternation on his face, and said, 'This is very unusual. They're not where they're supposed to be.'"

"I would think that for someone who has their life in good order things are pretty much always where they need to be. For you or me, it's upsetting but isn't entirely out of our experience. I bet he was fit to be tied."

"But we're not. We're one step further into the rabbit hole."

"Things are looking up or down depending on your point of view. So, we can hypothesize that someone got Ellen to get those files and then took care of her."

"Whoever we're dealing with is intent on covering their tracks."

"And they won't be so excited to know that we're trying to track them down."

"Yes, the forces of evil could have us in their sights."

"It's time we went over to the police station and talked with someone."

CHAPTER EIGHTEEN
The Police

WHEN I WAS sixteen I had the good fortune to be parked up on a hillside one night with Tricia Farmer. I was trying to work my way around the bases when there was a tap on my window and a police officer asked for my driver's license. Since it was after 10 p.m. he took me and Ms. Farmer to the police station. It was a very cold, brightly lit and dreary place. Neither my parents nor hers were overjoyed, but they thought the police had overstepped themselves, and we got off without further incident. Yet, I was left with an indelible mark: the police can take you away from your enjoyment of life.

The Santa Barbara Police Station was also Spanish Colonial and had its share of wood and tile. Not that I have much experience with which to compare it, but as police stations go it was on a par with the rest of Santa Barbara.

Eventually we got to speak with Lt. Flores. I tend to picture police officers as being older than I am, but Flores was in his early thirties. Good-looking, eager, and more interested in Rachel than in me. I couldn't blame him. I almost felt a duty to warn him about her, but figured it was best to keep that to myself.

Rachel told him about her relationship with her stepfather and our concerns about his well-being. He told us that an officer had already visited Cliff at the hospital and that when he regained consciousness they'd go back. Rachel then told him about our going to the clerk's office and asking Ellen about any signed papers.

"When we heard about her being shot we went back to the office and the papers that Cliff signed aren't there. The clerk I talked to said it was very unusual for documents to be missing."

"The documents that your dad signed are no longer there?"

"They're listed in the register so the clerk knows they were collected. But they aren't filed where they ought to be."

"That's out of the ordinary for them over there. We'll follow up on it. Thanks for letting us know. Anything else?"

"We're not alarmists," Rachel said. "But we want you to know that we think there's a connection between my dad being beaten and the clerk being killed, and that it has to do with that paperwork. If you can find that connection, you'll find who did this."

"That's very helpful. We'll certainly follow up on it. Now, I really have to go. Things are pretty busy here, what with it being Fiesta week."

"That went well," said Rachel.

"They didn't arrest us, so that's good. But what's Fiesta week?"

"I know the word, but I didn't know there was a Fiesta week."

"Let's find out what it is. And while we're at it, you know what we ought to do?"

"Yeah. Go figure out who took those papers."

We couldn't come up with anything we could do to figure out who stole the papers, so we opted to go back to the conference and learn something we could figure out.

Rachel wanted to stop by her hotel to get something. When she came back to the car she told me there'd been a note from John inviting us to "Join the rest of the family at the ranch to kick off Fiesta."

Another dinner date to put on my dance card. If I kept this up, I'd need to go to another conference to collect my credits.

CHAPTER NINETEEN

Mischief

BEING AT THE conference reminded me that I was supposed to be at the conference. I looked at the list of afternoon workshops and tried to guess which one Michael or Alan would attend. They were therapists. They were used to helping people get unstuck. Maybe they could help us figure out the Ellen/Cliff connection.

It was a draw between "Focusing" and "Building Intimacy the Old-Fashioned Way." Rachel opted for the former and I, the latter. I didn't take it as a particularly fortuitous sign when Rachel opted out of the intimacy workshop because she wasn't "fond of old-fashioned ways."

We agreed to meet later and off I went to upgrade my intimacy skills.

I wasn't that late so I was able to sign in and get three credits. Twenty-two down, fourteen to go.

Things were already underway when I entered into the room. Just as I noticed that Michael, Alan and Scarface weren't there, a woman came over to me, took my arm and said, "Oh, good. We needed one more. Please come with me." I was escorted to a chair facing a man who, on first look, promoted no desire to be intimate whatsoever. I felt a little bad for him as he was probably the guy who'd been last-picked more than once.

I admit it. I go a lot on first impressions. I'm not exactly sure what attracts me to someone, but if I had to pin it on one thing I'd go with a twinkle in the eye. I like someone who has some spunk in them. Some mischief. Someone who can step over the line a little bit. Not too much, but some. Not too often, but some. I couldn't see much of anything in this man's eyes, aside from relief. We smiled at each other and shook hands.

"We're supposed to ask each other three questions," he told me.

"Good enough. Who goes first?"

"That's your first question."

Okay, I didn't like him already and had an inkling why no one had chosen him for a partner.

"Since I'm one into it, why don't you ask one now."

"What's your name?"

"David. What kind of mischief have you gotten into lately?"

"Pardon me?"

"That's your second one," I said, trying not to sound too snotty but wanting to show him that two could play at that game. Which maybe had something to do with wanting to recreate some of that good old-fashioned thing that people who are intimate do—annoy one another. Those closest to us get to share in the best and rest of us.

"I'll repeat my second one. What kind of mischief have you gotten into lately?"

There was a pause. He didn't like me either, but I could see the wheels turning. I was hoping he'd say that he'd shot someone in a parking lot recently.

"I forged my wife's name. How about you? What kind of mischief have you gotten into lately?"

"I'm glad you asked. It gives me an idea. Lately my mischief has been under wraps, but I'm about to step it up."

"You didn't answer my question."

"You're right. Well, I did sort of say I was at a workshop when I wasn't."

"You what?"

Uh oh. He wasn't much of a rule-breaker, and for all I knew he was the guardian of continuing-education credits. It was time to double down on the mischief and lie to protect my ass.

"Okay, that's your fourth question. Happy to answer it. I was talking to some people in town about the conference and this very attractive woman told me how much she liked it when her therapist asked about her dreams. So I told her I'd just been to a workshop on dreams and would be happy to talk to her about hers. I hadn't been to the workshop but wanted to see if I could make some headway with the woman."

"Oh."

I can lie with the best of them when called upon. I'd like to consider myself a basically honest guy who can invoke situational ethics when required. However, you might be considering differently and I wouldn't blame you.

I don't condone lying as a way to build intimacy. Lying has been around since time began and we all have our secrets and personal truths. However, we build intimacy by sharing our truths. To build a relationship with this guy I'd eventually have to tell him I'd lied, but for the moment I kept that to myself.

When the workshop was over we were thanking each other when I noticed someone open the door, look in, see me, and close it. Scarface. I decided it was time to buddy up with my new friend. I chatted him up all the way into the hallway and then, when I thought the coast was clear, I told him that I had to go.

CHAPTER TWENTY
Marrying for Money and/or Love

I found Rachel, Michael, and Alan discussing the Focusing workshop. From what I could tell, you basically close your eyes and focus your attention on that place where you usually feel things, and see what comes up. I couldn't understand what the fuss was about, but they seemed to have been inspired by it.

Not one to go against the flow I said, "I know I asked you this before, but now that you're more able to tune into that place where you feel things, can you close your eyes and focus on what comes up for you in connection to any legal or quasi-legal things that Cliff has been up to recently?"

No one closed their eyes, but Michael—no surprise—had something to say.

"Marriage is still a legal matter in California, so there's that."

"Evidently, as of last week the marriage is on. Anything else coming to you?"

"The pre-nup," said Alan.

"Does anyone know what was and wasn't in the final version?"

"No idea," Michael said. "He wanted her to share everything. She wanted it prorated by year. The longer they were married the more he'd get."

"That seems fair," Rachel said.

"Not if you're planning on leaving soon," said Alan. "Hold on a minute. Was Cliff was in it for the money?"

"That's my take."

"Michael, do you agree?" Rachel asked.

"Yes and no. At one point he was in it for love. Or at least mostly. But lately there seems to have been less love. It could be that thing where couples get doubtful before they marry, but it was more than that."

"If he wasn't feeling that old-fashioned intimacy, she probably knew," I said. "Maybe that's why originally the pre-nup wasn't a big deal but as she dealt with the uncertainty of his love she wanted to protect herself."

"She, or maybe one of her family," said Rachel. "Thinking about that group and their respective spouses, I can see someone warning her about giving it all away. If her brother, sister, and father had better pre-nups, some of those marriages might not be intact."

I agreed.

"Okay, since you all focused so well on that, how about this. Who do you think would be the most likely candidate for stealing the papers Margot and Cliff signed?"

"Wait. Are you saying someone stole the records?" Michael asked.

"Yes, I am. We just found out. The plot thickens. Do you think the person who stole those papers wanted there to be a pre-nup or not? And here's a bonus question. Did they steal those papers to get the will, the marriage license, the property deed, the business license, or all four?"

There was a lot of focusing going on but not much commentary.

"While you mull that over I have an idea. I'm doing some sightseeing this afternoon. I don't know if you were planning on doing the late-afternoon workshop, but if not, why don't we all take a trip to the courthouse? It's on the tourist worth-seeing list."

I can't say there was much enthusiasm, but it seemed that we were united in our mission to discover what had happened to Cliff. It felt good to have a unifying purpose. Although, as with all missions, some bought in more than others and everything was open to interpretation.

Michael squeezed us into his Fiat and a-touristing we did go. We drove up State Street, which ran from the ocean and its hotels and bars to the courthouse, which was well within walking distance of Spalding Enterprises.

We parked in the courthouse parking lot and made our way to the main entrance. I took Rachel aside.

"What can we do to find out something? Any ideas?"

"It was your idea to come here. I thought you had a plan."

"Coming here was as far as I got with the plan. We could always go back to the county clerk's office and see if we can learn anything new."

"It's something."

"Hey, gang," I said. "Let's go over here first."

We made for the corner office and stood at the back of the line. The same guy was there along with another clerk. As luck would have it we ended up with the familiar face.

"Hi," I said. "Remember me?"

"Certainly. And Dr. Blum. Good afternoon," he said, looking at Michael.

"Glad you remember. And you know Dr. Blum as well?" I asked.

"Of course."

"Of course. We were wondering if there's anything else we ought to know. We're all very concerned about Cliff and Ellen, and want to do what we can to help out. Anything you can tell us?"

"I'm afraid not. I've spoken with the police and told you all I can."

"All right. Anyone have any questions for the gentleman?"

Nothing.

CHAPTER TWENTY-ONE
Team Meeting

I DON'T KNOW how this happened, but it happened. It's happened to me before so I shouldn't have been surprised, but I still didn't see it coming. I'd formed a posse. We were now an investigative team.

A team that needed a team meeting.

We went up some winding stairs to the four-faced clock tower that provided a 360-degree panorama. There wasn't a bad view to be had.

We found a spot facing the mountains.

"So, Michael, it seems that the guy at the clerk's office knows you," I said as innocently as possible. "That could be very helpful to us. How do you know him?"

"I was wondering that myself," said Rachel.

"Nothing very mysterious there. We swim at the same place."

"You swim?"

"Yeah. I love it. I used to run but it played havoc with my body so now I swim every day at the Y. I see Richard, the guy in the clerk's office, there all the time."

"They say swimming is one of the best forms of exercise," Rachel said.

"But it's exercise," said Alan. "I try to have my daily life provide sufficient nourishment for my body, mind, and, you know, soul."

"Nice speech," said Michael. "What he's really saying is that he chops wood for the winters up in Tahoe and fishes in the summer."

"That sounds like good exercise," I said. "I like that it's an organic part of your life. Sort of like our ancestors."

"Who lived well into their thirties," Michael pointed out.

"There were other factors involved," Alan said with a trace of annoyance. "What about you two, what do you do to maintain your well-being?"

"Yoga. Been doing it since I was a kid. And rock climbing. But now I'm in school they're both taking a hit."

"Rock climbing? Yikes," I said.

"It's challenging and scary. I like it. What do you do?"

"I'm mostly into stretching. I once heard that motion is lotion, so I try to remember to keep putting on the lotion."

"Motion is lotion… I like it," said Alan.

That was the end of the team meeting. Like a lot of meetings, it wasn't very satisfactory.

CHAPTER TWENTY-TWO

Spalding Ranch

Michael dropped off Rachel at her hotel and got me back to the conference in time to dress up for the Fiesta dinner. I'd not known to bring something in the spirit of a fiesta, so I took a shower to freshen up and put on my jeans, a dark-blue button-down shirt, and loafers. I drove over to Rachel's hotel and picked her up. She was wearing a light peach summer dress and looked fetching.

"Looking good," I said as she got in.

"It's an occasion. My introduction to the homestead."

"If it looks as good as you, you'll be suitably impressed."

"Thank you."

I wasn't really flirting with her, was I? Maybe, and she did look good. But I didn't want to dwell there.

"Did you notice that something Michael said was off?" I asked.

"Of course. I considered busting him, but thought better of it."

"Me too."

"That's such bullshit about the swimming."

"They could swim at the same place. But if you and I swam there and saw each other fairly often, after a while wouldn't you'd stop calling me Doctor? That seemed very weird to me."

"Yeah," she said. "I don't see Michael as that formal a kind of guy. If he goes into the clerk's office a time or two and signs some paperwork as Dr. Blum, then the title would make sense. Michael wasn't totally forthcoming."

"I agree with you. I don't like that he lied, for a couple of reasons. First, it makes us suspect him. And second, it makes me suspect the family less."

"There definitely are shenanigans there. But don't go overboard."

"I'll try but I'm beginning to see shenanigans everywhere."

"Let's just focus on tonight," she said, cutting to the heart of the matter.

"Okay."

"You need to do some snooping around while we're there."

"How come you said I do and not we do?"

"No one will be paying you much attention. I don't think I'll be able to slip away. I will if I can."

We were driving north, the ocean on one side and rolling hills on the other. We passed some ranches, but it was mostly open space with some grazing cows here and there. After about fifteen minutes, we turned off the highway and passed through an iron gateway topped with a good-sized wooden sign that had *Spalding Ranch* branded onto it. It took us a good five minutes to get to the hacienda, garage and barn. Given the long driveway and fancy gate, it all looked rather modest at first glance.

The simple adobe-style house may have been the original homestead. As we got closer, upgrades and additions stretched the house out so that it no longer looked so humble. Magenta bougainvillea and night-blooming jasmine covered much of the walls.

We parked alongside some Land Rovers and a Jaguar.

Elizabeth opened the front door. She was wearing a black cowboy hat, black pants, a turquoise shirt, a hand-embroidered black jacket, and a pair of snazzy boots that looked like they'd never been on the range. I guessed this was Fiesta-wear. We were certainly not dressed for the same gathering.

There was lots of horse memorabilia, along with leather furniture and wooden beams. It felt like it should have been darker given the abundance of earth colors, but there was a lot of recessed lighting.

She led us through the house to the backyard where the family was gathered.

The house was built for indoor/outdoor living. The living room extended into the backyard, which stretched as far as I could see. I caught a glimpse of horses in a corral, the ocean, and in the distance I saw cattle. They seemed far enough away from the house that whatever aromas they were creating were covered by the ocean breeze and jasmine.

Fiesta-wear flourished. Everyone except the mom wore a cowboy hat, boots and a brightly colored shirt. It seemed they'd been hitting up the liquor before we arrived.

I ended up next to the dad, whose name I actually remembered. Vic.

"Vic, how long have you lived here?"

"I was born in this house, as was my father and his father before him."

"That's pretty remarkable these days. Most families rarely stay in the same place that long."

"When you live in paradise, why move? I've traveled a fair amount and there are plenty of impressive places in the world, but I'm always happy to come home."

"Why not? You have a magnificent spread here. I see you have horses and cattle. I take it this is a working ranch."

"Has been for over a century."

"That's pretty impressive as well. In the offices downtown there were a lot of pictures of men on horseback. Some looked like they were taken at a parade."

"Those are the Ranchero Visitadores. We've been riding in the Fiesta parade since the thirties."

"Are there other things in the parade aside from horses?"

"There are antique carriages, wagons, a few floats for the officials, but it's mostly horses. Lot of horse people in this region."

"Are the Visitadores a business group like the Rotary Club?"

"We do some of that, but mostly we're about preserving the historic west. We also meet every May for a four-day ride. Sort of reminiscent of an old cattle drive."

At that point Eleanor joined us and said, "I'm not sure your ancestors had hookers, sex toys and catered meals on those drives."

"It was the wild west," Vic said, "but you might be right about some of that."

"Of course I am. This is all about boys being boys."

"So help me, please, what exactly is the Fiesta?"

"Since the twenties, we've been celebrating the Rancho period," Vic said, sounding like the chamber-of-commerce man he most likely was. "We like to honor the Old Spanish Days with the parade, a rodeo, music, mercados, and traditional dances."

"Mostly it's a chance for local businesses to make money off tourists, and for locals to dress up and get drunk for a week," Eleanor said.

"And don't forget this," said Brendon as he came up behind me and cracked something on my head.

"Cascarónes," said Vic with an approving smile.

"It's a local tradition," Eleanor said. "All year long, families make dime-sized holes in eggs and pour out the insides, then fill them with confetti. Then at Fiesta they sell the eggs and people take great pleasure in cracking them over the heads of unsuspecting tourists and their loved ones."

I wasn't sure that I liked the egg being cracked on my head, though at least it was filled with confetti. I also wasn't sure if I was supposed to let the confetti stay in my hair and on my shoulders. I brushed some off anyway. I'm a little too fussy to want eggshell on my head for long.. Confetti I can handle, but usually it's New Year's Eve and I'm drunk.

"Welcome to the club," Brendon said to me. "Walk all over town the next few days. There'll be confetti in banks and everywhere. You'll see. Soon you'll get some Cascarónes yourself and be sharing them with your friends."

"Perhaps. It does seem a fun tradition, just as long as I don't have to sweep up afterwards."

"We have people to do that," Vic said.

As we talked other people got gifted with confetti. There seemed to be a correlation between the number of drinks consumed and the harder the eggs were cracked.

Everyone was looking forward to the rodeo and parade. Well, some more than others. But all the family would be at the parade the next day to watch Vic and his boys strut their stuff.

I figured the tri-tip they were barbequing would take another thirty minutes. Maybe this was my moment to do some snooping. I excused myself to go to the bathroom.

While I delve into someone's private life when they're in therapy, I don't make a habit of it when I'm a guest in someone's home. I like to look at bookcases and pictures in public areas. But there weren't any bookcases and the art didn't hold much of my attention as it was mostly of men, cattle, and horses.

I had no idea what I was looking for, which made things a bit easier. I figured there wasn't a lot to be gained from looking in the bathroom so I kept going past it and down the hallway. Rooms that appeared to have once belonged to the children were now guest rooms.

I found what I assumed was Vic's office and went inside. There were a lot of horse statues and pictures of men on the range—maybe his father, grandfather, and great grandfather. One large group shot looked like it had been taken at his wedding. You could clearly see the two sides of the family. Aside from that one picture of Eleanor, I hadn't seen any others in the house. There were pictures of Margot,

Elizabeth, and John mostly taken in their younger days. Brendon and the Playmate were nowhere to be seen.

His desk looked a lot like John's downtown. No paperwork or writing implements that I could see. If anyone came in now I could say I was innocently ambling around. If I decided to open a desk drawer, they might think otherwise.

In for a penny, in for a pound. I opened a drawer. I don't know what I thought I'd find, but there was a revolver sitting right on top. I closed the drawer and went to the bathroom.

Maybe they had rattlesnakes or coyotes out here. Or perhaps that gun was for something else. I brushed all the eggshell and most of the confetti out of my hair and rejoined the group.

I don't know how it's possible to have a dinner conversation with eight people in which nothing worth talking about is talked about. We had a pretty thorough discussion about the weather, the Fiesta, and how President Reagan had gone riding with the Visitadores before he was president. Vic took a lot of pride in that. More so it seemed than he did in his family.

He tried to entertain us with stories about various parades over the years but it was easy to tell they'd been told too many times. As he got drunker he included some of the ribald tales from his outings with the Visitadores that included some sex toys. Those were marginally more interesting.

On the drive back, Rachel made it clear that she wasn't enamored with her prospective family. I told her about Vic's wedding picture and how, from the looks of it, Eleanor's family felt the same way.

"She's a cold fish," Rachel said. "I don't know who she was before she joined the family, but they've drained all the juice out of her."

"She seems to have retained a snarky tongue."

"To quote Oscar Wilde, 'Sarcasm is the lowest form of wit, but the highest form of intelligence.'"

"She's the brains of the operation, but if she's so smart what's she doing here?"

"I suspect she's a prisoner. Anything else you discovered aside from the wedding picture?"

"Not much. Lots of pictures of horses and men. No recent pictures of anyone. And there was a gun in one of the drawers."

"Really?"

"Yeah. Maybe it's for the occasional rattlesnake or coyote that shows up."

"Or…"

"Something else."

"What else did you find?"

"The gun scared me away."

"Then we have to go back."

"We do?"

"Certainly. But I made it easier. I left my lipstick in the bathroom. We can use it as an excuse. Let's go back tomorrow. Hopefully, they'll all be at the parade."

"Vic was certainly geared up for it and the entourage will be comfortably ensconced in a VIP seating area outside their offices. John told me that before, during, and after the parade there's going to be a party at their office, complete with margaritas, cascarónes and tacos."

"Good. We'll check out the house and be back at the party for some margaritas before it's over."

"Great," I said with no enthusiasm.

CHAPTER TWENTY-THREE

What Friends Can Tell You

July 30, 1983

WHILE I WAITED for my granola I read the *News-Press*, delighted that no one I knew had died recently. A lot of the paper was dedicated to the various Fiesta celebrations in town and the parade that would start at two.

I was finishing my breakfast in the hotel's restaurant when Alan came in. We made eye contact and I welcomed him over.

"Good morning," I said. "It's good to see you."

"You as well," he said as he slid into the booth. "Although the good comes after the coffee."

"I got the jump on you."

"I'll catch up."

"I'm curious. When and why did you move to Tahoe, and what's it like to live there?."

"I drive around the lake and think, There's half my salary."

"Meaning?"

"I'd easily make twice as much anyplace else, but I'm taking that half and putting it into being by the lake and the mountains."

"That makes sense. Living somewhere you love really makes

a difference. The last few months I keep hearing Randy Newman on the car radio singing 'I love LA.' I sing along because it's kinda infectious, but I can't really say that I love LA. I grew up in New York, so LA has never felt like a city. It's not a city but it's not the country. It's a bunch of suburbs loosely glued together. Having the beauty of nature surround you sounds very appealing."

"I grew up in LA, met Cliff and Michael at grad school there, but always wanted to be in the mountains."

"It must be kind of cool to be in California and live where you have four seasons. I miss those."

"It's a definite bonus. Although the winters are rough. I stay home and read a lot."

"That sounds very restful. While I'm fighting traffic you stay home, watch the snow from your window, read, and earn half as much for that privilege."

"That's it."

I was mostly listening to him, but saw Scarface come into the restaurant, scan the room, and leave. I can't say he left because he saw me, but it did unnerve me. I didn't know if he had anything whatsoever to do with me, but I certainly felt eerie every time I saw him.

"There's something magical in natural beauty."

"What? Oh, yeah. Nature. Indeed. Can I ask you something?" I blurted.

"What's that?"

"I know we're all very concerned about what happened to Cliff and, more importantly, what will happen to him. Between you, Michael and Rachel, I'm the least connected to him. And, yet, I'm very driven to want to find out what happened to him and to Ellen."

"I've noticed."

"So, there's something I want to ask you. When we were up in clock tower, Michael said something that sounded like a lie. I wonder if you know what I'm talking about."

"I do."

"Can we talk about that? Why did he lie? And what do you suggest I do about it?"

"Good questions. I don't really want to talk about it. But I will."

"Thanks. I don't want to make things awkward between you."

"He's already done that."

"So why did he lie?"

"Because he doesn't want Rachel to know he's been conducting some business with the city."

"Business with the city?"

"Yes, business with the city. It's his story to share with you as he sees fit."

"I understand and respect you're not wanting to out him, but maybe you could tell me why not let her know."

"I'm not going to answer that. If it's important to you, why don't you talk to him yourself? Maybe without Rachel."

"That sounds like good advice and good friendship."

CHAPTER TWENTY-FOUR
Reframing

I KNEW I'D confront Michael sooner or later, but I wanted to run it by Rachel first. Funny, I thought. I was behaving like a partner. The other times I've had mysteries to solve I've mostly done it by myself. Sure, there were people who helped, but I never had anyone I wanted to run something by.

As I've learned more about therapy, I've come to realize that while you don't always get to understand the why of things, you can understand the way of things. I'd had a would-be posse at the music festival and a confidant. Now I had another posse with Alan, Michael, and Rachel. And maybe a budding partnership with Rachel.

I'd never thought about having a partner. I'd always favored the lone-wolf detectives. But there was that Nick Charles reference, and Nick had Nora and Asta. And there were also sidekicks. The Lone Ranger had Tonto, Sherlock had Watson, and Batman had Robin.

Those relationships never quite stood on equal ground. With Rachel, I couldn't see her filing an application for sidekick.

I remember a Danny Kaye song called *Lobby Number* about a movie based on a book, that was extracted from a story, taken from a chapter, derived from a sentence overheard somewhere, and on and on. I thought about that as I sat in a workshop titled "On

Reframing." It was stretching things to put on a workshop based on a word that could easily be expressed in a sentence and detailed in a short paragraph. But I was getting three credits and upping my total to twenty-five, so I wasn't really complaining.

Put things in a new frame and get a new perspective. That's the sentence.

The words you use or the stories you tell about the people, places, and things in your life can be seen through multiple lenses. Instead of saying, "I'm stupid," you can say, "I've got something more to learn," or "I could have approached that differently." Same event. New frame to put on it. That's the paragraph.

So I could take Scarface coming into the workshop, looking around, and leaving in one frame and infer he was checking to see if I was there. Or I could see his actions through a different frame. Maybe he was looking for a friend, hadn't found them, and was looking someplace else now.

I didn't want to indulge the horribilizing frame, but my mind was whirring with questions about why he'd be interested in me. If he was following me, there had to be a reason, but I hadn't done anything to warrant it. Had I?

I tried to focus on the frame I was using to look at the events of the week. I'd initially seen what had happened to Cliff through its own lens. Then I'd seen it connected to Ellen's death. Now, I saw shenanigans everywhere. Everyone seemed suspicious to me.

Of course, none of us are fully known. But there wasn't anyone who seemed to be what they seemed to be. Alan perhaps. And maybe Rachel. But as soon as I thought that, my lack of suspicion made me suspicious. Perhaps my frame was a little too skewed toward paranoia and distrust. For a basically trusting soul to be suspicious of everyone might benefit from some reframing.

What if I looked at things through the lens of the killer? What were they seeing? What were they doing? What else did they plan to do? Had they finished their work or was there more to do? If I could see through their eyes what would I see?

You don't kill without reason... unless you're drunk or crazy, and even then there's some murky explanation. It was my guess that the person who'd done this had had a clearer motive, and something had happened that had prompted them to behave in extreme ways. What was that occurrence?

Something must have threatened them or been so incendiary that the only option had been murder. They hadn't wanted to murder Cliff but they had wanted to murder Ellen. Maybe this was really about Ellen, and Cliff was collateral damage. Maybe the person wanted to warn Ellen to keep her mouth shut about stealing the documents and Cliff had been a warning to Ellen that hadn't been heeded. Or maybe both had been a warning to someone else.

I could spin theories and questions endlessly and it was kinda fun until I had a disturbing thought. If this was all about the Ellen, I was looking in the wrong house. Maybe we should be going to the Ellen's. I didn't like that idea.

I don't know how you deal with breaking the law. As a rule, I try to limit it to speeding on the freeway, jaywalking and smoking a joint now and then. I know—I live a wild life. The idea of doubling down and becoming a two-time lawbreaker didn't appeal to me.

I didn't have to get involved, I told myself. I didn't have to put myself in any jeopardy. I didn't have to solve any mystery. I didn't need to be the hero.

Maybe Cliff would be better, and I could put the end frame on the sleuthing. But then this would be a short story or a paragraph, maybe even a sentence. Certainly not a book.

CHAPTER TWENTY-FIVE
Bending Integrity

I drove myself over to the hospital. There was only a little traffic on the roads and when I came to an intersection, people were in no rush and waved me to go first. It threw me off my game a bit. If I lived here I'd have to be nicer. I wasn't sure if I'd sacrifice half my salary for that, but throw in the beach, mountains, architecture, and some cultural activity? Maybe.

Rachel was there when I arrived.

"I have something to run by you," I said. Then remembered to say, "Oh, hi. It's good to see you. How's everything?"

"Hello. And?"

"And I'm considering… I was about to say confronting, but maybe just talking with Michael about his lie."

"You should."

"Good. I ran it by Alan and he suggested I ought to talk to Michael without you. Since he's your dad's friend, I thought I'd run it by you first."

"That's very thoughtful. By all means. Go talk with him and see what you can find out. It was weird."

"Alan implied it had to with you, so if I find out anything I'll let you know."

"Sounds good."

"So if you get a chance at some point, see if you can find a reason to go be with Alan and I'll see what I can do."

"Got it."

Dr. Novatt sounded like a broken record. Same delivery. Same news. Cliff was still unconscious but now the doctor was calling it a coma. He didn't think that the duration indicated an increase in severity. Certainly he'd have liked Cliff to be conscious, but whether it was a few days or a couple of weeks didn't seem to upset him. I'm not so sure you could say the same for the rest of us. We agreed to meet again the next day, same time. Rachel opted out of going to see him.

We were standing outside the hospital. Rachel asked Alan if she could have a private word with him and off they went. I could have said the same to Michael, but now that we were alone I was, naturally, happy to skip the foreplay.

"So, Michael, I want to ask you something. Why did you lie at the clock tower? We all know you did. I guess, to your credit, you're not a very good liar."

"Everyone knows I lied?"

"Yeah, we talked behind your back. People tend to do that. Sorry. But in this case it was helpful. I gather there's something you don't want Rachel to know. That's okay. I can keep secrets if you want to tell me. But if you don't, could you at least tell me why you don't want her to know what you don't want her to know."

"That's fair, but I'm not sure I want to tell you. I can tell you there's something I don't want Rachel to know, and if you knew what it was you wouldn't want me to tell her as well. You'll have to trust me on this."

"Okay, I can do that. But I gather that it has something to do with the clerk's office. Can you tell me anything about that?"

"Sorry, that needs to be private for now as well. I hope it won't have to be a secret for long, but it's a secret I can't reveal."

"You know, it's hard sometimes to deal with people who have integrity. I can't even get you to bend things a little?"
"I already have."

CHAPTER TWENTY-SIX
Spalding Ranch Re-Visited

"Trust the process" is what my graduate-school professor taught me. Ever since I heard him say that I've been a believer that this will lead to that, which will lead to this, which will beget that, and somehow or other it all works out.

If Michael needed to keep his knowledge private so be it. I wasn't going to get anywhere badgering him; I needed to let it go and come back to it later. Besides, I had illegal things to do—homes to break into—and needed to trust that process wouldn't get me thrown in jail.

The parade started at 2:00. Rachel and I figured that if we were at the ranch at 1:30 p.m. everyone would be gone. Given the relationship I have with time, we got there very close to 1:30. The last time we drove up to the ranch we were expected. This time we were anxious. It's one thing to snoop around someone's house when you've been invited in. It's another when you haven't. While we had the excuse of looking for Rachel's lipstick, that wouldn't hold up very well with Vic or in court.

The closer we got, the more misgivings I had. We had little reason to suspect that anyone in the family was involved with Cliff's beating or Ellen's death. Yes, I could feel shenanigans everywhere, but that was the case with anyone's life if you peered too closely. Heck, I was feeling shenanigans with Scarface and all he'd done was look at me.

Just because I wanted to find out what had happened to Rachel's dad and Ellen didn't mean that I wanted to go to jail for it. I was getting a better understanding of the term cold feet.

Rachel said there'd be a housekeeper and that she'd ask them to help her look for the lipstick. That would give me time to get myself into trouble. Rachel figured she could keep the housekeeper detained for five to ten minutes so I wouldn't have to worry about being discovered. That made me feel slightly, and only slightly, better.

We rang the doorbell and waited. And waited. It didn't look like the housekeeper option would pan out. I felt slightly worse. We made our way to the backyard where we'd eaten the previous night. There were some doorways into the house that were still open. Rachel opted to search the master bedroom and Eleanor's office while I got to revisit Vic's study.

The desk was still devoid of paperwork. The gun was still there. I gently lifted it and looked through the various papers below it. There were some old letters that looked to have been saved. I glanced through some; they were mostly from the kids when they were younger and away from home. Who knew that Vic was such a sentimentalist? I guess all those old pictures on the walls ought to have tipped me off.

I looked through the drawers, saw the usual bills and letters from the bank, and realized I wasn't going to find anything worthwhile. I was also anxious to get out of there. I went looking for Rachel. She was in a room that definitely belonged to Eleanor. The walls were painted a pale yellow. The art looked to be of museum quality. There was a bookcase with classics along with James Michener's new bestseller *Space*, Raymond Carver's *What We Talk About When We Talk About Love*, and Umberto Eco's *The Name of the Rose*.

The more I knew about Eleanor the more I didn't understand what she was doing here.

"Let's go," Rachel said, and I was all for that.

We got out of there as fast as we could.

"All I found was some old letters from the kids when they were away at camp and college. I hope you found something better."

"Well, I found my lipstick, but left it there for future expeditions."

"Great. Anything else?"

"Eleanor is a fish out of water. What's she doing here?"

"I've been wondering the same thing."

"She had an affair at some time. In the back of a closet I found some love letters with no envelopes or dates on them. They could have been from before she married Vic, but I don't think so. The guy who wrote them to her, Ryan, gushed a lot about his love for her and said he was sorry she found Santa Barbara so provincial and had no one she could talk with about things that mattered."

"What does that mean, 'Things that mattered'?"

"I was rushing. But from what I could gather, it wasn't just about how there wasn't a decent book club. She was involved in something and Vic got wind of it. And that's what's keeping her here."

She could be right, but equally she might just be one to buy into conspiracies a bit more than most.

CHAPTER TWENTY-SEVEN
Office Party

Getting a good parking space isn't always an easy thing during a big event that attracts locals and tourists. We had to park some blocks away. At UCLA I'd have considered myself lucky to park only this far away. I guess everything is relative. As we walked to Spalding Enterprises, I noticed the confetti and eggshells on the street. Merriment was in the air.

By the time we reached the building, the parade was still going strong. I don't know if Vic and his cronies had already passed this way, but once I'd stood on the street and seen a few groups of people riding horses and a couple of stagecoaches and wagons, I was ready to call it quits. We went up to the offices.

We came out of the elevator on the top floor and into a full-scale party. Rock music blared, confetti was everywhere, and there were people dancing, drinking, eating, talking. Some were clustered by the windows, watching and not watching the festivities below. I hadn't noticed it before but Spalding Enterprises shared the floor with KTYD, the local FM radio station, and they were blasting their live feed for all to hear. I had a hunch that things would not have been quite so festive if Spalding had had the floor to itself.

Rachel and I had devised a sketchy plan. I wasn't sure it would work but we figured we'd give it a try, experienced sleuths that we were. We knew where John's office was; perhaps we could do some snooping when the moment looked ripe.

We grabbed some margaritas and mingled. We went to one of the open windows and looked left down the main street. Palm trees and red-tile rooftops gave way to the harbor and the ocean beyond. It was a picturesque city. To the right, the street continued on into the hills and mountains, creating a high and powerful boundary.

In front of another set of windows, John and Elizabeth were half-watching the proceedings on the street and talking with Brendon, and John's wife, whose name I'd forgotten but whom I was now calling the Playmate. Eleanor was nowhere to be seen. Vic, I assumed, was still parading. Unless Eleanor was hanging out in John's office, this seemed as good a time as any to make our move.

The hallway leading to John's office was empty. A group of people were hanging out in one of the offices that we passed, but the party was primarily located on the other side of the building. We flipped a coin and Rachel lost. I stood guard a few yards down the hall from John's office but close enough that if I talked she'd hear me. She went in and did her thing.

My thing was to look like I had some purpose other than being a warning system. I do enjoy the timelessness of black-and-white photographs so I stepped closer to one and tried to look like I was intently engaged in it. Funny thing is, I was. It was a picture of the Visitadores riding in the parade. Vic was front and center. It was hard to discern the faces of the riders farther back in the pack, but one of them looked a lot like Cliff. I couldn't be sure, but I could be curious.

I looked at some of the other pictures to see if I could find Cliff, but couldn't. I was pretty focused on them when John came up beside me. So much for my lookout skills.

"Hey, Dave. What you looking at?"

"Hi, John," I said, too loudly. "I'm checking out the photos of the Visitadores at the parade. How come you're up here and not down there on the street? Aren't you a Visitadore as well?"

"It's a long story. But, no, I'm not."

"I was going to say that's too bad, but maybe it isn't. Is it too bad?"

"It was at the time, but I'm over it."

"All right. Sorry. But I guess it turned out okay. You get to be up here and party. It must be kind of cool sharing the floor with a rock station."

"Not really. We want to rent the whole floor. Heck, we want to buy the building, but all we've been able to do is rent these offices. One of these days we'll buy it. Fanciest building in town."

"Well, they are great offices. I have to admit, though, I found the courthouse pretty commanding."

"Of course. And the mission. Let's not forget the mission. They're iconic buildings. But this office building is the jewel of the business community."

"Well, good luck getting to buy it someday. In the meantime, let me ask you a question," I said, raising my voice again. "Take a look at this picture. Can you see in the third row there? That looks like Rachel's stepfather. Was he, is he, a Visitadore?"

"That's a long story too and best saved for another time."

While he was taking a close look, Rachel smartly came up beside him. I don't think he saw her coming out of his office, but I wasn't sure.

"Rachel," I said. "Look, there's a picture of your dad. John tells me there's a bit of a story connected with it. Maybe sometime we can get him to tell it to us."

"I'd like to hear it."

"Maybe someday Cliff and I will tell you."

Rachel and I tried to get into Fiesta mood, but I had other things on my mind. I wanted to know if she'd found anything in John's office. And now, more than ever, I wanted to talk with Cliff. Instead we got Eleanor. She was on the radio-station section of the floor, walking aimlessly. We sidled up to her.

"Good afternoon, Eleanor," I said. "Would it be all right if we ambled along with you?"

"Certainly."

"Thank you. Are you not a big Fiesta fan?"

"I like the dancers."

"Where do they dance?" Rachel asked.

"Every night in the sunken gardens at the courthouse. You should come. You might like it."

"I imagine if you like it, we'd like it," I said, kissing a little ass.

"They have all manner of different folk dances and troupes. People bring blankets and put them on the lawn and have picnics. That's what I like about Fiesta."

"You don't really seem like the crack-an-egg-over-your-head type," I said.

"It's fun. People like it."

"Can I ask you a question?" I said, preparing to skip the pleasantries.

"Yes?" said Eleanor

"Certainly, you don't need to tell us, but we're curious. What is it about your life that keeps you living it in the way that you do?"

"Excuse me?"

"Pardon me, but you don't seem all that happy. You're a smart woman and appear very capable, so I assume you're here by choice. And yet that doesn't add up."

"You're a very rude man. You ought to have better manners than to say something like that to anyone."

"You're right. I didn't express that well. There was no empathy or consideration and I apologize for that. It's just that I get curious about why people do the things they do. It really isn't any of my business why you make the choices you make, so I'm sorry. I ought to have kept my curiosity to myself."

"Please continue. I like hearing you scold yourself instead of me."

"I didn't mean to scold you. Maybe me. But not you. I guess I want to help you but I realize you didn't ask for that."

"That's a little better, but still insulting."

"Right again. I ought to know better that once I screw up its wise to shut up."

"Now you are correct."

"So before I shut up, let me just say this. Is there a reason you stay that you can't tell us? Not won't or don't want to, but something that you feel you must keep secret. How about answering that and then I'll shut up?"

She didn't say anything. But she didn't move away.

"Okay," I said. "One more thing. Rachel, how about you help me out here?"

"I don't know if I can, but let me try. Eleanor, how are you?"

"I've been better."

"I would think so. Anything you want to tell me about as a possible soon-to-be family member?"

"I welcome your being part of the family. It's not the best family, but it's a family. It has its secrets as all families do. Some are worse than others, but we keep them in the family. We don't talk about these matters to each other, and especially not to newcomers."

"Totally understandable. What David wanted to say to you is that if ever you'd like to talk about any of those private matters he'd be happy to listen and see if he could help."

"That's very considerate of him, and you, but I don't need it."

"Well done, Sherlock," Rachel said, when Eleanor had left.

"I pushed that one a bit too much. Thanks for bailing me out."

"I can see there's a need for that."

"I hope not a big need, but it's comforting to know you're there if I need you."

"When possible."

"Exactly. Thanks. What do you say we try to find Elizabeth, Brendon, or the Playmate?"

"You mean Kimberly?"

"You see her your way, I'll see her mine. Let's go see what we can stir up."

"Maybe this time you'll let me lead."

"Okay. Speaking of which, did you find anything of interest in John's office?"

"No, I didn't. Well, except he doesn't do much of anything in there. There was hardly any work- or play-related stuff. Although he has an impressively stocked bar."

"There's something to be said for that. But it's weird the office looks so unused. You did say that Vic doesn't hold John's business acumen in the highest order so maybe Vic still takes care of everything and John enjoys the view."

"Or maybe he has a work office and a show office."

"That could be, but why would he need that? I'm guessing he doesn't do much all day aside from drink and kick back."

"It's a job. Not sure I'd want that job, but it does have its benefits."

CHAPTER TWENTY-EIGHT
Office Party Too

ELIZABETH AND BRENDON were standing by a window, silently looking out at the street that was now empty of horses.

"Hi," Rachel said. "Can we join you?"

"Please," replied Brendon.

"It looks like the parade is over," I observed wisely.

"Thankfully," said Brendon. "To be honest, it's not really anybody's thing except Vic's. We're all rather a disappointment to him."

"Really?" I said before I remembered that the ball was supposed to be in Rachel's court. At least I hadn't slammed it yet.

"Maybe Margot likes it some, and John used to, but these days it's mostly just Vic's thing and we're here for moral and alcoholic support."

"That's very family of you," said Rachel.

I wasn't sure whether to log that on the kiss-ass or the needling side of things.

"Like Sister Sledge says, 'We are family…'"

"Can I ask you a question?" Rachel said.

I couldn't help but notice her phrasing. *She picked that up from me*, I said to myself with a small measure of pride. As a teacher/

therapist, I like to pass along things. Heck, we all like it when someone adopts something we do. Unless it's one of our lesser qualities.

"Sure," Brendon said, doing the talking.

"As a family member-to-be, I was wondering if there's anything you think I ought to know."

"You mean like, for Christmas Eleanor only likes clothes from Paris or New York and John is a large size?" Brendon said.

"That's very helpful, and I suppose all that kind of information is something I'll eventually want and need to know. But I was thinking of something else. I don't know how to say this, but it seems people are estranged from one another. Is there something going on that I ought to know about?"

Brendon looked at Elizabeth. I knew he knew enough to keep his mouth shut. He knew I knew that too.

Elizabeth was mostly looking out onto the street when she spoke. "You're very observant. We've never been the most touchy-feely of families, but lately we've been under a fair amount of strain."

"I'm sorry to hear that. That can't feel good," Rachel said.

I talk about being empathetic, but she was walking it.

"Thank you" is what it got her. Which is better than the "You're rude" that I got.

I could see it, Brendon could see it, and Rachel could see it. That was the end of the discussion.

CHAPTER TWENTY-NINE
Getting It On

We were learning more but it didn't feel like we were getting anywhere. Affirming and frustrating all at once. Rachel and I agreed we'd found out all we were going to find out and left the party. As we returned to her car, I could hear music and smell food.

"Want to go check out the Mercado?" I asked.

"I thought you'd never ask."

"You thought I'd just say 'Let's go get it on' without taking you to dinner first?"

"The thought had crossed my mind. But, to be truthful, I don't think you really want to get it on with me, and I'm mostly lukewarm on you too."

"I do have moments when I consider getting it on. But mostly I enjoy being with you and don't really want to mess that up."

"That's good. I know you like to finish your meal before you sit down, and perhaps it's better to get to the bottom line before heading for first base. So yes, it's unlikely we'll ever get it on. It's more likely we'll each have moments, but those moments won't overlap."

"Well, maybe once or twice."

"Maybe, but not this time."

"In that case, I like the looping-in-the-baseball reference so that's points for you. Now we can go to the Mercado and if I get a good portion of the taco on my shirt it won't blow my chances."

"Sounds perfect to me."

We were in agreement about not taking things to another level. At least for now. There was no overt pressure to have any connection other than the one we were forging. If it was good enough for her it worked for me.

Two rows of booths faced each other, and there was enough space between for people to sit, eat and look at the stage, where a Flamenco guitarist was playing. People danced in front of the band, and local stores and organizations were selling a range of Mexican foods.

I happily got sauce on my shirt and in an exuberant moment said, "Since we're not going to go make out, what do you say we try to find where Ellen lived and ransack her place?"

"Why sit here and enjoy the moment when we can put ourselves in harm's way?"

CHAPTER THIRTY

Summerland

SMALL-TOWN LIVING APPEALED to me. Ellen Withers' name and address was listed in the phone book. I had no idea why I could remember her name but not the Playmate's. I'm not good with names, but maybe having seen hers in the paper had helped.

We went back to her car and drove south a few miles to a place called Summerland. You won't find a lot of towns in the Midwest with that name. To me it said: This would be a good place to spend the summer all year round. Then again, maybe Bob Summer bought the land and named it after himself.

Summerland might have been a summer land before the freeway decided to bore right through it. Sort of took the charm out of the place. Just ask the Miramar. Still, anyone in the small houses on the hillside could glance over the freeway at the ocean extending to the horizon. The view was marred only by the occasional oil well.

We found her house. So had others. Perhaps they were having a memorial service or were just congregating in her home to comfort her family. Whatever the occasion, it didn't seem like the optimal time to sneak in.

We circled the street once, went back toward the freeway, and pulled into a gas station. Rachel asked the attendant to fill the tank with Premium. At $1.20, it was more expensive than in LA, though most of the gas stations in LA no longer had attendants. The hike in price following the oil crisis a few years earlier had made people less willing to pay for the extra service.

While the guy was cleaning the window I said, "I bet a lot of people were upset when they decided to run the freeway so close to the ocean and right through town."

"You bet. It messed with real-estate values, though it made it more affordable."

"I guess that's the silver lining."

"Well, that and the fact that they always stick it to you in the end."

"Excuse me," said Rachel.

"Sorry. Didn't mean to be offensive. It's just that the guy who founded Summerland in the 1880s was a big-time spiritualist and he built this town for his supporters. The spiritualist church was the center of the city. It had a séance room and everything. Now they'd call it a historical site, but what do they do in the 1950s? They destroy his church to put in the freeway. They called it progress. Of course, now no one cares. But it's history. You can look it up."

CHAPTER THIRTY-ONE

I Dunno, What Do You Want To Do?

July 31, 1983

ANOTHER DAY, ANOTHER early-morning workshop. I was nickel-and-diming my way to thirty-six hours. After this one, I'd have eight to go. I was sitting in a workshop called "I–Thou–We." Another example of a session that could have been expressed in a few sentences, but then how would we get enough continuing-ed credits?

The facilitator wrote "I–Thou–We" on the board and said, "I want to present this model to you this morning, and hope you find it of interest. What do you want?"

A few game people threw out some answers to which he replied, "Let me see if I understand what you want," and basically repeated what they'd said. Then he summed it up by saying, "I want this. You want that. What do we want to do?" That was the model in a nutshell.

It seemed simple enough. What do I feel? What do you feel? What do I think? What do you think? What do I want? What do you want? What are we going to do?

The facilitator had us form into two lines facing each other. He asked us to share our I-Thou-We for five minutes with the person opposite, and then switch and keep switching until we had spoken to everyone.

After doing the I–Thou–We a few times I ended up with Scarface.

"Hi," I said.

He didn't speak.

"I have to tell you, I'm feeling nervous talking with you. I've seen you a few times and I can't help but think you've been keeping an eye on me."

He remained silent. My discomfort kept me talking.

"I don't know what you want. But I want to know if you're following me, and if so, why."

He stared at me. He was much better at it than I was, and I averted my eyes. Usually I'm a pretty good reader of expressions, but his face didn't disclose much. I looked again, this time at the scar, and followed its line from the corner of his eye down to his mouth.

"What are you looking at?" he said.

"I was looking at your scar. It's hard to miss." I looked him in the eye, but found no comfort there so checked over his shoulder at the clock on the wall, hoping our time was almost over.

"I don't like it when people look at my scar."

"I'm sure. And if that's what you want—me to not look at it—I can endeavor to do that. But what about my question to you? Have you been following me, and if so, why?"

"I don't know what you're talking about."

"You're not the only one. So are you a shrink? What are you doing at the conference?"

"The same thing you are."

That was that. I'd learned nothing new. Other than he didn't like people looking at his scar and was at the conference for the same reasons as me. Did that mean he was getting continuing-ed credits or breaking laws, stepping on toes and trying to put the pieces together?

I didn't have any answers so after the workshop I went back to the hospital, hoping to gain some insight there.

When you get used to the status quo you expect things to be status quo. And they mostly were. Dr. Novatt was wearing a white smock. Michael and Alan showed up a little after Rachel and me. Cliff was still in his coma. Rachel went in to take a look, came back, and gave a bit of shudder.

We stayed a little while, exchanged pleasantries, and decided to absorb some Fiesta culture. We arranged to meet that evening at the Old Spanish Days Fiesta Stock Horse Show & Rodeo at the Earl Warren Showgrounds.

Michael and Alan returned to the conference. I turned to Rachel. "So waddaya want to do?"

"I dunno. What do you want to do?"

"I dunno. But this reminds me of when I used to go cruising with a friend and we'd talk about where we wanted to go. He'd always say, 'I dunno. What do you want?' Then I'd basically say the same thing. We'd do that for a while, and then he'd say, 'I don't care. You choose.' I'd suggest something and he'd say no. This from the guy who'd told me to choose. Eventually I learned to leave the suggestions to him. He was more likely to say yes to his own idea."

"Yeah. I know that dance. So waddaya want to do?"

"I dunno. How about we go check out Ellen's house?"

"I dunno. Maybe."

"Okay, how about we try to find out more about Brendon and the Playmate?"

"I dunno. Maybe."

"Okay. How about you make a suggestion?"

"I dunno… Just messing with you. Let's go see what we can find at Ellen's house."

CHAPTER THIRTY-TWO

House Hunting

WE STOPPED IN Summerland to get a hamburger at what looked like your typical beat-up ocean shack. The burger and fries fit the space. I filled Rachel in on my conversation with Michael and his telling me that something was happening, but that he didn't feel comfortable telling me what. He wanted to wait and have Cliff tell us. That didn't make her any happier.

By the time we got back to Ellen Withers' place, it was early afternoon and things were suburban slow. We drove around the block a few times to check things out. Unfortunately—and, I suppose, fortunately—the house looked empty and the streets were mostly deserted.

Still, I wasn't eager to break in.

"Remind me," I said. "What are we hoping to find here?"

"You're the one who suggested it. You were talking about reframing things—how maybe my dad wasn't that much in the picture, and that Ellen was killed because of her involvement in something fishy that somehow or other connects to him."

"That's what I was thinking. But what do you think? Maybe we should talk about it some more."

"Go on in."

"Yeah, that's what we think. Since I was the lookout before I'm guessing you're going to opt for a repeat. But I'm happy to trade."

"Thanks for the offer. You can be the insider this time. I'll keep a watch and honk the horn if you need to skedaddle."

"Thanks. Just make sure you honk loud as I've had some issues with that before."

"Well, I can't go blasting away. I'll do a discreet beep as though I inadvertently hit the horn."

"Okay, but if you don't see me hauling ass down the street before anyone comes in the house, throw in a couple more."

"Will do. Anything else?"

"Aside from the files, what am I looking for and where would you look?"

"Could be anything. It's a small house so there may be a desk or table where she writes checks and takes care of household matters. Or somethings hidden in a closet or…"

"All right. If for some reason I'm spending time this afternoon in the jailhouse, will you try to arrange bail without telling my parents? This isn't what they were hoping for me."

"Quit stalling. It'll be fine. If you have to get out quick, go out the back. Use the alley behind the house. Go there and I'll pick you up."

"I just thought of something. I have no gloves. I have no burglary gear. Maybe we ought to stop by a hardware store first?"

"Put your shirt over your hand and smash a window. And use your shirt if you have to touch something."

"I know there's really no difference in a judge's mind between breaking a window and just lifting it up, but I'd like to think they'd be a bit more lenient if I didn't destroy any property."

"I'm sure they'd commend you for your thoughtfulness. Now quit dragging your feet and get going."

I tried to look like I knew what I was doing. In California, we've come to understand that how you look is very important. I strode casually up to the house and knocked, hoping and not hoping that the door would be opened. When it was obvious no one was coming, I meandered to the back, trying to appear natural, like I was just checking to make sure that someone wasn't gardening in the backyard. I opened a side gate and proceeded to trespass.

This looked like the kind of neighborhood where people felt comfortable leaving their doors open because a goodly number of residents were home and looking out their windows for troublemakers like me. Unfortunately, the back door was locked. Fortunately, the backyard had a good-sized fence that obscured my presence.

I found a window that didn't need to be broken, and climbed in. Not that climbing through a window four feet off the ground was a skill I needed to master, but if there were ever a burglar's Olympics, this would be an event where I could enter.

As soon as I was inside, I felt horrible. There were pictures of Ellen, candles and cards, and food stacked up everywhere. Now I really felt like I was intruding into someone's private life. Not that I don't do that for a living, but it usually comes with approval and assurances. Now, I was in the home of someone who lived there no more, whose family was in the throes of mourning her death.

In my heart, I wanted to do a cursory job and just get out. I found the desk and gave it a good going-over. I didn't see anything of note, though it's not that easy sorting through things when your shirt's off and you're using the sleeves as gloves. Then I found the bank book and the ten-thousand-dollar deposit from the previous week.

That was enough to justify my getting out of there ASAP.

Back in the car and heading for Santa Barbara I shared the news.

"We don't want to jump to any conclusions. It could have been an inheritance, a lucky weekend in Las Vegas or any number of things."

"Or it could have been a payoff for deeds done," Rachel said.

"Let's just say someone did pay her off to thank her or silence her. Why kill her?"

"We don't know that the person who paid her is the person who killed her. And while we're throwing out options, maybe someone paid her because she was blackmailing them."

"Oh, that's good. Now we have a veritable cornucopia of conspiracy theories. She knew something and told someone that if they didn't pay her she'd out them. Was there something in those files worth ten thousand? Is that what you're thinking?"

"I don't know what I'm thinking," she paused. "Well, I know one thing. That's dirty money. It came to her because she was in cahoots with someone or she was pressuring someone. Could be that the person who paid her killed her, or someone else did. We don't know. But I'm going to rule out Vegas and grandma dying."

"Why not? It adds to the plot, gives us 423 fewer options to consider while at the same time opening up another line of inquiry."

"And what's a mystery without misdirection?"

"Boring."

"Exactly," she said with a smile. "So waddaya want to do?"

"I don't know what do you want to do?" I joked. "What do you say we follow the money. Isn't that what they do in mysteries?"

"Yeah, but how do you know where it went or came from?"

"We could ask the guy in the clerk's office if Ellen had any new expenditures, but I'm guessing that how it got to her is more important than where it went after she got it. So how do we find out where that money came from?"

"If we knew that," she said knowingly, "we'd have way more skills than we do."

"Right. What do you say we let go of following the money for now and instead try to figure out what the 'it' was she was getting paid off for? What's the thing that got signed, sealed and delivered to that office that's causing all this commotion?"

"Let's do it. How?"

"I was hoping you could answer that."

CHAPTER THIRTY-THREE
Ice Cream

When in doubt, eat. That must be written somewhere other than my psyche. It certainly seems to be part of our collective unconscious. It seemed an appropriate way to celebrate breaking the law, not getting caught, and finding a potential clue. Possibly the police were working this angle as well—who knew? I wanted Lt. Flores to know about our suspicions, but not how'd we come to have them.

We dropped by the police station but Flores wasn't there. I started to write him a note:

Sorry, we missed you. Just wanted you to know that regarding the death of Ellen Withers we couldn't help but wonder if she...

I tore it up and we left. If we couldn't tell him why we thought she stepped over a line there was no reason for him to suspect her. He'd just consider us a nuisance. Or worse. Not that people didn't feel that way about me anyway, but I saw no sense in going out of my way to prove it. We could come back when we had something of value that didn't involve our breaking the law.

Instead, we found a local ice-cream place that made their own. Two surprises awaited us at McConnell's. First, we weren't the only ones who needed an ice-cream break. The Playmate was there.

Seeing her sitting by herself, eating her cone, made me like her a little more. I didn't know whether she'd spend the next two hours working off the fat or if this was just a treat she'd given herself for enduring whatever it was she needed to endure in this life.

"Hi," I said. "Is it okay if we join you?"

"Sure."

"Great. Any recommendations?"

"I like the vanilla."

I was about to say *Of course you do* but thought better of it. Besides, I like vanilla. Not as much as chocolate mint or coffee, but it's right up there. Rachel opted for the strawberry and I went with a double cone of chocolate mint and coffee. We joined the Playmate.

"How are you guys doing?" she asked.

"As good as can be, given the circumstances," Rachel replied. "I'm worried about my dad. He's still in a coma, and while the doctor tells us that isn't necessarily a bad sign, it doesn't feel like a good one."

"I'm so sorry about that. I'm sure it must be stressful."

"Yes, but there isn't anything I can do about it aside from worry so I'm trying not to focus on it. How about you? How are you doing? You enjoying Fiesta?"

"It's not really my thing. John used to like it, but now even he doesn't care. We'd get out of town as many locals do, but it means so much to Vic that John feels we need to stay."

"I can understand how a couple of these would be enough if you're a local," I said.

"I'll say."

"How come John soured on Fiesta? I thought he'd be right out there in the parade with the rest of the Visitadores."

"It's a sore subject."

"Oh, sorry. Was he ever a Visitadore or was that just not something he was into?"

"He was into it big time. Once."

"Did something happen?" I asked.

"We're not supposed to talk about it."

"Okay, but isn't Rachel's dad also a Visitadore?"

"I don't really know your dad, but I did hear about him and John."

"Since I may not get to hear from him, can you tell me what happened?" Rachel asked, her voice full-on sugary.

"I suppose that would be all right."

"Thank you. It would mean a lot to me."

"I don't really know much about it. And, as I said, we don't talk about it."

"I understand."

"But, evidently, at this year's outing things got out of hand. It's kind of hard to understand why that was a problem because from what I've heard, things always get out of hand. That's partly why they all join up."

"Did John and my dad get kicked out?"

"That's not the word they'd use. They were 'encouraged' to resign. It was a big deal. Vic wanted John to stay and weather the criticism. But there was a lot of pressure. Oh well."

"Do you know what they did that caused the uproar?"

"I don't know the details. It wasn't so much that they were out of line, more that there was some incident and they tried to interfere but got on the wrong side of things. All I know is, John got disillusioned and that was the end of that."

"Are John and your dad friends?" I said to Rachel after the Playmate had left.

"I wouldn't think so, but it surprises me that Dad was a Visitadore. They seem like an old-money good-old-boys club."

"Yeah. I get that impression as well. But maybe he joined for business reasons. Although not a lot of those guys would be lining up to get into therapy."

"They ought to be."

"That's another matter. It's possible your dad and John had some business dealings."

"Why don't we ask him?"

"Given what the Playmate said, he won't be at the rodeo, unless that's another one of those family things where attendance is expected."

CHAPTER THIRTY-FOUR

Old Spanish Days Fiesta Stock Horse Show & Rodeo

We were due to meet Michael and Alan at the Earl Warren Showgrounds. Built for equestrian events in the 1950s, the arena held a couple of thousand people and enough uncomfortable seats to ensure you'd leave after the show. The place was three-quarters full. Outside of the arena were some food booths.

We couldn't see Michael or Alan, though we'd gotten used to arriving before them. What we did see was Elizabeth and Brendon having a heated discussion. We tried to get close enough to overhear but they spotted us. They looked a little embarrassed but waved us over.

"We were just squabbling," Brendon said.

Normalizing being one of the things that therapists do, I said, "Couples do."

"Every year we have the same argument. We've taken to calling it our rodeo ruckus."

"You'll be pleased to know it's normal for couples to have perpetual fights, something they argue about over and over. I guess this is yours."

"It's one of them," he said.

His openness ran against the family grain; I needed to get him alone and see what secrets I could persuade him to unload. I hadn't been overly successful the last time we spoke; he clearly knew how far he could pull the leash. Still, if at first you don't succeed…

"Will the family be in attendance tonight?" Rachel asked.

"Fiesta is a family love fest," Brendon said.

"Seems that way. So I have a question. I know Vic is a Visitadore. What do you have to do to become one? Is it open to anyone or do you have to be invited in, or what?"

"It's invitation only," Elizabeth said. "They have about five hundred members. Once you're invited you have to ride with them a few years before they grant full membership."

Thanks Joe Friday. Always good to get the facts and nothing but the facts. She wasn't a big one on the extras.

"They have a fair number of guests if you ever want to go, Dave," Brendon told me. "They've yet to see the light and include women, but I'm told they had Walt Disney here one year."

"He actually was a member," said Elizabeth. "Along with Reagan."

"So you don't have to be local?"

"No, but it helps."

"Oh," I said spotting Michael and Alan. "Here come some friends of Rachel's dad. Let us introduce you."

Soon after introductions were made, John came over. Another round of introductions ensued before John said he needed a private word with Elizabeth and Brendon. They excused themselves but invited us to sit with them in their reserved seats. Evidently, Spalding Enterprises bought a lot of seats and usually had extras. If I'd have been going to do business with Vic, perhaps I too would've developed an interest. Otherwise I couldn't see a lot of people being bothered. But I live a sheltered life.

Michael and Alan had something they wanted to talk to us

about privately. We found our own quiet spot, of which there were quite a few.

"We've been talking about Cliff," Michael said. "There are some things you ought to know about your dad, Rachel. We'd prefer him to tell you, and when, or if, he recovers, he's going to want to talk to you for sure."

"Thank you. I'm very interested in knowing more. I want to hear what you have to say, and I've got a lot of questions."

"There are some things we don't feel comfortable telling you, but given the circumstances, it's only fair that we share them. We know Cliff intended to tell you so it's not like we're completely out of order."

"I understand."

"There are two things we want you to know now. One of them has to do with the lie I told you. It's been bothering me, but I don't feel I can be forthcoming about that just yet. I'm going to continue to withhold that information, but acknowledge that my holding back isn't okay."

"That feels better. While I'd like to know, I'll trust your judgment."

"Thanks. Tomorrow Alan and I want to take you somewhere and show you something."

"Very well. Want to give me a hint now or is this a surprise?"

"A surprise. It's something your dad's working on. What do you say you meet us in the Miramar lobby tomorrow right after the early-morning workshops?. We can show you before we go to the hospital."

Not many animals at a rodeo are happy to be there. Like in circuses, they're there for our entertainment. Which I guess is better than being there for our dinner. That comes later in their lives. While I can appreciate the athleticism of the competitors and the perpetuation of skills and culture, I'd prefer it if the animals were out on the range.

I was sitting in the section reserved for Vic et al. There was a lot of beer and hooting in play—some of the family's ranch hands and livestock were in the show. I knew it was a small town when the announcer said that the winners of the team roping competition included Dr. Gary Novatt. Who knew that the ER doctor was a cowboy?

I sidled up to Brendon. "Big rodeo fan?"

"The biggest. You?"

"Right there with you."

"How you doing, brother?"

"I'm good, but if you could help me out I'd feel even better."

"Glad to give you a hand," he offered. "Does it have to do with which kid to bet on in the seven-and-under mutton-busting competition?"

"Yeah. That's a tough one. I like number three. He looks like a winner to me."

"Good choice. I have my eye on number five. He'll be moving up to calf-riding next year."

"You obviously have a keen eye and some valuable experience in these matters, but I'm going to be rooting for number three regardless."

"As well you should."

"Thank you. Even though I could profit from some rodeo insider tips, that's not the help I need right now. Rachel's dad is still in a coma and that's not necessarily a bad sign, though I know even less about that than I do about mutton-busting."

"I'm so sorry. I'm sure the strain and worry are hard. I have some valium, if that's what you want."

"No, but that's good to know. I want to understand why John and Cliff were booted out of the Visitadores. And I have a follow-up question once we're done with that."

"You know I'm not supposed to talk out of school."

"I know. You know I know. And, come on, we know it'll be fine if you tell me. I'm not going to out you. I just want to find out why Cliff was beat up and whether it relates to what happened when this Visitadore incident occurred. By the way, when did it happen? And why? Come on, tell me."

"Oh, look. Your kid has the early lead. He was riding that sheep a good five seconds."

"Yeah, I thought he looked pretty solid."

"He's ahead, but my guy is going to go the whole six seconds."

"In the meantime, want to help me out?"

"My friend, look around you. Does this look like the kind of place I'd even begin to have a discussion like that?"

"I can see that. Where would be suitable?"

He jumped up. Yelled, "Go, go, go!" and gave out a big woo-woo-woo. Then he turned to me and said, "My house, two o'clock. I'm in the phone book. Brendon McDaniels."

That was the highlight of the evening. Well, that, my kid getting a ribbon for second place, and the churros.

I stopped the car in front of Rachel's hotel. I turned toward her, and she gave me a look that said let's not make this awkward. I nodded. She said she'd meet me, Michael and Alan in the Miramar lobby at ten. We said goodnight.

CHAPTER THIRTY-FIVE
Target on the Back

August 1, 1983

I HAD TWENTY-EIGHT credits and was about to get another three. I really needed a workshop in how to turn thirty-one into thirty-six. While there was some light at the end of the tunnel, I'd abandoned my carefully planned out schedule and was now hoping I could squeeze in the rest.

As luck would have it, the morning workshop was about procrastination. I don't consider myself much of a procrastinator because I've learned that even if I wait till the last minute, the task doesn't get any easier. I prefer to get things over with as soon as possible.

I take that back—maybe I do procrastinate about some things. Like with the continuing-ed credits. Maybe I talk the talk but don't walk it so well. Given the choice, I'd rather do the things I want to do than the things I don't. Until I have to. Or it's too late. So, yeah, I procrastinate.

The facilitator had us share stories of times we'd procrastinated, and when it had worked out and when it hadn't. There were some not-so-well stories that I hoped would never happen to me, but there were some really positive accounts that explained, in part, why we all were in the room. Procrastinating, like most everything, has its pros and cons.

One thing I couldn't procrastinate about was managing the rising anxiety that I felt when Scarface, true to fashion, arrived late. He opened the door, looked around, saw me, and sat nearby.

Given his tardiness, I could understand his interest in learning more about procrastination. He did seem quite intent on the material when I stole side glances at him.

I wondered whether my proclivity for intrigue was causing me to create mystery where it didn't exist. As long as he was facing away from me, it was easier to hold that thought.

Was my focus on Scarface and what had happened to Cliff an example of how I was procrastinating about attending to my own life? I hadn't really thought any more about what dream I wanted to come true. And as long as there was no dream, there was no dream that would come true.

Truthfully, I wasn't totally sure if what I was doing with my life was what I wanted to be doing. Yet I'd been willing to procrastinate and wait for my midlife crisis to sort it out.

In the meantime, I knew that I wanted to be the hero and solve the mystery. But all I had was the essence of intrigue. No real suspects. No real motive. No evidence. I could be making a proverbial mountain out of a molehill and freaking out about Scarface when all he wanted to do was learn how to be on time.

Honestly, trying to find out what had happened to Cliff, and Ellen Withers, made me feel good. The conference was continuing, Fiesta was in full force, cascarónes remnants were everywhere, and I needed to get the rest of my continuing-ed credits.

I was in the lobby, waiting. Rachel showed up first. Her jeans were stylishly faded, and her blouse muted, but the rest looked pretty spry considering the wear and tear of the week.

"Good to see you," I said. "How you doing?"

"I'm okay. You?"

"I'm doing all right. Curious about how things will evolve. I wish I had more of a plan. I seem to be going from one thing to another without any guidance system."

"I hear you. It's not like we're bloodhounds following a scent."

"Yeah. But we are. We just don't have their nose for it. We get a supposed lead, follow it until we can't get any further, then wait for the next lead to come along and follow that till it dead-ends."

"What are you saying?"

"Maybe we could do something proactive. We keep reacting to the circumstantial things we learn, and don't get very far. We have possibilities on top of possibilities, but at this point everything is possible and that's not going to get the job done."

"So?"

"So it's time to stop procrastinating. Time to focus on making dreams come true."

"I have no idea what you're talking about."

"Neither do I really. And I don't like saying this, because I know what it means, but we have to get the responsible people to show their hand."

"And how do we do that?"

"That's the thing I don't want to think about. I haven't really thought about it until this moment and I wish I wasn't."

"Come on. Let's hear it."

"We have to let people know we're about to figure out what happened."

"Are we?"

"I'm not. Are you?"

"Not really. So we just pretend we know more than we do?"

"I've been doing that for years so that won't be a problem on my end. How about you?"

"I'm good. So who are we telling?"

"We don't know who to tell so we tell everyone. But we need to be subtle so people think we don't want them to know. It just slipped out and because they're so smart they caught it."

"Okay. I get the art of deceit and I'm up for it. But why? Why are we doing this and what are you thinking is going to happen?"

"The why is to flush them out. We need to prioritize what we want and go for it."

"Have you been at a workshop this morning?"

"Yeah. Well, maybe I got a little revved up. I wasn't really paying full attention. It was about procrastinating and I've decided I need to be more rah rah and go for things. Make the dream come true. You know, that sort of stuff."

"I still have no idea what you're talking about, but I'm glad you're fired up."

"Me too. But the not-so-good part is that if we flush out someone, they might want to flush us out. And I don't really want to think about that part."

"I can see why you were hesitant to suggest this. I know you like to push ahead and you don't want to be bouncing from one thing to another, but let's take this a step at a time. Let's see what Michael and Alan have got. Then we go to the hospital. And then you go talk with Brendon. I don't really know why I can't come."

"It's a guy thing. He and I have some rapport. He kinda trusts me. Not that he wouldn't or doesn't trust you, but we don't need an extra measure right now. Maybe you can follow up on something and then we'll go eat at the Mercado and watch the dancers."

"That almost sounds like a pleasant evening. Much better than walking about with a target on our backs."

CHAPTER THIRTY-SIX
The Vision

Michael drove for about twenty minutes up into the Santa Ynez mountains. We were four thousand feet above the ocean below. It wasn't a Colorado high, but it provided an excellent overview as the road switched back and forth. Close to the top of the peak, he turned off the pass onto a road called Painted Cave that ran across the crest of the mountain. There were a few structures and homes along the road but this was mostly wide-open space. After about half a mile of weaving alongside the mountain, he turned off. There was a mailbox with the number 3030. There were no buildings. He drove down a dirt road for another fifty yards and parked in a space barely large enough to turn around in. We all got out.

"Take a look," he said, and we did.

As the crow flies we were less than ten miles from the ocean. The view was striking—Santa Barbara and the Channel Islands beyond. There were lots of oak trees, bushes and boulders. Off to the side was what looked like a hot spring. Nothing much else. It was very quiet and peaceful.

After we'd all had some moments to take it all in, I turned to Michael. "And…"

"And this is Cliff's secret."

"This piece of property?"
"That's the start."
"And the finish?"
"Have you ever been to Esalen?"
"Sure. In Big Sur. It's one of my favorite places."
"Cliff wants this to be Esalen South. He wants to build a center for people to come together. You know, a place to integrate mind, body and spirit, to build community and grow together to make the world a better place. Not too kumbaya. Not too serious. But a healing place for all."

"Sounds great. It has the hot spring so that's a good start. And it's hard to beat the view."

"There are lots of trails up here for people to hike to streams and waterfalls. He envisions environmentally gentle buildings so people can stay here, take workshops, swim in the pools and replenish themselves."

"Sounds wonderful," said Rachel. "Was this the secret you wanted him to tell us?"

"It's one. He's been working on this for some time. We thought it was just a dream at first, but it sounds like he's been able to get funding. Some of the paperwork he recorded might have had to do with the 150 acres."

"It's a special place," Alan said.

"Very much so," I said. "I'm sure it costs a bundle and you don't build a center on a therapist's salary. Or maybe I need to raise my rates."

"We're curious about that too. He's been very open about the vision. We've been up here before and he's pointed out where the various buildings and pools would be located. He's obviously put a lot of time and energy into the whole thing. As open as he's been with us, he's been very evasive about the funding. He told us he had big news he wanted to share, and this is what we thought it was about."

"I'm in awe," said Rachel. "I sure hope he can pull it off. It's a great location and Southern California doesn't really have anything like Esalen so I'm sure he'd be able to get enough people to come to make it work. Wow."

Michael ushered us back to the car. "Hopefully, when we get back to the hospital, Cliff will be able to tell you about his vision for this place. And maybe soon he'll bring you up here himself."

"I'm curious about something. You said this was one of the secrets. Are you going to tell us the other? And how come you told us this now?"

"I'm not glad you asked, but I'm willing to answer. This is all I'm going to tell you at the moment. Alan can explain the now bit."

"We thought this was the time."

"Because…"

"Because life is a judgment call."

"That's very profound, but I'm more of a nuts-and-bolts kind of guy. Can you boil that down to something I could get a better grasp on?"

"Yes, he could," said Michael. "But for now, let's just let it be."

Another day. Another update. The wounds were healing nicely. Cliff was still unconscious. Michael and Alan went back to the conference. Rachel went in again, stayed a bit longer and, once again, kept her own counsel. I wasn't sure why she didn't want to talk more about what it was like to see him. After all, we're therapists. We talk about things. But I elected to honor her lead.

"What do you think of your dad's Esalen South idea? Pretty great, huh?"

"Very. I'm impressed and depressed at the same time. I really want him to pull through, but I have to tell you, each day I get closer to fearing I'm going to lose him."

"I hear you. I'm sorry you feel that way. It's harder to stay hopeful with each day that passes. There's also a part of me that's becoming resigned."

"I get it."

"We're just protecting ourselves in case things go south," I said in my therapist voice. "You know the cliché—prepare for the worst and hope for the best."

"I suppose so. Not only do I want to get to know him and spend time with him, but I also want his dream to come true."

"That would be great. I'll sign for my CE credits right now. You can help run the place if you want. That would be cool."

"In the meantime, good luck with Brendon. I'll see you at the Mercado at six. Then it's off to the sunken gardens at the courthouse."

CHAPTER THIRTY-SEVEN
The Beach House

BRENDON WAS RIGHT. His address was in the phone book. They lived in a place called Hope Ranch, which once upon a time was a grazing spot for sheep but was now divvied up in multi-acre lots. The ranch entrance told me right away that I was entering rarified land. I passed under a sizable yet tastefully designed iron gateway to see rolling fields and a constructed lake that almost looked natural. In the distance were homes, most of them considerably above my pay grade.

As soon as I turned in the driveway, I knew I'd have been delighted to move into Elizabeth and Brendon's place. It was a two-story Cape Cod-looking house nuzzled up next to the beach. Off-white cedar panels covered the sides and two sizable chimneys stuck out of a steep roof. Pretty ideal in my book. I could easily see why Brendon had become stuck in his rut.

He was jauntily attired in khaki shorts, a yellow polo shirt and docksiders, and greeted me warmly. The house was full of light and bleached wood that looked older than the house. I was told they'd had the wood shipped from the east coast because they wanted the house to have that Nantucket–Cape Cod feel. I guess it's good to be rich. Certainly different. The furniture looked less comfortable than I'd like, but everything was very tasteful.

Just so I could fully embrace my envy, Brendon took me out onto the porch, where we sat in wicker chairs under an umbrella, looking at the stretch of empty beach and ocean.

"Okay," I said. "You convinced me. Why do anything to risk losing this? I get it."

"I rest my case."

"As I would too. Very hard to beat, but I think I can."

"I'm intrigued. Let's hear it."

"I'm not going to appeal to your conscience, your obligations to society, or anything other than your basic survival instinct."

"That's good of you. My conscience and my obligation to society thank you, but I beg to differ. You say I'm at risk? I don't agree. I'm only at risk if I talk to you."

"That's true. And it's not. You know, in California, appearances count. If it looks like you've gone off-leash, that would be just as bad as if you really had."

"Now you're blackmailing me?"

"No no no. I'm not going to tell anyone about our conversation. So long as I'm out in a sufficient time, this meeting can be strictly between the two of us."

"Exactly. So if you aren't going to out me and I'm not going to out me, why do you think I'm at risk? That bothers me."

"It would bother me too. I don't mean to scare you. I actually want to help make you as safe as anyone can be these days. I want you to live a long and fruitful life in the comfort of your humble home."

"That's very kind of you. I fully intend to do so. Which brings me back to the fact that you haven't convinced me it would be of any value if I were to tell you any more than I already have."

"Let's look at some facts. I know you have way more insider information than I do, but here's what I know. Rachel's dad was beaten up and dumped at the courthouse. And right now, he's possibly more dead than alive. Ellen Withers, the county clerk, was killed.

Not beaten up, just shot. Why? Why was she shot and Rachel's dad beaten? Did it have anything to do with a trail put in place when John and Cliff got booted from the Visitadores? I don't know, but perhaps you do."

"Perhaps. What has that to do with my safety?"

Since I wasn't really it had anything to do with his safety, I decided to ignore the point. "Perhaps what you know is part of a puzzle that, if put together properly, will put someone in a place where they can do you no harm. Perhaps the beating and murder had nothing to do with any of this and I'm just a curious, misguided guy looking for pieces of information."

"I'd say pushing not looking."

"I'm not pushing that hard because you know I'm your best chance. Look, it doesn't take Miss Marple to know something is off with this family. It feels to me like everyone is being deceitful, and for that to happen there must be something to be deceitful about."

"I hate the thought that you're my best chance."

"I know what you mean. But from the looks of things, it needs some nosy outsider to shake things up."

"You are that. But I'm not sure you have the rest of the requisite skills."

"Me neither, but Miss Marple is busy elsewhere at the moment."

"I need you not to tell anyone what I tell you. That includes Rachel."

"Agreed," I said, and tried not to cross my fingers behind my back.

"If the subject ever comes up, you'll deny to your dying breath you heard anything from me."

"Someone would beat me up to my dying breath? Like they did to Cliff?"

"It was just a figure of speech."

"I won't tell anyone. Ever. Unless you tell me I can. How's that?"

"Fair."

"So waddaya got?"

"Not that much. You're right—this family has not always taken the higher path. We've all trespassed in our own ways. But what John and Cliff did was to trespass the other way. A couple of months ago they called out the wrong person for something they'd done on one of their rides. A big stink was made and it was better for everyone if they stepped aside."

"That's the whole story?"

"No, that's the outline. If you want the whole story you'll need to talk to John. I don't know if he'll tell you. It's a big sore spot with him and Vic. They've been estranged ever since, and everyone's had to pick sides and manage their relationships under the table."

"I get that. Can you tell me who it is he rubbed up against?"

"That's something Miss Marple will have to help you find out."

"You sure? It would be helpful if you told me."

"Helpful to some, hurtful for others."

"Thanks for the heads-up. It seems Vic is really big on the cowboy stuff. To not have John follow in the family's footsteps must rankle him."

"It's not cowboy stuff. It's a way of life. A creed. Something bigger even than Vic. For the rest of us, it's a generational thing. We humor him with it and he belittles us. For him, John's a disgrace. A disgrace that will haunt him the rest of his life."

CHAPTER THIRTY-EIGHT
More John

I WAS SURPRISED to discover that the mischief Cliff and John had gotten into was actually the moral high ground. I guess if you were going to create a Spalding Education Center it helped to have a decent moral compass. I wasn't so sure it was advantageous for John, but he did still have a corner office on the top floor of the tallest building in town and a Playmate wife.

I couldn't see how getting kicked out of a club for doing the right thing could have led to Cliff getting beat up a few months later and to Ellen being killed. Maybe there was no connection, but Brendon had been willing to say more than he'd wanted to because he knew something was brewing that could possibly bite him in the butt. Beatings and killings can do that to you.

I had time before meeting Rachel at the Mercado. I went to see if the guy in the corner office had time for me. He did.

"Thanks for taking the time to meet with me, John. I expect things are pretty busy."

"Not this week. This week's about trying to get over the hangover soon enough to get to the office. Then making sure you're not too wasted to drive home. It's rough, but someone has to do it," he said as he went over to the counter and poured us a couple of shots of Don Julio tequila.

"Viva la Fiesta!"

"Viva," I said and downed my shot.

That shifted things.

"John, would you like some small talk for a bit before I get into why I came here, or should I just go for the gusto?"

"Go for it."

"Is there any update on Margot? Have you been able to reach her?"

"Nothing. I just talked to Françoise again and she hasn't heard anything."

"I gather that's not unusual."

"No, it's not. Margot's been known to be out of touch for weeks at a time. But hopefully we'll hear from her soon. I'm sure she'll want to be here when she finds out what happened to Cliff."

"Speaking of which, I'm trying to help Rachel work out what happened to her dad. We can't figure out why anyone would beat him up so badly."

He noticed me glancing at his knuckles and I noticed him smirk at me.

"It truly is a horrible thing. I gather he's still in a coma."

"Same prognosis today as yesterday, although him being in that state wears on you."

"I'm sure. But that's not why you came here."

"Right. I came to talk to you about your relationship with Cliff. I gather you were both in the Visitadores."

"That's not exactly true. I was a member. He was a guest for a couple of years. You have to go through a probationary period before you get voted in."

"And he never did become a member. And you ceased to be one. Want to tell me about that?"

"Values change. Life moves along. What seems important one day is less so the next."

"I hear you. And yet I also hear you two didn't exactly leave on your own terms."

"That's not true either. We left entirely on our terms."

"Was that because you and the group didn't see eye to eye?"

"You could say that. Or you could say that whatever faults Cliff and I have we couldn't stand by idly and let a travesty be committed."

"That's a good fault not to have. You obviously have integrity. That's not so easy to find these days."

"Thank you."

"The way I see the world, anyone who wants to get ahead needs to look the other way at some point. You need to forgive and forget something that's on the darker side of things. That wasn't your time."

"That's understanding of you. I get that we all overlook things and say this when the truth is that, but sometimes you need to stand up for something you think is right."

"That's admirable of you. Really. I'm not just kissing your ass. Well, maybe a little. But there are times in life when we need to take a step forward and be proud of ourselves. You took a chance and did something to make a difference. It's good to be proud of that. I'm happy for you."

"Thanks."

"So, I don't know who you pissed off because I heard this didn't go down so gently, but do any of those people have lingering resentments or any other reason to want to hurt Cliff or you?"

"Apples and oranges. The one has nothing to do with the other. Yeah, we ruffled some feathers and gave people something to talk about for a while, but it's over. Whatever happened to Cliff was its own thing."

"So what was it? Why did someone beat him up so badly?"

"He must have made someone awfully mad."

"Are you friends with him? Do you keep up with him regarding the goings-on in his life?"

"You mean did he tell me about Rachel? Yes, I heard about her a while ago."

"Anything else going on with him out of the ordinary?"

"Not that I can think of."

"Very well. Before I leave, is there anything I can do to find out who did this to Cliff?"

"I'd ask his therapist friends. They'd know more."

"Good idea," I said, back to my ass-kissing ways. "They said they liked meeting you and it was too bad they hadn't got to hang out with you."

"That's very nice to hear. Bring them along when we have our Fiesta blowout party in a few days. It's a hoot. We usher Fiesta out with a blast."

CHAPTER THIRTY-NINE
Dancing at the Sunken Gardens

On my way to the Mercado it occurred to me that while John had said what had happened with the Visitadores was old news, I wasn't so sure. A second opinion would be nice. It also occurred to me that Rachel would ask me how my afternoon had gone, and I'd have to choose the moral high or low ground.

Would I keep my promise to Brendon and not tell her what he, and by default John, had told me? Or would I weasel out of it and disclose only what John had said?

John hadn't seemed particularly concerned about where I'd heard of the events on the ride. There'd been hundreds of witnesses—too many for him to suspect one person of outing him. Yet Brendon had been hesitant.

I wasn't sure what to tell Rachel. I'd figure it out when I saw her.
But I didn't see her.
She wasn't late yet, but I was used to her being on time.
At five after I started to worry.
At ten after, my blood pressure upped.
At twenty after, I began to horribilize. Could she be dead? Beaten up like her dad? What was wrong?

While I waited and worried, I figured what the hell and got a couple of tacos. Food being the temporary salve that it is.

At 6:45, I gave up my post and made my way over to the sunken gardens. Maybe Rachel was there. If she wasn't, she'd figure out that I was and hopefully join me with case-breaking news.

If I'd been an architect, I'd have liked the sunken gardens and the surrounding courthouse on my résumé. The Spanish Colonial revival architecture was elegant and bold, yet warm. The simplicity of the open space complemented its white and earthy deep-red palette and tiled archways. There was no stage per se, just an extended entry under a large archway. In the gardens there were blankets, chairs, and families enjoying the evening's mild weather.

There are advantages to being old money—reserved seats.. Not that there were seats exactly, but someone had set up a cluster of chairs and blankets in the front for the Spalding clan and friends. Most of the coterie was in attendance.

Rachel wasn't there. There was an empty chair next to Eleanor.

"Good evening," I said. "Is it all right if I join you?"

"Certainly. That's Vic's seat but I doubt he'll be coming."

"Why's that?"

"Dancing is to him what the rodeo is to me."

"Say no more. I want to apologize again for blundering in the last time we spoke. It was an insensitive thing to do and you were right to say I was rude."

You have to give a little to get a little, and I'd been truly out of line. And likely to be again.

"Apology accepted. Is there any update on Rachel's father?"

"Nothing new. It's disconcerting that he's still in a coma, but according to Dr. Novatt we shouldn't be overly concerned."

"That's not too comforting."

"It is and it isn't."

"Yes."

"What do you think happened to him? Any idea who might have done this to him?"

"Not really."

"I was talking with John about the incident with the Visitadores and whether he thought there was any lingering bad blood. He said it was old news. Do you agree?"

"I tend to agree with him."

"It sounds like they ruffled some feathers. I know the group has some powerful people in it. Could that be at play?"

"I really wouldn't know."

"Okay, let me change the subject. I know Spalding Enterprises owns a lot of land. Was Cliff involved with any land deals or something like that?"

"You'd have to talk to John or Vic about that. I stay away from that end of the business."

"Are you involved in other parts of the business?"

"Just the philanthropy side. We do a design house every year and I'm actively involved in that."

"A design house? What's that?"

"It's a fundraising activity for our non-profit. We find a house that could benefit from some sprucing up and we bring in various designers, contractors, and architects to give the place a good going-over."

"That must be a lot of work. I knew a couple who were remodeling their home, and they told me a therapist ought to be assigned to every project. There were a lot of fights, frustrations, overruns… you name it."

"That about sums it up. Now multiply it by fifty for all the designers and people you have involved. It can be a nightmare."

"I bet, but I'm sure it's a lovely home when all's said and done."

"Yes, the owners go through hell. But they get a lot of services at a price they could never afford, and their property value goes up considerably."

"Oh, so this isn't some remodeling in a needier part of town."

"No, these are the upper-end houses that haven't kept up."

"So do people come knocking on your door to have their home selected?"

"They do."

"Do you ever consider building something from scratch?"

"We've actually been considering that for the past couple of years. No firm plans, but perhaps."

I wanted to ask her if that had included building a center for her new family member, but since Michael and Alan had said that the center was a secret, I didn't want to bend that bit of integrity.

Some officials made announcements that I didn't pay much heed to. Then brightly dressed dance troupes came out to the delight of the audience. A fair number of the participants seemed to have family members in the audience cheering them on.

I preferred the dancers to the rodeo and horse parade but still wasn't all that engaged. Eleanor seemed to delight in it all; I could see the pleasure she took in being swept away. Unfortunately, I wasn't sharing in it.

Where was Rachel? Was she following up on a lead? Had there been news from the hospital and she'd rushed over there? As the evening progressed, my horribilizing increased.

I could excuse myself and go look for her, but aside from dropping by the hospital I had no idea where to look. I knew Eleanor wouldn't take kindly to my leaving before events concluded, but I wasn't sure I could take kindly to my staying.

Be in the moment, I told myself. You'd think I'd have been able to walk some of the walk I talked, but worry has a way of overruling other functions. The dancers were festive, the audience appreciative, and I was counting the minutes till I could make a graceful-enough getaway.

I remembered a basketball announcer once talking about how rookies in pressure situations tended to rush. I waited a little longer, then told Eleanor I was looking forward to seeing her and the family at the blowout party, and bade her farewell.

CHAPTER FORTY

Where's Rachel?

I WENT TO the one place I thought there might be news. Of course, it could be good news or not-so-good news.

Rachel wasn't in the waiting area outside the critical-care unit. I asked a nurse if Cliff Anderson had been moved. She looked at some paperwork and directed me to another floor. I took that as a good sign, then realized he could be in a surgery room or somewhere they put the patients who no longer had to worry about their bills.

I stepped outside of the elevator and read the sign: Neurology. I wasn't sure what to make of that. On my way to the nurses station I passed a seating area and saw Rachel. She wasn't sobbing, which I took as a good sign.

"Hey," I said.

"I'm so sorry I stood you up, but the hospital left a message at the hotel. I rushed over. He woke up. I'm so relieved. He's awake, he's aware. He can't really talk yet and when he does it's jumbled. The doctors say it'll take time. I can't believe it. I'm so happy."

With that she hugged me, and kept hugging me until the tears had come and gone. It felt so good to have her feel so good. The dread that had been hanging over the week had been lifted. At least for us. I'm sure Ellen's family wasn't feeling any relief.

"This is great news," I said. "I'm so happy for you and your dad."

"It's incredible. I hate to say it but I'd given him up for dead."

"I know. We were bracing ourselves for bad news."

"He's not out of trouble yet, but things sure look a lot better now. Hopefully as he regains strength all his faculties will come back."

Elizabeth came rushing up to us.

"I'm sorry I didn't get here sooner. How is he?"

"Hi," Rachel said, and embraced Elizabeth, who seemed to welcome it.

"He's awake. Barely, but he is. He can't really talk yet and I only got to see him for a moment. I was told to come back tomorrow but I haven't been able to leave. It's just so good to be here and know he's all right."

"That's wonderful news. I was—we were all—very worried about him."

"I know. We were just saying the same thing."

"So we can't see him till tomorrow?" she asked.

"Yeah. You're welcome to come. We meet here at eleven, but I'll be here earlier, if I leave at all."

"Yes, it's good to be here and know he's safe."

"It's a relief," I said, just to say something.

Elizabeth looked at me as if noticing me for the first time. I felt superfluous and she seemed to agree.

"I don't want to be rude as I know this is a moment of celebration, but there's something I'd like to ask you, Elizabeth," I said.

"What's that?"

"Are you involved with your mother's design houses?"

"What a strange question. No, I have nothing to do with those. I go to them, of course, but that's her thing."

"Why did you ask that?" Rachel said.

"I was wondering if Eleanor had any plans for a design house that involved Cliff."

"What?" asked Rachel.

"I wouldn't know anything about that," said Elizabeth

"I'm just curious."

"Are you talking about the center?" Rachel asked.

It seemed the strict guidelines about not sharing that information weren't commonly held.

"I was just thinking out loud. Maybe I ought to keep my thoughts to myself," I said, hinting to Rachel that it might be prudent to shut down the conversation.

But her relief seemed to have trumped my moral high ground, and she said, "Is Elizabeth's mother going to build the center for my dad?"

"Well, that's a possibility. What do you think, Elizabeth?"

"I certainly wouldn't know anything about that. It sounds like a lovely idea, but she's never built a home, just helped remodel and redesign them."

CHAPTER FORTY-ONE

Doing Nothing

August 2, 1983

I COULDN'T RESIST the morning workshop "Doing Nothing." Plus, the three credits would get me up to thirty-four. In the grander scheme of things, so much of what we do is really nothing. I wondered what it would be like to purposefully do nothing. Turned out it wasn't much different.

I lay on the floor with my eyes closed and listened.

"You're in a workshop called 'Doing Nothing,'" the facilitator said. "For the next twenty minutes, I want you to do absolutely nothing. But don't worry; you'll be getting full credit for lying here and doing nothing. I want you to do nothing as best you can. The ground will hold you up without your having to do anything. In twenty minutes, I'll tell you to stop doing nothing and we can talk about it. Now, please, do nothing."

Since I was lying on the floor doing nothing, I was doing something. It was kind of like meditating, which is another form of doing nothing. Relaxing the mind and body and letting the spirit free. I wanted to clear my mind and drift away. Instead, I looked around the room to make sure that Scarface had better things to do. Not seeing him, I closed my eyes and tried to relax.

Unfortunately, even though I wasn't concerned with Scarface, I couldn't do nothing. I kept wondering what Cliff would say when he could say something. What if he didn't want to say anything? What if that beating had been a message for him to shut up? And, if he didn't want to say anything, would I let it go and get on with my life, be in the moment and do nothing?

Not in my mind. My mind wasn't interested. My mind kept asking, *What do I do now?*

When I was finished doing nothing, I went back up to my room. Rachel had left me a message: she would be at the hospital early and would meet me there later. With her father on the mend, I could understand her wanting to be there. He had stories to tell. If he'd tell them.

I drove over to the hospital. I decided to stay in the usual waiting area as I figured Michael and Alan would be there. I hadn't seen them at the conference in the morning and assumed they'd had better things to do than nothing.

When they arrived, the three of us went up to Neurology. Rachel and Elizabeth were waiting there. We exchanged banalities until Dr. Novatt showed up. He told us Cliff was continuing to mend and we could all see him, but not touch him. He suggested that Rachel and I go first, followed by Elizabeth. Michael and Alan would go last. He didn't want us taking more than ten minutes in total as what Cliff really needed was rest. We were welcome to visit Cliff again at 5:00 p.m.

Rachel had gotten used to seeing him, but I immediately understood why it hadn't been comforting. He looked pretty bad—all bandages, IVs and bruises. He lit up when he saw Rachel and managed a smile, but that was about it. She talked to him and he mumbled something to her, but it was indecipherable to me. She introduced me and he gave me a little smile. Either he'd understood what she'd said or he just liked to smile.

I could tell she wanted to stay but after a few minutes she stepped outside. Elizabeth came in before I'd had a chance to leave. The glow that came over Cliff was striking. I could have sworn he even raised himself up a little.

Five minutes later Elizabeth came out with some spring in her step. She didn't know how to divide ten by three. Nobody else seemed to notice but time's my thing, and in my book Elizabeth had suddenly become more interesting.

When Michael and Alan were done we all debriefed and agreed to meet back outside his room at five. Elizabeth excused herself. Rachel looked surprised when I told her I had to go do something and would see her later.

Elizabeth's Silver Land Rover was in the hospital parking lot. So was mine. That made things easier. I needed to know more about Elizabeth and the easiest way to start was to follow her.

I'd gone to the Automobile Club before I left LA and had gotten a local map, but I'd shuttled back and forth enough in town to know without checking it that we were headed for the mountains. I'd been on this winding road before and knew the way to Cliff's house.

I wasn't alone in that.

She pulled into his driveway and I parked my car down the street, just far enough so I could still see her car, but not so she could easily spot mine. I'd just stepped out of the car when I caught a glimpse of her going back toward hers, carrying her purse. I scurried behind my car and hid. It was a mostly empty stretch of road so I wasn't worried about someone seeing me. Well, other than her.

Had she tried to unlock the front door and given up when it hadn't opened? Had she foregone the backdoor/open window option? Or had she gone in, quickly grabbed something, and left?

I was putting my money on the latter—that she knew what she

was looking for and where it was. Was her seeing Cliff and coming directly here cause and effect? If she'd known where something was, she'd either had prior experience with it or Cliff had told her. Would he have told her something but Rachel nothing? If so, what had that beating beaten into him?

Once back in her car, she made a U-turn and drove back to town. I followed.

I was full of questions. What had she gotten from his house—some documents, the unfinished letter he'd written, the autographed Babe Ruth baseball? And why now? Cliff had been in the hospital some time. She could easily have gotten what she wanted at any time. And what exactly was their relationship? On paper she was a married woman and he was betrothed to her sister. But that look in the hospital had spoken of more.

I had to wonder whether there was some hanky-panky there. But if she was worried about having any of her belongings in his house, wouldn't she have pulled them out earlier? No, she wasn't retrieving her lingerie. So what was it? Something of his?

I didn't know what had motivated her but knowing that something had motivated me. I didn't know if it was a lead, but it wasn't nothing.

She drove home. I parked down the street a bit, watched, and thought. What now?

CHAPTER FORTY-TWO

By the Pool

I WENT BACK to the Miramar. Maybe I could take time to lie down outdoors, read a book, nap, take a swim… do the kind of nothing that meant something to me.

I was strolling by the pool on the way to my room when I spotted Michael. He was lying in the sun, wearing something that looked too close to a Speedo.

"Hey," I said. "All right if I join you?"

"Why not? Just soaking up some rays."

"It feels good to be out in the sun. Not too hot, but nicely warm."

"Precisely."

"I can't stay out here long because my complexion is the result of centuries of inbreeding by people who rarely saw the sun."

"We all have our burdens to bear."

"I have a question for you about that property we saw. Well, not the property. The concept. Can you tell me more about what Cliff had in mind?"

"Sure. Cliff had the original idea to build the place. That was some years ago when he, Alan and I went to Esalen. We were sitting in the hot tubs overlooking the Pacific and talking about how there ought to be a place like that in Southern California. It will never be as idyllic as Big Sur, but just because you can't beat it doesn't mean you can't emulate it."

"I get that. I've always thought Esalen was the world the way I'd like it to be. People are friendly, open, supportive, encouraging, and invested in making themselves and the world a better place. If you can take that energy and replicate it in any way, that's a real service. It's a great idea."

"Yeah it was. Is."

"So how did the idea blossom to where it is today?"

"That's a more complicated story."

"I got a good five, ten minutes more before the sun has its way with me."

Michael told me how the three of them had indulged in fanciful, idealistic, and wonderful conversations. Then they left Esalen—Alan went back to Tahoe, he to LA and Cliff to Santa Barbara—and got on with their lives. Occasionally they would catch up and talk about their shared vision.

Last year Michael moved to Santa Barbara. He and Cliff had continued to meet and talk earnestly about the project. What they hadn't done was work out how to pay for it.

Then Cliff met Margot. As the relationship evolved Cliff spent less time with Michael. Some of that was natural. Whenever someone falls in love they forsake time with friends for time with the love interest. It's often a bumpy passage, as friends can feel displaced. But this was more than that. At first Cliff talked about Margot and her wealth, and how she might help. But after a few months he shut down.

"What happened when he stopped talking about it?"

"It was okay at first. The conversations had become stressful. But over time I realized that he was excluding me, and it upset me. Eventually I asked him what was happening and he said that he was managing it and didn't want to talk about it."

"And then what?"

"And then he got beat up."

I got out of the sun before I regretted having been in it. What Michael had told me added a new dimension to things. Something was brewing about the property. Was Cliff getting the money from marrying Margot? It certainly looked like her piece of the pie could pay for a good chunk of it.

However, if she bankrolled the center, would a share of it become hers? Cliff, Alan and Michael had each owned a third of the idea in its original conception. But who owned what now?

If some of those signings at the clerk's office had to do with the center, Michael and Alan might have been left at the starting gate.

Until that moment I hadn't figured on Michael or Alan having anything to do with Cliff's being beaten up and Ellen killed. I hadn't seen any bruised knuckles on either of them, but if Michael or Alan had wanted Cliff beaten up for having stolen the idea from them, they would hire someone to do the job. We're all six degrees of separation from someone who'd carry out that task, no questions asked, for the right price.

CHAPTER FORTY-THREE

By the Ocean

Why be in Southern California if you don't spend some time at a pool and the ocean? Since the hotel was by the water, I went back to my room, put on my bathing suit, reacquainted myself with my suntan lotion, and headed out.

The beach was fifty yards wide where it met the ocean. Some people were lying on blankets. Others were wading, swimming and bodysurfing in what little surf there was. A transistor radio played Donna Summer's "She Works Hard for the Money."

One guy held a fishing pole. He was standing in the water up to his knees, casting his line. I looked a little closer—it was Alan. He was intent on his task and didn't notice me. I put my towel on the sand along with my shirt and room key, and waded out to him.

"Hey, Alan. How you doing?"

"Life is good."

"I didn't know you fished like this."

"I don't really. I'm more a stream-and-lake guy, but when I come here I like to hit up the ocean a time or two."

"It's both similar and different at the same time."

"As with most things."

"Yeah. Well, you picked a lovely day to be out here. Cliff seems to be healing, although we didn't get much time with him."

"It's more than we had. Makes you appreciate what you got."

"There is that. I was talking with Michael about the center and how you three hatched the idea up at Esalen."

"That was a special time."

"To hear Michael talk, you bonded over it. And yet it seems as though after you left Esalen it was he and Cliff who carried forth with more of the conceptualizing."

"That's true. We'd all talk on the phone now and then. But it wasn't like we were sitting down and talking about it like we had at Esalen."

"Michael told me that things seemed to have shifted recently. You have any sense of that?"

"Some."

"Some?"

"Yes, some. I gather you want more than that."

"If you will."

"Michael is certainly closer to it than I am, but I talk with Cliff and Michael on the phone now and then. Michael worries we're getting squeezed out. He's convinced Margot is going to provide sufficient funds to make it happen at the expense of our share."

"What did Cliff tell you?"

"He didn't. He didn't want to talk about it and told me not to worry about it."

"Did he say 'trust me'? That kind of thing?"

"Not so's you'd feel comfortable. Something was off."

"What?"

"That's the question."

Something was up with Cliff, and both Michael and Alan had cause to be concerned. Once trust is compromised people get uneasy. How uneasy they were, and what they'd done with that unease, I wasn't sure. All I knew was, now I had a reason to suspect them.

CHAPTER FORTY-FOUR

Rodeo Too

Why have a mystery if you can't suspect everyone? Last night I'd asked Eleanor about whether her philanthropic efforts might include building something from the ground up, and she said they'd been considering it. If Margot and she were involved with Cliff and the center, wouldn't Vic be close at hand? I hadn't planned on going back to the rodeo but there were no other special evening events scheduled so I figured I'd give it a try.

Vic was back in the same seat but I didn't see any family members with him. This looked like a gathering of the good old boys. There was a lot of hooting and hollering along with beer swilling and tri-tip devouring. I observed the group from afar and asked myself whether this was really how I wanted to spend my evening. It wasn't, but sometimes ya gotta do what ya gotta do. I didn't really have to do this, but I guess my obsessive tendencies were getting the better of me. Vic was unfinished business. I didn't figure I'd get much business conducted with him but when you have obsessive-compulsive tendencies you need to finish something even if it makes no real-world difference.

I sat some distance from the group and glanced back and forth between them and the proceedings in the arena. I'll say one thing for the Old Spanish Days Fiesta Stock Horse Show & Rodeo organizers: they seemed to understand that any one of these activities would hold limited interest for most people, and moved along quickly from one thing to another. Dr. Novatt appeared in various events—quite the enthusiast.

Vic finally lost the battle of retention with the beer and made his way to the bathroom. I followed him. There was a little wobble in his step, which I hoped would translate into a loosening of his lips. He was cut off from the herd; it seemed a good time to make my move. But first I let him relieve himself. I'm a humanist, after all.

I caught him on the way out.

"Hey, Vic," I said. "It's good to see you."

"Hey. What are you doing here? I thought you city slickers would have had enough after one night."

"I like it. I thought I'd come back for more."

"That's great. You can learn a lot about life watching a rodeo. Why don't you come and sit with us?"

"That's very kind of you but unfortunately I have to leave."

"Hot date with Rachel?"

"Nah, we're just friends. This is some other stuff."

"Okay. Well, hope to see you at the blowout," he said as he started to make his move to go.

"I'll be there, and Rachel too. Did you hear that Cliff is out of critical care? He seems to be mending, albeit slowly."

"I heard. That's great news."

"Can I ask you something before you go? I know Cliff was a guest on the Visitadores' ride this year. What the hell did he do to get everyone so pissed off?"

Vic took a close look at me. Even though his eyes were a bit glossy, they still conveyed anger.

"Look, I don't really know you so I'm not going to get upset. But that's not something you ought to be asking. If you want, you can ask Cliff, but he's not gonna want to talk about it either."

And with that he weaved his way back to his seat.

Had Cliff's beating been a reminder from Vic to keep his mouth shut? If I asked Cliff, maybe he'd wince and that would tell me what I needed to know.

I was ready to put the rodeo behind me, but maybe there was someone else here who could help me out. I went around to the back of the arena. This wasn't a big city arena where you needed a VIP pass to access backstage. There were a bunch of stalls and corrals. Some of the rodeo participants were milling about. I spotted Dr. Novatt sitting on a bench, taking a breather.

"Hi. Mind if I join you?"

"Suit yourself. I'm sorry, I can't remember your name."

"I'm David. I'm a friend of Rachel's—Cliff Anderson's daughter."

"Yeah. I knew that. He does seem to be progressing."

"That's good to hear. But I didn't come over here to talk about that or to see if I could get some free medical advice. You deserve your off-time and I respect that."

"Thank you."

"No problem. But I do have a question for you. Are you a Visitadore? I figure with all the rodeo stuff you'd be a natural."

"I'm not a member, but I go on their rides. I'm their ride-along doctor. In fact, we just went on one a couple of months ago."

"That sounds like a good job to have. I gather they live it up on those rides. Do you have hangover cures? I bet those would be popular."

"I'd be retired if I had that."

"Do you remember Cliff from a ride? I gather he was a guest once or twice."

"Yes, a memorable guest."

"I heard that something untoward happened. Care to tell me what it was?"

"Some of the guys were being stupid, which happens, and he and another man stood up to them."

"That's it?"

"It was a big deal. Nobody stands up to Mr. Parmacelli."

"Who's Mr. Parmacelli?"

"Parmacelli Wines."

"Oh, that Parmacelli. I thought it was an Italian winery."

"Italian grapes that he brought over to the Santa Ynez Valley from the homeland. Very similar growing conditions, but they don't produce the same quality here unfortunately."

"I'm not much of a wine drinker, but in my grad-school days, when money was at a premium, I recall some bottles being passed around. So he's a local?"

"Well, he's not Santa Barbara local, but the Santa Ynez Valley's just over the hill."

"So how come no one messes with him?"

"He's been the president of the Visitadores for some time. No one runs against him. The last guy that tried met with an unfortunate accident and had to withdraw as he wasn't able to ride anymore."

"So Cliff called Parmacelli out?"

"You could say he didn't know better as he was a guest, but we all know better. Parmacelli casts a large shadow. But Cliff wasn't alone. Another man took up his side, someone who knew better."

"Are we talking about John Spalding?"

"We are. He knew better than to open his mouth, but he was drunk. It's not like most of us didn't agree with Cliff and John, but just since he was right didn't mean he needed to say so."

"So Cliff wasn't invited back and John was kicked out?"

"Pretty much."

"Did Parmacelli have Cliff beaten up?"

"He certainly has people who could do that, but I'm not going to say that. In fact, we never had this conversation."

CHAPTER FORTY-FIVE
Mr. Parmacelli

August 3, 1983

I'D LIKED AND not liked hearing about Parmacelli. He could very well have been responsible for Cliff's beating. Seemingly, he didn't shy away from taking care of matters the old-fashioned way. It was good to have a viable suspect. What wasn't so good was that I'd need to investigate him.

I tend to shy away from people who cause unfortunate accidents to befall others. That said, I was curious. I know, curiosity killed the cat, but I was only planning on being a little curious.

Maybe if I'd had a good night's sleep my curiosity would have been gone in the morning. But it wasn't. In fact, I'd had a restless night because of it.

I figured I could take the forty-five-minute trip to Santa Ynez, meet with Parmacelli, and be back for the 11 o'clock meeting at the hospital. I was taking a risk by missing the morning workshop, but hoped I'd be able to make up the credits in the afternoon. It was a very iffy schedule.

The drive over the mountains into the valley ought to have been relaxing. The prospect of an unforeseen accident put a damper on it. In the midst of summer, the hills were brown and the air on the other side was dry and hot. I guess grapes like it that way.

It wasn't hard to find the vineyards. They were planted alongside the highway for what seemed like a mile, and extended into the foothills and beyond. There was a rather unattractive but hard-to-miss sculpture of grapes covering the entrance to Parmacelli Wines.

Driving down the quarter-mile entranceway, I wondered how to meet Parmacelli. I didn't exactly have references and wasn't expecting him to be behind the tasting bar. It wouldn't behoove me to mention Cliff, John or even Vic. Neither did I want to throw Dr. Novatt under the bus, but he was all I had.

From the fake grapes at the entrance to the faux old bricks that framed the buildings, the place was both eye-catching and garish. I was supposed to be transported to Tuscany, but that wasn't my destination; I was going to the tasting room. Turned out it hadn't opened yet, which was just as well as I wasn't keen on tasting. There was a gift shop, though, so I went in and struck up a conversation.

"Hi, these are lovely grounds."

"Yes, they are," said a middle-aged woman in a smock patterned with grapevines.

"Are all the buildings part of the winery?"

"Yes, all the ones here. The houses up on the hill belong to the family who live on the property. We're a family-owned business," she said with the lack of enthusiasm one can generate after having repeated something too many times.

"When does the wine-tasting part open up?"

"Ten. You'll have to wait an hour."

"That's fine. I'll just look around some."

"Please. Just don't pick any of the grapes. Of course, I say that to everybody, but nobody listens."

"I didn't hear what you said," I said as I stepped out.

As I drove up the long private road toward the houses, I expected to run into a barrier, something to keep the riff-raff out. But I guess when people know enough not to mess with you there's no reason to protect your enclosure. There was a large circular driveway with a fountain in the middle. It had been sculpted to look like grapes. I didn't like it any more than the one at the front gate, though it had been done more tastefully. The bricks and façades looked like the real deal too.

I knocked on the door. A small child opened it, but before she could say anything a housekeeper came up behind her.

"I'm sorry," she said. "Sofia is always curious."

"Hi, Sofia. I'm David. I'm glad to meet you."

"You should be. I'm a princess," she said, and skipped off to attend to her royal duties.

I smiled at the maid. "Hi. I was hoping I could speak with Mr. Parmacelli. I'm here on behalf of Dr. Novatt."

"Please wait," she said, and pointed toward a bench just inside the door.

I wondered if some people took a seat here with their heads bowed, waiting for them to be chopped off.

The housekeeper came back and said, "Come with me." I followed her down a tiled hallway. The walls were a combination of rock and brick and looked very solid but cold. I didn't know much about wine storage but the pictures of cellars I'd seen always looked like this.

Toward the end of the hallway, the housekeeper ushered me into an office. A massive picture window looked down on the valley's vineyards. In front of the window was a desk that looked every bit as solid as the house. The man behind it was equally sturdy.

Sixty-five-ish. Two hundred and twenty pounds. Wavy gray hair and a face that maybe his mother had loved. He looked up when I came in.

"Good morning. Thank you for seeing me. I met Sofia at the door. You have a lovely granddaughter."

"Daughter."

"Yes, a grand daughter. A delightful young lady."

"Dr. Novatt sent you?"

"Not exactly. We were talking at the rodeo last night and your name came up. He told me how much he enjoys riding with the Visitadores and that he's there to provide any medical assistance needed."

"He's a valuable resource."

"I'm sure he is. I thought maybe I could be as well."

"How so?"

"I'm a therapist. Wait, before you laugh, let me tell you why I can be helpful. Gary told me that in addition to being sore and having minor bruises, people sometimes have conflicts with each other. Even though everyone is out for a good time, things can go south. Having a therapist at hand to smooth out any rough edges might help."

"No thanks. We don't need any shrinks."

"I agree. You don't most of the time. But every now and then, when things boil over, it's good to rely on someone who knows how to handle these things so nobody walks away too upset."

He was quiet. Maybe he was thinking I had a point. Or maybe he was thinking he ought to have someone beat me up. I couldn't tell. Not being skilled at waiting, I pushed some more chips out onto the table.

"We don't know each other so I don't expect you to say yes right now. This is just an informal suggestion for you to consider. For all I know, as president of the group you're fully able to help resolve any differences and don't need outside help. It's just that I'm interested, I have some skills of value, and I can mail you a résumé and cover letter if you'd like."

I can tell when people can't figure out what to make of me. They sense I'm bullshitting but aren't sure. Maybe I'm naive or just stupid. Had I said he was able to handle conflict because I knew how he did that? Or had I said it to kiss his ass? But he was sure of one thing.

"Thank you for talking with me. Sandra will show you out."

He must have had some bell system under his desk, for no sooner had he spoken than she showed up. I was out the door and on my way in plenty of time to get to the hospital. At least I wasn't recuperating there alongside Cliff.

CHAPTER FORTY-SIX
Update

Michael, Alan, Rachel and Elizabeth were in the waiting room when I arrived. Dr. Novatt had yet to make his appearance. I wanted to catch up with Rachel. For a couple of days we'd been in tandem, but since her dad had awakened from the coma we hadn't been in touch much. It reminded me of what Michael had said about Cliff when he met Margot and how their friendship had taken a backseat. Cliff certainly was Rachel's priority but it's not as though she'd been sitting in the waiting room the whole time.

When Dr. Novatt finally appeared, I got a bonus nod of recognition from him. Otherwise things were pretty much the status quo. Cliff was talking a little but it was jumbled and he had no memories of what had happened to him. The doctor didn't want us querying him. The police had been in earlier, which had exhausted him. We needed to keep it light, breezy, and short.

Rachel and I went first. Again, I stayed in the background while Rachel talked about how happy she was that he was feeling better. I wanted to ask him about the financing of the center and his experience with the Visitadores but that didn't fit the doctor's orders. There wasn't a Babe Ruth baseball or any personal stuff to be seen, but then Elizabeth hadn't been in yet.

When our time was up, I lingered again. Elizabeth and Cliff had something going on. I don't encounter those gaga looks often, but I know them when I see them.

Brendon didn't seem like the possessive type—happy enough as long as his rut was safe and secure. I wondered whether he knew about his wife and Cliff.

After Elizabeth's turn was over she told us that she had an appointment and said goodbye. I was about to follow her when Rachel said she wanted Michael and Alan to have lunch with us. It was as good a plan as any and I was hungry. We ate again in the hospital cafeteria. If you ever want to eat someplace where people are more stressed out than you, it's a good choice.

Alan had a questionable-looking Reuben sandwich. The rest of us opted for a wilted salad, which matched the mood in the room.

"He doesn't remember the beating," Michael said.

"You asked him?" said Rachel, her tone scolding.

"Of course. He doesn't remember much about anything. He said he knew he'd been beat up and yet wasn't really feeling any pain. I told him they've got him on a lot of first-class meds."

"We don't know how far back he remembers," said Alan.

"We didn't ask anything else," Michael said. "He sounded pretty wobbly and tentative."

"Selfishly, I hope he gets better fast," said Alan. "I'd like to see him back to himself before I go home."

"Yeah, I have to leave after the conference is over too," I said.

"You'll be here, Michael," Rachel said. "And I can easily stay a few days. And, of course, I can drive back up anytime."

Rachel decided to stay at the hospital, Michael and Alan went to collect some credits, and I headed over to Elizabeth and Brendon's house. I parked far enough away so no one would think my car was connected to their house, and strolled over to their not-so-humble abode.

If Brendon was home I'd feel him out about Elizabeth and Cliff.

Maybe I'd tell him; maybe I wouldn't. Would you want to know? I would, though I'm not sure how I'd feel about the messenger.

If Elizabeth was home I'd do the same.

If neither were home, I'd try to find what Elizabeth had taken from Cliff's house.

CHAPTER FORTY-SEVEN

Searching

I RANG THE bell and waited a suitable amount of time. Tried again. Then I put my stealth skills into play and went around to the back, looking for a way in.

When you live on a private beach you don't expect a lot of visitors coming in via the beachfront. I'd noticed residents in Santa Barbara didn't seem overly concerned about their home being broken into. The local paper had run a front-page story about a pedestrian who'd been hit by someone on a bicycle as they stood on the street. With front-page news like that, I guess you can keep your doors unlocked.

It was an impressive home. Beach chic. If it hadn't already been featured in *Architectural Digest* it would be one day. As much as I'd have liked to sit on the couch and soak it all in, I was on a different mission. I looked to see if Elizabeth had an office, a place to call her own. She did. I went in and strode straight for the desk. Not so much a secretive place to hide something as a convenient place to put something.

Convenience is convenient, but not always satisfactory.

It did occur to me that if she had taken something from Cliff's it had fit in her purse, which meant a lot of potential hiding places.

I surveyed the room—if I were smaller than a purse, where would I hide? If it was paperwork she'd taken, there were too many places to stuff it.

I stepped up closer to the bookshelf.

"Excuse me," said Brendon.

I turned around and, lo and behold, there he was, holding a gun on me.

"Hey, hi. I'm glad you're home. I was just waiting for you and got curious so I was taking a look at the books. I like to read, you know."

I babbled nervously, trying to look of good cheer, which isn't that easy when a gun's pointed your way and you've been caught with your hand in the cookie jar.

"What are you doing here?"

"Like I said, waiting for you."

"I didn't see your car."

"It's down the block. I wanted to take a little stroll. When I got here, I figured it would be fine if I came in and waited for you. I knew if you knew I was waiting outside you'd have said, 'Oh, you should have come in.' So I came in. Thanks."

"I don't like the look of this. I repeat: What are you doing here? Why do you want to see me? And why are you searching through Elizabeth's stuff?"

Not good. He'd probably seen me, left, and got the gun. My excuses were running away from me.

"Can we talk? That's the reason I came here. I want to talk with you."

"So talk."

"I don't really want to talk with the gun pointing at me. It doesn't really allow me to feel like my best self."

"I can put it down," he said.

He stepped over to a bureau, opened a drawer, and took out some handcuffs. They didn't have a fuzzy sex-shop look about them.

He put me in a chair with my arms behind me. While the gun was no longer pointing at me, I hadn't exactly upgraded my position.

"Okay, let me start by saying I want to put you at ease. I'm of good will. I came to speak with you about something I've learned, and want to know if you know it too."

"Let's hear it."

"Why don't you pour yourself a drink? Relax."

"What the hell are you talking about?"

I'd been unsure about sharing my thoughts about his wife and Cliff but I'd been thrown off my game and needed to balance things out.

"I've been visiting the hospital the past few days. I've seen Cliff a couple of times. You know who else has seen him?"

"I heard he was better. I have no idea who's visited him. Could be anyone."

"Anyone in your family visit him?"

"If Margot were here, she would, of course. I thought you'd have got it by now—we're not that kind of family. We all leave each other alone."

"Well, someone visited him."

"That's nice to know. We're not all heartless."

"Yeah, some maybe. But not all. Maybe each of us is in our own way."

"So that's what you came here to tell me. One of the clan has a heart?"

"I came to tell you that the someone is your wife."

"My wife? I don't think so."

"Yes, I saw her there. Twice."

"Well, good for her for representing the family."

"Yes, good for her. But there's more than that."

"What are you talking about now?"

"I'm talking about how your wife has a deep connection with Cliff that goes beyond the hospital visits."

"That's crazy. She doesn't love me, I'll grant you that, but the woman isn't capable of love. She has no interest in being with another man. It would just be another burden to bear."

"I don't know about that. The way those two look at each other is the way we only hope someone would look at us."

He left the room. Came back with a bottle of Macallan Scotch. He looked shaken and stirred. He didn't love Elizabeth but he was her husband and didn't want her loving another in the way we'd all want to be loved.

I watched him drink and ruminate. He went through all the stages—denial, anger, sadness, bargaining, and acceptance. I might as well have been in session.

Finally he looked at me and said something I've heard a time or two before. "I don't know what to do with you."

"I'll tell you what you should do. Let me go. I found out about them. And I found out something else you'll want to hear. I also want to find out more about what she and Cliff are up to, and I can't do it while I'm in handcuffs. They could be having a romantic thing, but it could be something else. I'm not sure. What I do know is that there's more there than just the gaga eyes."

He didn't like my saying any of this out loud. It's one thing to dwell on something. It's another when it gets spoken. Makes things a bit more real.

"So tell me."

"Not until you let me go. It's a trade. You let me go, I tell you. Then we're working together to find out what's going on."

"I don't know."

"Come on. I'm not a thief. You know me. You know how to find me. Let's help each other out and call it a day."

"Tell me first."

"No no no. That's not how it works. I'm at a great disadvantage here. You have to even things up a bit."

"Maybe I'll just call the police."

"Let's not make this more than it is. You're upset. Justifiably so. You're going to be mad and sad, feel one way then another. Look, there may not be a there there. But, truthfully, I'm sorry to say, I think there is. It certainly warrants a discussion between the two of you. But that's your business. I'm not going to tell you how to run your life."

That wasn't quite true because it's exactly what I was doing. But let's not get picky.

"You do what you want. But let me go and I'll tell you what I know. It'll give you something up your sleeve if you talk with Elizabeth. You'll know something about her that she doesn't know you know. Trust me. It'll be a good thing."

Of course, if he were a client I'd never tell him to trust me. I'd say, "Trust yourself." As much as I was trusting myself at that point, I didn't trust him. I was just hoping to sway him to my side.

"I'm going to let you go on two conditions. One, you tell me whatever it is you have to tell me. And, two, you help me deal with it."

Telling him the thing wasn't an issue; the help-me-deal-with-it was. It sounded too much like a therapy contract, and I didn't want to take him on as a client.

"How about I tell you, but instead of my helping you deal with it, you help me."

"What?"

"If I tell you, you'll do something which will lead to something which then has a life of its own. That's your business and I don't want anything to do with it aside from wishing you well. But if there are things you know that could help me, I want you to tell me."

"Forget that," he said as he freed me. "You tell me and then get out of here."

"Okay. Immediately after Cliff broke out of the coma and Elizabeth visited him, she drove to his house, went in for thirty seconds, and came back out. She had her purse with her so maybe she took something from the house and put it in there."

"Or took something out of her purse and left it there."

"I hadn't thought of that."

"The one is as likely as the other," he said.

"See, I said you could help me."

"God knows, you need it. But I don't know what she'd take or get from there. It makes no sense to me."

"There could be any number of things and she could have moved them for any number of reasons. I don't know if you're interested in finding out, but I am. I don't know if it's linked to Cliff's being beaten up but the more I find out, the more suspicious I get."

"They call that paranoia."

"Well diagnosed. It's weird. One day, I'm a regular-ish guy. The next, I'm a conspiracy theorist seeing indicators everywhere."

CHAPTER FORTY-EIGHT
Back at It

Driving away from the beach house, I had second thoughts. If someone thought your partner was fooling around, would you want to know?
Yes.
No.
Probably.
Maybe.
All of the above.
Sorry for the multiple choice. Sometimes I fall back on my teaching habits.
I wasn't sure if Brendon was thankful or not. I'm not sure I would have been. I regretted not asking him some foreplay questions that would have told me whether he wanted to know that his wife was likely cheating on him.
What was done was done, and whatever Brendon did now was on his table. I hadn't found out what Elizabeth had taken from Cliff's house, but I'd found out she could just as easily have taken something there. But what?
I didn't have anything better to do so I decided to check Cliff's

house again. I wasn't optimistic about discovering anything useful, but at least I didn't have to worry about being caught.

Cliff's house was as I'd last seen it and there were no cars parked close by. I parked down the street and hurried up to the house. It was a peaceful area although I could hear crows squawking. Not sure why other birds sing and crows squawk, but the crows came as close to singing as I do.

The trusting folk of Santa Barbara needed to consider locking up their homes now that I was in town. I seemed to be making a habit of breaking and entering. I snuck in the open back door. The inside looked very much as I'd left it. As for identifying a missing slip of paper, I had about as much chance of success as I did of singing at Carnegie Hall. Instead, I looked for additional paperwork or some new souvenir that was now calling this place home.

I was working my way through the papers on the desk when something caught my attention. It felt like a gun barrel at the back of my head, but maybe it was just a crow that had flown in through the open back door.

I don't own a gun. How many people do? Probably too many.

Was it something she kept in her purse for those times she felt like killing someone? I didn't know. Was this the thing she'd come to pick up or drop off? I didn't know. But I did know that Elizabeth wasn't happy to see me.

"What are you doing here?" she asked.

"Truthfully, I'm not sure."

"What?"

"Obviously I'm looking for something. I'm just not a hundred percent sure what it is."

"What are you talking about?"

Since I'd already thrown one other person under the bus, I wasn't worried about adding another. Besides, Dr. Novatt might like the company.

"Rachel asked me to drop by and find something."

"What?"

"That's the problem. She wasn't entirely clear. Maybe you can help."

"I don't think so. I'm not feeling inclined."

"Maybe I could help you with that."

"What?"

"I'm a therapist, after all. I help people."

"I don't know what you're talking about."

"I get that. Let me help you. But, first, what do you say you put the gun away? You know me. I'm not some random burglar."

"No, you're a deliberate thief."

"That sounds a bit harsh. Come on, waddaya say? You put the gun away and maybe together we can find the thing I'm looking for."

When the teamwork approach didn't work I went for best defense is offense. "Speaking of which, what are you doing here?"

Wrong question. However ill at ease she'd been with finding me there, she was more distressed by my questioning her. I felt the gun pressing a little further into my skull. Since I could still feel it, I was on the better side of things, but I'd preferred it back in her purse.

"I'm glad you're here, actually," I said, scrambling. "I could use your help. I don't know how familiar you are with this place, but if Cliff has important papers, where would they be?"

"Even if I knew I certainly wouldn't tell you."

"Okay, maybe we can look together. So, can you put the gun away? It's not easy sitting here with it pressed into my head."

"Put your hands up."

While I don't always do as I'm told, this seemed like a good time to do so.

"Keep them there," she said as she stepped away but kept me in view. She went into the alcove. "Don't move."

She was out of view momentarily. I guess I could have run, but she was between me and the door so that wouldn't have been an optimal option. Besides, I wanted to talk to her. I just didn't want to have to do it with a firearm barreling into my skull.

She took that concern away from me when she reappeared with some rope. With some difficulty, she tied me up—not the most professional roping job. Vic would have been disappointed. I'm sure Dr. Novatt could have given her some tips. Still, like those calves, I was roped in.

She kept the gun handy, but at least it wasn't aimed at me.

Whatever the record is on number of times restrained in one afternoon, I was over my average. At least they were keeping it in the family, although it wouldn't be to my advantage to let Elizabeth know that Brendon had beaten her to the punch.

Maybe it was time to go back to the teamwork approach. "Here's the thing. Do you know why Cliff was beat up?"

"Of course not."

"Right. But we have to go on the assumption that somebody was mad at him about something. But what? What could he have done that would bother someone so much?"

"I have no idea."

"Well, there's Mr. Parmacelli, who evidently wasn't happy with Cliff a couple of months ago."

"That's old news."

"So I've been told. But he's not someone to be messed with, and people like that can hold a grudge."

"You don't know what you're talking about."

"That's partially true. But if not Parmacelli, who? Want to guess?"

"No, I don't want to guess."

"Very well. How about I guess and you tell me if I'm hot or cold?"

She didn't answer. I'm used to that.

"How about your dad? You think your dad was pissed at him?"

"That's crazy. Dad hardly knows him."

"What about your mom?"

"Don't be stupid."

"I'll try. John?"

"There's no one in my family who would have any reason to hurt him."

"What about Margot?"

"What about her?"

"Maybe they had a lovers' quarrel. She had him beat up and took off. That happens."

"That's ridiculous."

"All right. What about Brendon? I know he wouldn't do it himself. None of these people would get their hands dirty that way. But maybe Brendon had a beef with Cliff."

She hesitated a moment, then said, "That's crazy."

I could see that she was worried I knew more than she wanted me to know.

I don't always invest in the commerce of information. I can keep things to myself. But, like most people I like having knowledge of something and then showing it off. Sort of like how news channels like to get the scoop on something. Getting those recognition points for being the first to know fuels gossip.

I knew something she didn't know I knew, but now suspected. My ego wanted to brag. I knew better than to let it have its way, but sometimes I can't help myself.

"I gotta believe Brendon isn't happy with what's going on with you and Cliff."

That got a rise out of her. She picked up the gun and put it right in front of my face. I could see the little front sight and got a deeper appreciation of what gun metal actually looks like.

She held the weapon there. I didn't hold outing someone about having an affair a capital offense, but we all dispense justice differently.

"Look, I don't care what you and Cliff have going on. I just want to find out who beat him up. I'm pretty sure it wasn't you. Don't you want to know?"

"You better not tell anyone. What we have is a special thing and I don't need you gabbing about it."

"I have no plans to tell anyone," I said, which was true at that moment.

She put the gun back down and I found my breath.

"I have to think that his being beaten up had something to do with the legal papers that were filed last week. Do you know anything about that?"

"No, I don't, and if I did I wouldn't tell you."

I read that as she did know something and wasn't going to tell me. It made no difference one way or the other unless I could find a way to get her to tell me.

"Here's my concern. Cliff could have been beat up as a warning. The clerk in the register's office either didn't get that warning or had done something that warranted being killed instead of beaten. Whoever was responsible for one most likely was responsible for both. Needless to say, they're willing to do whatever's required to protect their interests. If their interests have something to do with Cliff, you could also be of interest."

She lifted her eyes and looked out past me.

"If we can find out what Cliff was doing that was so important, we might be able to figure out who else thought so too."

I don't have the kind of powers that allow me to see behind someone's eyes, but something was going on there. I wanted to think she knew who the interested party was, but that was wishful thinking. We tend to see what we want to see.

What she didn't want me to see is what, if anything, she'd left or picked up in the house. She untied me, escorted me out, and watched me get in my car. Then she got in hers and followed me back to town. Whatever had brought her to Cliff's house had been interrupted by her discovering me. That meant there was unfinished business back there.

She followed me all the way to the Miramar, then took a turn and peeled away from me. That's when I made a U-turn and followed her.

CHAPTER FORTY-NINE
Over the Hill

SOMETIMES YOU NEED to do something even though you know it's wrong. It sounds stupid and I don't subscribe to it, but I do occasionally do it. I wasn't sure that following Elizabeth was wrong but I couldn't think of anything better to do, and in the split second it took me to turn the car around a decision was made. Of course, I could have stopped at any time, but my OCD tendencies push me to finish what I start.

Following someone isn't the most difficult job. Most of us don't pay close attention to what's happening behind us. Sure, I check now and then for the police, but that's about it. As long as I didn't tailgate her, I figured I'd go undetected.

And I was curious.

You ever hope someone will give you a particular birthday gift yet don't want to get your hopes up high? But when you see a box that's the right size for what you want, your hopes bump up a little.

When Elizabeth drove out of town and up the hill, I got excited. Was she going to look at the property Cliff wanted? I didn't know what that meant exactly, but it was something in the plus column. When she didn't take the turnoff, it moved over to the minus side.

As she went down the mountain toward Santa Ynez, my hopes shifted. She couldn't be, could she?

She could. She did. She drove right under Mr. Parmacelli's sour grapes and up the driveway. Would I? Dare I?

I stayed a few hundred yards behind but there was no one between us. She drove past the tasting room and right on up to the main house. I drove into the parking lot by the tasting room, parked the car, and had a good talk with myself.

Elizabeth and Mr. Parmacelli were connected. I hoped not in the Mafia sense of the word. Though they could be that too. Whether they were or weren't, Elizabeth was now seriously in the mix. I could hold that information and safely take my leave.

Or…

I drove the car up to the main house. There was Elizabeth's Land Rover. And there was the front door.

I knocked. A scene from *Gunga Din* flashed before me. Cary Grant, knowing he will be captured, dashingly enters an enemy encampment to save others. As I recall, he went in singing. I didn't quite feel as heroic or musical, but the image stayed with me.

The housekeeper opened the door and had me wait. Soon, Elizabeth came storming down the hallway.

"What the hell are you doing here?" she yelled.

"I followed you."

"You can't do that. What are you doing? First you break into Cliff's house and now you follow me here. I could call the police and have you arrested."

"That's true, I suppose. But it's not like I'm doing anything illegal. I just wanted to see where you went after you stopped following me. If following someone is illegal, I'd say we're even on that."

At that point, Parmacelli stepped outside his office and said, "Come here."

We came.

He sat at his desk and offered me a chair opposite him. Elizabeth stood at the end of the desk.

"What's going on here?" he asked.

"This man broke into Cliff's house and followed me here."

"He did, did he?"

"I didn't really break into Cliff's house. I went there at the request of his daughter to pick up something. If anyone broke into his house, it was her."

"Let's not squabble. What are you doing knocking on my door and coming into my home?"

"I don't mean to be disrespectful of your home in any way. It's just that Elizabeth and I were talking, and as I told you, I'm a trained therapist. I know when people are upset. I could tell she was in a troubled state, so I followed her to make sure she was okay. When she came here I felt some relief as I know you're a man who knows how to take care of things. So I knocked on the door to see if I could be of any help to you."

There was a lot of bullshit there, but you know how it is—once you've started, it's easy to get on a roll. I doubled down.

"I'm friends with Elizabeth's sister's fiancé's daughter. I hope that makes sense. Anyway, Elizabeth and I know each other and have spoken a few times. As I told you before, I'm good at helping people resolve conflicts and I know Elizabeth is having one. Maybe she came here to tell you so you could help her with it. You certainly can do that and if you have it all handled I'm happy to leave and let you two take care of matters."

"You're not going anywhere," Mr. Parmacelli said, and took a gun out of a desk drawer. This gun business was getting repetitive.

What's a guy to do? You'd think given my recent experience in these matters I'd have no worries. But Mr. Parmacelli was the kind of guy who made worrying worthwhile. I could be ground up fertilizer for those grapes in no time.

"I've met some bullshit artists in my life, but I gotta hand it to you. I haven't figured out your angle, but I know you're angling for something. And whatever it is, I'm not inclined to give it to you."

"Nor should you be."

I've learned in situations like this that it's important to start on points of agreement and build a level of trust.

"I don't have a lot of time to waste here so I'm only going to ask once. What are you doing here?"

"I don't want to waste any of your time. I think you'll find our time together will be well worth your while."

Build trust and show how they'll benefit. It's very important in therapy and sales. Especially if you're trying to sell your continuance on earth in forms other than compost.

"If you're going to spin it, you better do it well."

It was *Rumpelstiltskin* where the maiden spun hay into gold. I was rooting for some of that magic.

"What I said is true. Elizabeth is upset. Have you told him why yet? Do you want me to tell him, or do you want to do it?"

He looked at her. I looked at her.

She said, "You can tell him your lies."

"I'm sorry you feel that way. Mr. Parmacelli, you can judge for yourself. Elizabeth is closely involved with Cliff, who happens to be the very fellow who called you out on your ride a little while ago. Now, I don't care about any of that, but you might. Elizabeth is involved with him in ways I suspect you wouldn't want your wife involved with another man. So, Elizabeth is here today, in part, because she knows her secret could be exposed."

I paused to see how close my head was to the block.

"I don't know if she's going to ask you for help regarding that or not. And, frankly, that's not my concern. My reason for being here is to reassure her that I'm not going to tell anyone other than you, Mr. Parmacelli. I'm also here to let you know that if you need assistance in trying to resolve any of the issues related to this matter, I'm here to help. I'm a professional. I get paid to help people out when the world isn't treating them the way they'd like. I'm here if you want my help. And if you don't, I'm happy to leave."

He was cogitating.

The last part of what I said is actually close to the truth. I'd been working with clients in and out of the office for some time. Sure, I'd framed it a little differently, but I was still working within the scope of my practice, give or take.

"You're a shrink, right?"

"Right."

"You got confidentiality like a lawyer, right?"

"Mostly right."

"So if you hear something, you gotta keep it private, right?"

"Unless it involves a threat to yourself or others."

"Okay, I'm hiring you. Keep what you heard to yourself." He reached into his pocket, took out a wad of dollar bills, and handed me a hundred.

"Ah…"

"Good. Now here's what I want you to do. Get out of here and never bother Elizabeth again. And if I ever see you here again, I'm going to feed you to the plants."

I'd been right about the fertilizer. I wasn't sure about having Mr. Parmacelli as a client. He'd be the first one I called by last name only, and we hadn't really talked about my fee. I guess continuing with my life was a living wage. I was happy to honor what he wanted. Well, sort of. I wasn't sure about the not-bothering-Elizabeth part. Or the not-seeing-me-back-here again thing.

CHAPTER FIFTY

Documents

I DROVE BACK toward town. As I got close to the top of the mountain, I saw a sign for the Cold Springs Tavern. I was due to meet everyone at the hospital at five, and had a little time on my hands. So why not? I turned off the highway and soon found myself at a rustic watering hole. There was a historical sign that said the place had been built in 1865 and was a resting stop for the stagecoach as it went over the mountain pass.

I don't know what it looked like back in the 1860s, but the place didn't seem to have changed much. I ordered a beer and looked at the walls—lots of mounted animal heads and old-time pictures. Then I noticed the liquor license. I had one of those *aha* moments.

I polished off the beer and sped back to the clerk's office, hoping I'd get there before it closed.

My therapist's license was on my office wall. The tavern's license was on its wall. That meant they were public records. I don't know why Ellen Withers had initially been reluctant to show us Cliff's records. Maybe it was because we hadn't asked directly. Maybe that reluctance was connected to her murder. When I'd talked with the tight-assed man I'd only asked about the filing for Cliff and Margot; he'd confirmed documents had been filed. I'd assumed they'd both signed everything. However, while they'd filed the marriage license, maybe she or he had filed something else separately. You'd think I'd know better about making assumptions.

The same by-the-book looking man was in the office along with another clerk. I stood in the short line and waited my turn. Soon I was standing in front of Josefina Martinez. I asked her what I needed to do to see Cliff's and Margot's marriage license, business license and any other recent documents. She gave me a form to fill out and I made two separate requests. One for the marriage license, property deed, will and business license for Cliff Anderson, and another for Margot Spalding. It wasn't long by bureaucratic standards before I was face-to-face with the documents.

Margot and Cliff had indeed signed their marriage license the previous week. Aside from finding out their middle names, there was no new information. Well, there was one thing. On discovering there was a marriage license, I'd initially assumed they'd gotten married, but then realized they could have taken out the paperwork but not done the deed. The license in front of me confirmed that they'd been married the previous week.

My personal view is that when you get married it's preferable to go on the honeymoon together. Maybe she'd gotten a head start and he'd been going to catch up with her, but we hadn't seen any plane tickets in his house.

There were two other documents of interest, and one not so much. I hadn't been given access to the will so I didn't know whose it was or wasn't, but I did have the other documents. The property at 3030 Painted Cave Road was co-owned by Parmacelli Incorporated and Margot Spalding. She owned fifty-one percent. The sale had been completed the previous month. But filed only last week. There was also a filing for a Fictitious Business Name: The Center. Margot Spalding and Cliff Anderson were the sole owners. I asked if they'd make me a copy of the forms. They did, for a dollar.

CHAPTER FIFTY-ONE

Cliff's Memory

I DROVE OVER to the hospital. Michael was already there, reading an old *Time* magazine.

"Hey," I said.

"Hi there. How are you?"

"I'm good. You?"

"Much better now that Cliff is on the mend."

"I hear you. Hopefully he'll soon be able to shed some light on the mystery of who beat him up. Speaking of mysteries, are you now able to tell me about what you were doing at the clerk's office?"

"It's why I moved up here. I'm opening a small clinic, but it's still in the planning stages so I haven't said anything to anyone."

"That's great. I hope it works out for you."

"Thanks. There's a lot of paperwork and I'm just getting started, but hopefully it will all come together. I planned to tell Cliff and Alan at the conference, which is why I didn't want to talk about it the other day."

"Okay, I won't say anything. Has Cliff said anything to you about The Center? Have you spoken with him about any of that stuff?"

"We're on the same wavelength. I thought I'd ask him when we go in. I'm curious what he remembers. Very curious."

"Me too."

Rachel showed up soon thereafter, along with Alan. Elizabeth hadn't made it back yet. Dr. Novatt gave us the update. Things were progressing along slowly but steadily. Cliff's speech was almost a hundred percent but his memory was still spotty. We were allocated fifteen minutes. Given that there were only two groups, Rachel and I had a good seven to eight minutes with him.

Rachel hadn't thrown any hard balls at Cliff—hadn't questioned him about his love life, his work life, or why someone had beaten him up, but I could see she was starting to warm up.

"Dad, have the police talked with you?"

"Yes, they've been here a couple of times."

"What did you tell them?"

"I told them I don't remember anything about being beaten up. Obviously, I know I was, but I have no recollection of it at all. The police and doctors say that isn't uncommon and my memories ought to come back. But so far, not so much."

"I'm sure it's got to be frustrating."

"Yeah, it is. I don't like not knowing what happened to me, but right now I'm not feeling one way or the other about it."

The wonder of painkillers.

"So, Dad, what's the last thing you remember?"

"Everyone's been asking me that. It's strange. I remember things but I'm not sure if one thing happened before or after another. My memory is slowly coming back together, but it's pretty ragged."

"That must be eerie," she said with a shudder. "What's the most recent memory you have of us?"

"I certainly remember that lovely walk we took on the beach. Not so sure how long ago that was, but that seems to be about the time my memories are starting to come in glimpses."

"That was a couple of months ago. Do you remember what we talked about on the beach?"

"No, honey, I don't. I wish I did, but I have a lousy memory and it's not getting any better."

I thought I spotted disappointment on Cliff's face when we left and Michael and Alan went in. If Elizabeth didn't show up soon she'd have to wait till morning.

"Want to do something tonight?" Rachel asked.

"Sure. What have you got in mind?"

"How about something normal? A movie. Dinner and a movie. You up for that?"

"Is this date night?"

"I'm feeling better than I've felt all week. Sure, I wish Dad would remember who did this to him, but I'm so relieved and happy to see him improve."

"Yeah. It's comforting. So what movie?"

"We don't have a lot of choices, but *Risky Business* just came out. Seems appropriate."

"That's perfect. I saw that if we watched the movie and went to a discussion group in the morning we'd get a credit."

"Sounds like a win–win."

CHAPTER FIFTY-TWO
Evening Activity

"I have to talk with you," I said.

"I'm here," Rachel said as we each ate our own tacos at La Supa Rica. I'm a believer that a good restaurant is worth repeating.

"Here's what I found out today. Your dad and Margot got married last Friday. We knew about the license, but it seems strange that they'd get married and then she'd take off. Maybe your dad was going to join her, or they were going to honeymoon later. Or maybe they had a big altercation and she took off. Either way, it's odd. But it's not the oddest thing I learned. You know that property up on Painted Cave? I found out it was sold last month. Want to guess who bought it?"

"No. Just tell me."

"Mr. Parmacelli."

"What? The wine guy?"

"Yeah, the wine guy. But he didn't buy it all by his lonesome. He had a partner. Actually, a partner who owns fifty-one percent of it. And her name is Margot Spalding."

"No way. Michael did imply that Dad had found a way. It's a strange way, but his wife is the majority owner so I guess that's good."

"I guess. But I wouldn't exactly want to be partners with Mr. Parmacelli. He's not the silent-partner type."

"Even so, they own that property. That's wonderful news. Sort of. Mostly. I'm not sure. I'll have to ask my dad."

"And congratulate him on the marriage. I wonder why he didn't invite you?"

"Yeah, that's strange, but we're just getting to know each other so maybe he thought it was too soon."

"Maybe. He got married at the courthouse so it could've been one of those Elvis weddings."

"Elvis weddings?"

"Perhaps not the best example. You know, you pay the clerk $25 and someone witnesses it, then bingo, you're married."

"I guess. I'd like it to be bit more romantic than that."

"Who knows? Someone might have sung "Love Me Tender." And there's something else. There's a fictitious-business-name license for an enterprise called The Center, and that name is owned by Margot and your dad."

"My dad is making his dream come true. It's so great."

"He'll be real happy to know it once he remembers or hears about it. He may not know he got married."

"That's so weird."

We ate dinner, swapped life stories, saw Tom Cruise dance in his underwear, and then we were back in the hotel lobby. It was one of those moments where you want to do one thing even if it's wrong, but think you ought to do something else even if that's also wrong. I felt awkward and uncomfortable so I kissed her.

It was an awfully good kiss. Soft, hard, long, and too short. We looked at each other closely.

"Do we or do we not want to do this?" I said.

"Yes, that's the question."

"What's the answer?"

"The answer, my friend, is not blowing in the wind," said Alan as he approached us. "I'm sorry to interrupt your love fest, but there's something we need to talk about."

Saved or not saved by the bell.

"What's up?" Rachel said.

"As Dave knows, we asked Cliff what he remembers about the center. He recalled our coming up with the idea in Esalen and some conversations with Michael but not much else. He also remembered visiting the potential site, and some talks about the financing, but that's it."

"Wow. That's very interesting," Rachel said. "When he spoke with me he talked about a walk we took a couple of months ago when we first got together, but nothing else. I'd hoped he'd have remembered more."

"That's what we thought too, since we've been having ongoing conversations for a couple of years."

"I don't know much about concussions and comas but I guess one could have selective memories."

"That's what he has," said Rachel. "I hope things start falling back into place for him. I know I'd hate it if there were blanks in my memory."

One thing I knew, or at least thought I knew, was that Cliff had gone forward with the center without Michael and Alan's knowledge. Had he really lost the memories or was he purposefully keeping secrets?

Neither Rachel nor I thought it prudent to mention what I'd learned at the clerk's office, but when Alan left we talked about our next steps. Would they be to my room, back out on the case, or to parts unknown?

I wasn't sure what to do with Rachel, who looked like she wasn't sure what to do with me. The mood surrounding our kiss had been dispelled. We talked a little more about her father and his memory and, in doing so, pocket-vetoed our romance for later.

I think we both felt a combination of disappointment and relief.

CHAPTER FIFTY-THREE
News

August 4, 1983

I DIDN'T KNOW who was or wasn't going to be joining me for breakfast so I went ahead and ordered my granola and coffee. The front page of the newspaper had gone from Ellen being shot to a pedestrian being run over by a bicycle. Today we were back to shootings.

This time the victim was Elizabeth Spalding.

I had to read the headline twice and take a moment. I'd talked with her only the day before and now I was reading about her being shot in the offices of Spalding Enterprises.

This wasn't good news. When anyone loses their life "before their time" it's horrible. Life is precious; to lose it too soon is tragic.

My thoughts went to Brendon, John, Eleanor, Vic, and Margot. This was devastating for them. It's bad enough when tragedy strikes people you don't know. It's something else entirely when it happens in your family. I flashed on the Fiesta blowout party that was scheduled for tonight and wondered if it would go ahead.

I've never felt comfortable talking about death. I'm not alone in that. What do you say? What do you do? Do you want to be sincere and yet not get too involved or do you really want to be there for others in whatever ways they need? With friends, I want to be fully there; with the Spaldings, I wasn't so sure.

Spending time with them would mean forgoing my agenda and just being there for them. I'm not the best at that. But there were condolences to pay, questions to ask, reactions to assess, and a killer to find. I'd have to do it a little more delicately, which is not always my strength.

But first, breakfast.

Rachel strode into the restaurant saw me and came over. She looked good.

I started to lament the path not taken. But this wasn't the time for that. I could save the self-recrimination for later. Now, I had something I needed to tell her. And the newspaper front page to show her.

"Hi. Good morning. You look great. But that's all the niceties for now as I need to tell you something before Michael and/or Alan show up. I realized something that's embarrassing but truthful: just because I don't know something it doesn't mean that somebody else doesn't know it. I may not know what's on the menu—although by now I do—but it doesn't mean that you don't know."

"You just realized that?"

"Well, in a new way. I'm aware that many people know way more than I will ever know or care to know."

"Get to the point. So, the embarrassing revelation is…"

"Just because we couldn't access Cliff's and Margot's documents doesn't mean that other people didn't know they were in the public domain. And I'm talking about the other people coming to the table now. Who knows how long they've known."

"Good morning," said Michael as he slid into the booth. "Hope everyone had a good night.""Good morning," Rachel and I said in unison.

"Hey," said Alan.

"I hate to be the bearer of bad news, but I'm going to be."

I lifted the newspaper, displaying a picture of Elizabeth and the story of her body being found at Spalding Enterprises.

"Oh my God," said Rachel.

"That's dreadful," said Michael.

"Rough," said Alan.

"I don't know any more than the headline. There's no story—I guess it broke right before going to press."

Tears formed in Rachel's eyes. "This is horrible. I feel so sorry for everyone. We were just with her. I can't believe it."

"It really is hard to digest," said Alan.

"Right," Michael said. "Why would anyone do such a thing? It makes no sense."

"Maybe she came into the offices when someone was robbing the place and they shot her. There's that possibility," I said without conviction.

"Or maybe the person who killed Ellen killed her," said Rachel wiping her eyes. "It's just so sad."

"It is. But it's good to have a conspiracy theory," Alan said.

"If the same person killed them," Rachel said, "there's a reason that they both were killed and not anyone else."

"Yet," said Alan.

"And then there's your dad," Michael said. "The same person could have beaten him up."

"Yeah," I said. "We don't know if the person who did the beating did the killings. The modus operandi is different, yet they've all happened within a short window and seem connected."

"If one person did all this, they would need to be strong enough to beat up my dad and cold enough to kill two women. Or maybe they hired someone who could do those things."

"In that case, we're looking at someone who has the funds and connections to make that happen. Which conveniently leaves you out, grad student that you are," I said.

"Thank you for not thinking I had my dad beat up," Rachel said.

"We've all had that thought about our parents at one time or another," said Michael.

I wasn't sure about that, but got the point.

"So, let me ask you," I said. "We're all in the same business. Why did someone do this? Can we agree they were driven by something aside from their parents not loving them enough. What would motivate someone to the extent they'd be willing to do this with their own hands or hire someone else to do their dirty work for them? Who are we looking for?"

"Someone did someone wrong. Big time. Broke their heart," said Michael.

"Rejection is the key," said Alan.

"Greed," said Rachel. "I could see the broken heart and rejection for Elizabeth, but that's not what got Ellen killed. Maybe it got my dad beaten. It has to do with money. That's what they say in mysteries. Follow the money. Who profits from this?"

"John and Margot get a bigger piece of the inheritance," I said.

"That's disgusting," Rachel said.

"That doesn't work for Ellen," said Alan.

"I'm guessing it has to do with the property," I said. "Ellen is connected to legal matters. The property is a legal matter and Cliff and is connected to the property."

"That fits," said Rachel.

I didn't know how well it fit. Margot and Mr. Parmacelli owned the property. I couldn't see any connection between Elizabeth and the property but I knew she had gaga eyes for Cliff. I didn't know if Michael and Alan knew what I knew, and couldn't make up my mind whether to put it on the table. At one point I'd thought of us as a team, but that was before I became suspicious of everyone.

So far, they'd given me no indication that they knew who owned the property or who'd filed the papers for The Center. If they'd been lying, they'd done a good job of it. Although, we hadn't specifically talked about who owned the land. Theirs could have been the sin of omission. In which case, why commit it? Why not be forthcoming with me? Either they had something to hide or they didn't know.

"Do either of you know who owns the property?"

I couldn't spot a tell. They both shrugged and Michael said, "Some family's owned it forever, but Cliff thought they'd sell it to him."

If they didn't know, there didn't seem much need for me to burst their bubble. If they did know and were able to contain their lie well enough for me not to notice, then maybe it wouldn't be too much of a leap for them to keep other things unnoticed as well.

CHAPTER FIFTY-FOUR

Movement Therapy

IT WAS THE last day of Fiesta and the last full day of the conference. If I wanted to be the hero my time was running out. My dissertation—I'm sorry to mention it, but it'll be brief—was about how the task expands and contracts to fit the time available. If the case needed to be solved by tonight it would happen tonight. If it could be solved tomorrow, it would be done tomorrow. Or so the theory went. As we know, theory and practice don't always intersect.

I had two more units to go to get my continuing-education credits. Discussing *Risky Business* would give me one. I needed to find time later today or in the morning to finish up.

I'd thought we were going to discuss the movie, but I was wrong. We were going to dance to the soundtrack.

Movement therapy's in the textbook right next to art therapy. It's what they call an expressive therapy. Not that you don't express yourself when you're sitting down, talking to your therapist, but we can be guarded in our talking in a way we may not be in our movement. Being left to express ourselves in free-form while music plays provides an opportunity to experience ourselves in a different way. I'm usually up for anything that will enhance and expand my experience of life, as long as I only feel a little awkward and don't have to put my life at risk

I was moving along to Bob Seger's "Old Time Rock and Roll." Tom Cruise didn't need to worry about any competition from the group, but we were having fun and I was feeling loose. Until Scarface came into the room. They say you can tell a lot about a person by observing their non-verbal behavior. Scarface had no interest in loosening up.

Soon I was moving around like I'd been starched. I couldn't focus on being free in the moment, so I focused on my plan for the evening while I kept a discreet eye on Scarface.

I couldn't visualize getting all the suspects in a room, turning up the music and having them dance their way into the big reveal, but the notion had given me an idea. I tend to favor the big reveal. There's power in groups that can help you get to the truth. I had a hunch there was something I could do at the Fiesta blowout—if there were still going to be a Fiesta blowout—that might just get the suspect—if they were in the room—to reveal themselves.

But first I needed to go to a record store.

I drove to Discount Records in Isla Vista. One of the guys behind the counter looked familiar.

"Do I know you?" I asked.

"You're the shrink from the US festival, right?"

"Right. I remember you. You're Hale."

"Good to see you again. What's up?'

"I'm hoping you can help me. I need a song I can play for someone who's died. It doesn't have to be a slow song, as I'd like people to able to move to it, but it does need to be respectful of the moment."

"You have two choices. Both Jackson Browne. You can go with 'For a Dancer' or 'For a Rocker.' When Belushi died they played 'For a Dancer' on *Saturday Night Live*. It's slow, but he wrote it for a dancer friend who'd died, so it moves. 'For a Rocker,' well, he wrote that for the guitarist for the Pretenders and it rocks."

"Good choices. I have both those albums, but not with me. Any chance you have them on cassette and can sell me a cheap but good player?"

"You bet. I'm here to help."

It was nice seeing Hale again. He certainly knew his music and if he stuck it out he ought to do okay for himself. In the meantime, I needed to get to the hospital.

CHAPTER FIFTY-FIVE
Another Hospital Visit

Rachel, Michael, and Alan were sitting in the waiting area. Rachel had spoken with Eleanor and, while she was very upset, she'd said they were going forward with the party to honor Elizabeth's life. We all agreed to meet there at seven.

It wasn't long before Dr. Novatt showed up. We asked him whether we could talk to Cliff about more recent events and he said it would be fine but to stay away from anything that would be emotionally provocative. That left off telling him about his marriage to Margot, and Elizabeth's death. Rachel and I got fifteen minutes with him, as did Michael and Alan.

Cliff was looking better. His wounds were healing and he seemed to have more energy. Rachel lobbed him soft balls so as not to upset him. I wasn't sure she'd be happy if I upped the ante, but we needed more information or I'd be going home with no hero merit badge.

"Cliff, can I ask you something?"

"Sure."

"I went over to the courthouse the other night and watched the dancers. It really is a lovely place, and watching the dancers was quite enjoyable."

"I've never been much of a fan of Fiesta but sitting on a blanket, having a picnic, watching those dancers is something I try to do every year."

"Yeah, it's certainly a feel-good activity. I toured the building and bumped into some people who worked at the clerk's office. We got to talking and they mentioned that they knew you and that you'd been there a few times recently. Do you have any memory of what you were doing there?"

There wasn't any music playing so I couldn't see how he danced around the question, but I could see he was uncomfortable.

"I can't say I do."

Us shrinks, we listen to words. "Can't say I do" didn't mean he didn't remember. Just that he couldn't or wouldn't say. Maybe I was reading too much into it, but I thought he knew more than he was letting on. Of course, his memory was spotty and that could have made him hesitant to say anything until he was certain.

A look from Rachel told me I'd used up my quota of questions. However, I'd only learned some of what I wanted. My gut said Cliff was lying. Why, I wasn't sure. Maybe he wasn't ready to tell Rachel about the marriage or the property. Maybe he didn't know about the property. I needed to ask a follow-up question.

"That's okay. One other question. We wanted to let Margot know what happened to you, but she's in Europe and so far unreachable. Do you have any idea how we can get a hold of her?"

"She does like to travel and be off on her own. There's a key to her house on a hook on the coatrack by my front door. You could go check her place and see if she left her itinerary. Even though she goes off the radar, she does generally plot out her travels."

"That's great. I'll go do that. Do you have her address, or I can look it up in the phone book?"

"That easy. She lives on Mountain Drive, over by the reservoir. 1050 Mountain Drive."

Rachel and I left Cliff's room, and I told Michael and Alan I'd meet them at the ranch that evening. Rachel opted to stay at the hospital and go to an afternoon workshop later.

I was disappointed as I'd wanted to do the Margot-sleuthing with her, but she seemed as intent on her own agenda as I was on mine.

CHAPTER FIFTY-SIX

Margot's Place

I TOOK THE winding road back up to Cliff's house, figuring there'd be no surprises this time. The key was on a lanyard hanging on the coatrack that was otherwise empty. I was anxious to get to Margot's, but since I was already at Cliff's I decided to search again. I went up to his desk and re-read the note that was still there:

> Someone is going to kill me. I have done a terrible thing and deserve to die. If you read this before you hear of my death, do not contact the police. They'll only make things worse. The only thing that can help me is me.
>
> I am truly sorry for my actions as I know I have seriously hurt people. To those people and their families, I do not seek forgiveness but understanding. I did what I did because at the time I saw no other path. Now I do, but I fear it is too late. I have begun to make amends, but there is more to do. I am going to try to do that, but may not have enough time. I will

Had Cliff typed that note, or was it the person who'd beat him up? What had he done that was so horrible he deserved to die? He hadn't killed Ellen or Elizabeth. He'd married Margot. While that certainly could have been a terrible thing, most bad marriages are not grounds for murder, and those that are take a little longer to get there.

How had he known someone was coming to kill him? And if they'd found him, why hadn't they killed him? I was no closer to answering those questions than when I'd first read the note.

I surveyed the house once more but nothing garnered my attention. I got back in my car, took out my trusty AAA map and found my way to Mountain Drive.

I wasn't used to walking in the front door with a key. Well, that's not right. I was used to it. I just hadn't done it in a while. I don't how much room a single person needs, but Margot had the over pretty well covered. The house was in the foothills and didn't have a gated entry, but it could have had. Instead, a long driveway took you out to a point with a decent view of the south coast. The place had a similar feeling to Cliff's. His was the starter-kit version. I'd known it before, but seeing Margot's home affirmed that she wasn't after Cliff for his money. In fact, it seemed he was after her for hers. He'd certainly be living in a better house, and if it got burdensome he could always confer with Brendon.

Margot's home had a minimalist look. There was a lot of open space; Cliff's looked cluttered in comparison. The entranceway led to a cathedral-vaulted living room. Oversized windows framed the deck and the boundless view beyond. If she wasn't coming back any time soon I wouldn't have minded splitting my house-sitting between here and what had been Elizabeth and Brendon's home.

I began by looking in the places where I'd keep my own travel plans. Of course, mine weren't in the same league, but plane tickets, passports and other related material would likely be in one space.

I found what looked to be her study. It had a large picture window with a window seat that was more like a sofa. You could easily nap there if you were so inclined. There were shelves along the wall that were mostly void of books, just small groupings by topic—horses, travel, architecture and some fiction—interspersed with pieces of art. She had a good eye—at least, I liked what she'd collected. The items had an international flair and had likely been picked up on her travels. I didn't see anything you'd pick up at an airport gift shop.

A large half-circle desk looked like it had been custom-built. There was an Eames desk chair that cost more than my car. The desk was tidy by most people's standards—just a typewriter and some piles of paperwork. I looked through them but didn't find anything noteworthy, and was relieved there was no note in the typewriter warning of her demise.

I don't spend a lot of time in the kitchen, but if I did, this too, would have been a good place to hunker down. There was a six-burner stove, and a refrigerator big enough to hold all the bronze pots that were hanging over a wooden island with stools for casual eating. On the refrigerator there was a shopping list of things she needed at the market. I decided she wouldn't mind if I kept her list. It was a good reminder that I needed to stop at the grocery store before I got home.

At the top of the stairway was a landing with more picture windows. Upstairs I arrived in a space that I wouldn't have bothered leaving if it had been mine. The whole of the top floor was an oversized bedroom, bathroom, and closet.

The bathroom contained a tub that could just as easily have been called a pool. Okay, you couldn't actually swim in it, but you could turn on the jets and let the Jacuzzi push you around. She'd opted for a Scandinavian look—bleached wood, a sauna, and a shower that jetted spray from all sides. I could see why Cliff was drawn to become a member of the rut club. If you weren't going to love your spouse you could at least live in the lap of luxury.

The closet was an obsessive-compulsive's dream. Everything was arranged by color. It seemed to me that she was the type who bought what she liked not only in multiple colors but also in duplicate.

There were matching dresses, blouses, pants, shoes, socks and hats. I didn't see any gaps in how her clothes were arranged. Just a few empty hangers. And there were three luggage bags on a shelf, enough to handle most trips.

I moved back into the bedroom. The bed was massive and festooned with pillows. There was a stone fireplace, sitting area, and another desk that looked to have gotten a bit more attention. No typewriter here, just papers, magazines, books, and a large calendar with a picture of the Eiffel Tower.

It was open at July, and there were entries for almost every day— lunch with the Junior League, dinner with Jacqueline, date nights with Cliff, and appointments for the dermatologist, hairdresser, and masseuse. What wasn't there was a wedding date and honeymoon in Europe. Plus, unlike the previous week there were appointments for the current week that she hadn't crossed off.

Margot seemed to use her calendar, so it seemed odd that she'd omitted her wedding and an overseas trip. I knew the marriage-license issue had been an on/off thing so maybe the ceremony had been spontaneous. But would that seizing of the moment have been followed by deciding to pack up and take off by herself?

I didn't know where Margot was, but I had a hunch she wasn't in Europe. Not unless she had a second passport. One was in a drawer right next to some Michelin guides.

Maybe the horrible thing Cliff had done was marry Margot and then knock her off. If he was in it for the money, that would relieve him of having to live with her long enough to go through a nasty divorce for which she could afford better lawyers. If Cliff had killed her, why send me to her house? Unless he'd forgotten he'd killed her. Was that possible? He'd forgotten he'd gotten beat up. Or had he? I wasn't so sure what to think anymore.

I looked at the books on the desk, because I'm curious that way. Danielle Steel's *Changes* and Jackie Collins' *Hollywood Wives* were on top. Below them was a leather-bound journal—her diary. I opened it up and read the last two entries:

> *July 19: I hate Elizabeth. She always wins. She always gets what she wants. She may have stolen Cliff's heart but he will never marry her. Brendon took care of that and I have taken care of him.*
>
> *July 21: We're going to have it out. This feels like the showdown at the O.K. Corral. We're meeting at the property and I'm taking my gun.*

I scanned back. Evidently Elizabeth and Margot had a longstanding hatred of each other. I'm not familiar with much of the research on twins, but having a twin means there are going to be issues. We barely get enough attention as it is; the rivalry and having to half things could easily make it more hate/love than love/hate.

I didn't know who she'd met at the property. Elizabeth? Maybe someone else. Regardless, a showdown had been on the cards. And she was bearing arms.

CHAPTER FIFTY-SEVEN

Center Property

NEXT STOP WAS the property. I drove down the dirt road until it ended, and parked. When I'd come here with Rachel, Michael and Alan, we'd stood close to Michael's car and looked out over the 150 acres and beyond. The view was just as palpable now, with the Channel Islands some thirty miles away. My attention, however, was focused more on the ground. I had no idea where the property line was or what 150 acres looked like, but it was time to take a closer look.

If something untoward had gone down here it had likely occurred relatively close to where my car was because that was the only reasonable parking area. If you killed someone and needed to move their body, how far would you go? You could take it back to your car and dispose of it elsewhere or you could look for closer options.

Margot didn't look like she weighed that much so someone could have thrown her over their shoulder and carried her some distance. But when they stopped they'd have needed to dig a grave. And, you know, it's not like everyone keeps a shovel in their trunk. The main reason to have a shovel in the trunk is because you expect to use it.

I started searching, my eyes to the ground. The property seemed to extend along and down the mountain. There were oaks, agaves and other trees and plants that lived without water most of the year. Boulders and rock formations sheltered a small stream with pools of steaming water that someday might be filled with paying attendees of The Center.

Outdoors, in the great unknown, I felt like a hunter and wanted to catch my prey.

I didn't like the idea that it might involve a grave.

Unfortunately, it did.

I found a spot where it looked like the earth had been recently dug into and piled back up. I didn't have a shovel in my trunk, and after scooping up some handfuls of dirt I lost interest in digging. I might be a hunter but, evidently, I wasn't a gatherer. I'd tell Lt. Flores and let him gather the evidence.

I could have been wrong. Maybe someone killed a coyote and buried it. Maybe there were giant gophers or some other acts of nature in play. Despite knowing the pitfalls of assuming, I decided to assume that Margot's body had been left on the property that she owned.

Had she bought this land with the intention of being buried on it? In that case, had she used up all her money on the property and left none for an actual burial site? I figured it was safe not to assume that.

But wait. No, she hadn't bought this land. According to her journal, she'd come here for the showdown on the twenty-first. Those papers were signed on the twenty-second. How could she have signed the papers if she was already dead? Unless it wasn't Margot who'd been buried. It could be it the person Margot had been meeting.

I'd thought Margot was meeting Elizabeth, but if they were meeting here and Elizabeth was buried here, she'd been doing some excellent afterlife-experiencing. If Margot was buried here, she too had been the beneficiary of an excellent afterlife. If it was someone else entirely, I had no idea how their afterlife was proceeding.

Most likely it was Margot. And if that was the case, who had Cliff married the next day and who had Mr. Parmacelli bought the property with?

Elizabeth.

Had Elizabeth come up here and killed Margot, posed as her for the paperwork and gotten herself killed at Spalding Enterprises for her efforts?

Had Margot come up here and killed Elizabeth, posed as her when called upon and gotten herself killed at Spalding Enterprises for her efforts?

Or had Margot come up here and killed someone else, or been killed by them?

Questions upon questions.

I don't like admitting this, but I'd felt excited on seeing that grave. That hunter/gatherer part of me high-fived my ancestry. Once I was in the car, though, the adrenaline subsided and I started to feel the pain of it.

This morning I'd read about Elizabeth's death. Now I was wondering whether her sister was dead too. Tragedy on top of tragedy. My thoughts went to Eleanor, Vic and John, and the devastation they'd soon feel. Horrible enough to lose one child.

This wasn't what anyone wanted. Except for one person.

I suddenly didn't want to go to the Fiesta blowout. The dread and agony in the room would be overwhelming. And yet that's where I needed to be. To help console.

And to reveal.

CHAPTER FIFTY-EIGHT
Checking In

Lt. Flores was neither pleased nor displeased to see me. He listened to my story, asked some questions, and then said, "This is a serious matter. The Spalding family has suffered a tremendous loss, and what you're telling me, well, that isn't what anyone wants to hear. I'll have some officers go up there and check. Make sure you leave your information with the sergeant out front."

Before I left I also shared some thoughts about my client, Mr. Parmacelli, that bordered on a breach of confidentiality. I didn't name names, but there weren't many vintners in the Santa Ynez Valley and I figured Flores would know how to reframe what I told him.

I didn't know what kind of priority the lieutenant would put on going to the property as it was the last day of the Fiesta and the town was bulging with tourists who were doing a lot of last minute Viva La Fiesta-ing. I certainly would not be saying anything to the Spaldings until they heard from him.

It was early afternoon. I had some time before heading out to the ranch and a few things to do. My civic duty done, I went back to the conference and looked for Michael and Alan. Michael wasn't at the pool, but Alan was back fishing in the ocean.

"Hey," I said as I came up alongside him again. "Any luck?"

"I haven't caught anything, but I'm lucky to be here."

"That sounds about right. Most people who fish feel lucky to be fishing. It's like the bumper sticker that says, 'A bad day fishing is better than a good day at work.'"

"Just being outside is good medicine. Fishing and watching a baseball game are my two favorite outdoor activities."

"I can relate to the exertion quotient."

"There's that. Plus, you never know how the game will turn out. And the water is like your unconscious—you throw your line into it and don't know what it's going to catch."

"I like that. I have a question for you. Any breaking news from your time with Cliff this morning?"

"Not much. Basically the same."

"Does he remember anything more about the property?"

"After hearing about Elizabeth, we didn't really want to push him. Reality is tough enough when you're at full strength."

"That's for sure. I have a question I've been meaning to ask. When you told Michael and me that the hospital called you because your number was in Cliff's wallet, how did that happen? I don't have my friends' numbers in my wallet, how come he had yours?"

"It was a lucky break. Last time I'd seen him I'd written down a note for him on the back of one of my cards and he still had it."

"That was fortunate. Well, good luck with the fishing. See you tonight. Won't be the blowout party anyone wanted."

"Not sure I should be there. I won't stay long."

"I hear you. I'm going to share a little something so I hope you stay for that."

"Share a little something?"

Leave it to a therapist to reflect back to you what you say.

"Yeah. You'll find out. It's a surprise."

CHAPTER FIFTY-NINE

Hospital Visit

I WENT BACK to my room and took out Margot's shopping list. Then I compared it with the copy of the marriage license, property deed, and business license. I'm no handwriting expert, but it didn't look to me that Margot had signed any of those forms.

It gave me no comfort. I had a hunch who Cliff had married and done the paperwork with, but like my graduate advisor used to tell me, I needed to check my sources.

You'd think if you did something often enough you'd get good at it. I was hoping experience was the best teacher as I got in the car and drove over to Brendon and Elizabeth's place. I needed to find a writing sample.

Fortunately, Brendon was doing his mourning away from home. I went around to the beachside and made my way back into the room where he'd come upon me before. I had two choices: one sensible one impulsive. I could find something she'd written, steal it, and compare it with the documents when I was no longer breaking and entering. Or I could find the sample, compare it with the documents I'd brought along and not steal anything but information. The second option would take longer and put me at more risk but allowed me not to have to take anything away. The first option was the wiser way to go, as I'm not one to linger. I found some notes she'd written and took out the documents. I couldn't compare signature to signature, but the writing looked to be the same. Since Elizabeth had looked like Margot it would have been easy for her to say that she was. I'd like to think I'd be able to tell my intended from her twin. But she could easily have fooled the clerk and most everyone else.

Had Cliff known they were forging the papers? Was that the horrible thing he'd done? Would someone want to kill him or beat him up for that? It was hard to tell. It was time to talk to Cliff.

I managed to get myself out of the beach house without being caught and drove over to the hospital. It was Saturday afternoon and the place looked pretty much the same. There aren't a lot of off-days at a hospital.

There was no one standing guard outside his door and no one else looked like they'd care, so I went in.

He looked pretty much as he had in the morning. I could tell he was a little confused to see me as he only knew me in connection with Rachel.

"Hi. I thought I'd come and see you by myself. Is that okay with you?"

"Sure. It's not like I've got a lot going on here. It's pretty boring actually. I just nap and take drugs. Today I got up and went to the bathroom. Pretty exciting."

"You do get to appreciate anew so much of what you take for granted when it's taken away from you."

"Whatever fantasies I had about lying around all day have been pretty well dashed. I can't wait to get out of here and complain about the usual stuff."

"I'm sure. There's a reason I came without Rachel today, and I'm hoping we can have a bit of a discussion."

"If you're coming to ask me about marrying her I'm afraid I'm not going to be much help there. Even if I gave you my blessing, Rachel has a mind of her own."

"You're right about that. But that's not why I came. I actually came to talk with you about your wedding."

"My wedding? I married her mother a long time ago. Fortunately, my long-term memory has yet to completely fade."

"That's good to know. But, no, that's not the wedding I meant. I want to talk with you about your wedding to Margot."

There was a pause, and enough awareness behind his eyes to warrant my pushing him a little.

"Dr. Novatt doesn't want us talking with you about anything that would up your blood pressure, so I don't want to upset you. I just want you to tell me why you married Elizabeth and had her sign the documents as Margot."

That didn't do wonders for his blood pressure, but it eased mine. He gave me a look that said he knew his bubble had been burst.

"You know about that?"

"I do. But if it's any consolation, I'm the only one who does. That's why I didn't want Rachel here. I want you to help me understand why you did it."

"Thank you. I'm actually glad you found out. I've been besieged by worry and regret."

"I don't know if I can help you, but I want to try. If you're comfortable enough, why not tell me the story and let me see what I can do."

I could see his desire to come clean outweighed his good sense. He ought to have clammed up but, just like clients in therapy and parishioners in the confessional, he needed to unburden himself. Plus, he was on a lot of drugs.

So he told me.

I didn't know if his story would line up with Elizabeth's but since she wasn't going to be forthcoming, his version got to stand unless proven differently.

His relationship with Margot had been going well and he'd had every intention of marrying her. Yes, for her money, but also because he'd loved her. But as he spent more time with her and the family, he'd become enamored with Elizabeth. Despite knowing better, little by little, they fell in love.

Brendon had managed to secure himself a tidy pre-nuptial so if Elizabeth divorced him she'd take a serious financial hit that wouldn't be recuperated until she received her inheritance. Cliff needed serious money now to buy the property and build his dream so he'd needed to marry Margot. Their realtor had told Cliff a couple of months earlier that someone else was interested in the property and if he didn't buy it now he'd lose it. That's when Cliff and Elizabeth hatched their plan.

Margot had been getting cold feet about the wedding, feeling increasingly like she was losing his affection and being used. Elizabeth had convinced him to go through with the ceremony and said she'd stand in for Margot. She'd told him she'd take care of Margot. He hadn't been sure what she'd meant by that, or how she'd accomplish it, but he'd let his desire overcome his judgment.

Being familiar with that impulse, I could understand it. He pretty well knew how she'd take care of things, but I didn't press him and he hadn't pressed Elizabeth.

It was a pretty sketchy rendering, but I guessed his guilt and his still spotty memory were playing a part in the storytelling. He still couldn't remember his being assaulted so he was either still regaining him memories or telling me what he wanted and not what he didn't.

When I left the hospital, my suspicions were confirmed. His reasons, his fear, and his truth made sense. That's one of the problems with being a therapist. You can empathize with people, understand why they do the things they do. Your heart can open to someone, but your brain can't always condone their actions.

I wanted to help him make The Center dream come true. But he'd crossed some lines and I wasn't yet sure what to do about it.

As I drove away, it occurred to me that it hadn't been hard for me to get into Cliff's hospital room. Anyone else could just as easily have spoken to him. Maybe someone had advised him to be quiet or to spin the story one way and not another.

CHAPTER SIXTY
Quality Time with Mr. Parmacelli

I NEEDED ONE more piece of information before I put the mystery together. I didn't want to go talk with Mr. Parmacelli, but since his name was on the deed I figured I'd better.

He wasn't any more pleased to see me this time than he'd been last time. I wouldn't charge him extra for the house visit, but decided it was worth reminding him that he was my client.

"Thanks for seeing me. I'm sure you're busy and I only want a few minutes. But since you did hire me as your therapist I thought I'd better come and talk with you."

"Half the time I don't know what you're talking about. The other half I know you're full of bullshit."

"That sounds about right. But let's not quibble about percentages. There's something I found out and you need to know about it."

"Spill it."

"First, let me ask you. Are you planning on going to the Spalding's house tonight?"

"Of course. It's a horrible thing that happened."

"Yes, it is. And that's in part why I'm here."

"I'm waiting."

"Okay. I don't know how close you are to Vic and Eleanor. I know Vic, like yourself, is a Visitadore, so I'm sure you two go back."

"We do."

"If the subject of the property on Painted Cave comes up when you speak with him, well, I thought you ought to know that the information relating to its sale and ownership is in the public domain."

"I know that. But who knows about the property and how the hell did they find out?"

"That I can't tell you. I just happen to know that the information is out there."

"What do you mean you can't tell me?"

"Like we discussed before, I get paid to keep confidences, but I thought you'd want to know that the information is going to be shared."

Something was wrong. He told me to get out and on the way I asked him for a favor. I knew it would put me in his debt, but it was a debt I was happy to bear.

Until it was payback time.

Had Elizabeth fooled him? Had he thought he was buying the property with Margot or had he been in on the deception?

Or had I put the wrong frame around it?

What if it was Margot who'd made the deal with Mr. Parmacelli a month ago? Maybe she'd liked Cliff's idea, decided not to be his bankroll, and instead make it happen herself. Maybe she'd take his idea and leave him. She wouldn't have been the first.

Michael and Alan had said that there was a fatal flaw with all of Cliff's girlfriends. Perhaps Margot had had some larceny in her. Or perhaps she'd found out about Cliff and Elizabeth and was vengeful.

If Margot planned to take Cliff's idea and make it her own, she might have wanted to look outside the immediate family for financial assistance. Mr. Parmacelli, an old family friend, could bankroll it. He could also take care of any problems that came up.

If Elizabeth had got wind of Margot's dealings and knew they would screw Cliff over, she might have decided to do unto Margot as Margot planned to do unto Cliff. That would explain why Cliff had been willing to look the other way if Elizabeth took permanent care of Margot. Maybe that's what the showdown on Painted Cave had been about.

As I drove back over the hill my thoughts went to Rachel. She'd just been welcomed into a family and discovered she had sisters. Then suddenly she didn't. My heart went out to her, and yet my thoughts went back to how Cliff had reached out to her about the time of the Visitadores ride and invited her back into his life. She'd told me that he wanted her to help him. Was she helping in ways I didn't know?

CHAPTER SIXTY-ONE

Dressing the Part

Elizabeth had most likely been killed by either Margot, Mr. Parmacelli, Brendon or unknown persons. Margot seemed an unlikely candidate, as she'd likely died before her sister. Perhaps Brendon was the jealous husband who'd killed after I'd divulged my suspicion that she'd betrayed him. Or maybe Elizabeth had told Mr. Parmacelli that her goings-on with Cliff were no longer secret. If he thought things were unraveling he'd take care of any loose end, like perhaps he'd done with the clerk and the paperwork.

To solve the whodunit before the night was through I'd need to know more… or find a way to make the truth reveal itself.

As a therapist, I get paid to help people speak their truth, and come to terms with it. The killer wouldn't have my help coming to terms with their deeds; I'd let the police and the judicial system do that. What I needed was something to nudge the killer(s) into confessing.

The power of groups appeals to me. There are things we do when we're with other people that we don't do alone. Groups create a space for social pressure and can influence behavior. I could use that.

Since everyone seemed to have secrets but were disinclined to share them, a rise in temperature was required—some finger-pointing, name-calling and raised voices. Things I usually advise against, but which get the blood flowing and lips loosening.

I needed to do one more thing before the blowout. I needed something appropriate to wear. Southern California is casual, but I have east-coast roots. I found a Robinson's on Upper State Street and got myself a dark sports jacket and slacks to complement my blue shirt and loafers.

To work therapeutic magic, I'd need to look the part. That's very important to us here in Southern California. If you don't look the part, people will have a hard time believing you.

I know what anyone has to say is more important than how they look, that the truth is the truth. But we all also know that's only partly true. Job seekers, political candidates, workshop presenters, and therapists dress up because it projects a more professional presence. It can take longer to see through the veneer. I was hoping the jacket and slacks would buy me some time.

CHAPTER SIXTY-TWO
Fiesta Blowout

I DROVE TO the ranch on my own. Rachel had suggested that we drive together with Michael and Alan, but I wanted the freedom that comes with providing your own transportation. My first dose of that came when I learned to tie my own shoes. Getting my driver's license came next. The independence that came with those events was a big deal. Now, my shoes, my car and I were cruising up the coast.

Cars were lined up along the driveway. I didn't do a count, but it looked like there were close to a hundred. There were college aged kids doing the parking, but I wanted to park myself. I needed to leave the car headed out, with room to move, just in case.

I took my time approaching the house and was surprised to hear a Mariachi band playing. Parts of the original blowout plan were still going ahead, despite the wake, but the mood was somber. People were standing in groups, talking quietly, commiserating and occasionally gently laughing. The alcohol was flowing, the hors d'oeuvres circulating, and I was glad I'd bought the jacket. This was a well-heeled group.

I took a mini quesadilla from a passing tray and noted the kicker of jalapeno hidden within. I needed something to drink. In other circumstances, I'd have opted for a beer, but my evening was delicately woven and I needed to be on my game. I took a Perrier.

Rachel was with the Playmate. They both looked the worse for wear.

"Hi. How are you both holding up?" I asked.

"It's been pretty grim for everyone," Rachel said. "It's just so shocking. Nobody can understand how something like this could happen."

"This is a small town," the Playmate observed. "These things don't happen here. Not to people you know. It's very disturbing."

"I'm sure this has come as a shock. It's horrible news and my heart goes out to everyone."

Having talked the talk, I skipped walking it. "Why would someone do something like this?"

"Because they're crazy."

"That's for sure. You were close to her. Do you know if she was involved with anyone questionable?"

"Elizabeth didn't get involved with people like that. She was like the rest of us."

"Yes, I'm sure. Would you please excuse me a moment so I can talk privately with Rachel? Just for a couple of minutes."

"Okay. I'm going to go get a refill," she said, and stepped away.

"Why'd you do that? I was having a good conversation with her."

"I'm sorry. I didn't mean to interrupt. Well, I did, but I didn't mean to be rude. I know you're interested in getting to know the family so I'm sorry. I wasn't being very considerate."

"No, you weren't. What's so important that you needed to interrupt us?"

"Nothing really. I just haven't seen you since this morning and thought we might catch up."

"That would be good. Why don't we do it tomorrow?"

Was she pushing me away, ending our "conference romance"?

Maybe I was being overly sensitive. Or insensitive. While I could understand Rachel's wanting to spend time with her new family, I couldn't conceive that the conversation with the Playmate had been all that engaging. She didn't seem to have any insight into the murder, and that was my priority. I didn't like that I was so dismissive of her, but my task-oriented OCD was kicking in. I was on the clock and for a time-minded guy that can cause social-skills slippage.

Of course, Rachel's and the Playmate's priorities were different and deserved equal respect. They were hurting and needed each other.

"Okay. Tomorrow it is. In the meantime, I have a favor to ask."

"Go on."

"I'm going to try to find out who killed Elizabeth, who beat up your dad, and who took care of Ellen. And I'm going to do it tonight. I have most of the pieces. I just need to put them together."

"You are? That's great."

"Yeah, I guess. But I may need some help from you."

"How so?"

"That's the tricky part. I'm not entirely sure. I'm hoping that at some point I'll get the central characters in one room and do a little group therapy."

"What?"

"Well, not so much 'How are you feeling?' therapy. Although there may be some of that. More like stirring things up, getting some truths flying. When people start talking, anything you can do to keep things afloat would be helpful."

"Keep things afloat. I got it. I'll do what I can, but I have to get back to Kimberly as we were in the midst of a significant conversation."

CHAPTER SIXTY-THREE
Fiesta Blowout Continues

There were people all over—in the study, kitchen, living room, terrace, and out in the yard. I could see the family members, all surrounded by others. I wanted to speak with each of them, but would need to wrangle them from the herd. Maybe Dr. Novatt could help.

He was standing by a table, working a bowl of guacamole with some chips.

"Doctor, it's good to see you."

"Hello there. I was hoping you'd show up."

"Oh, yes? Why's that?"

"Because you flouted my instructions. I gather you went to see Cliff during my off-hours and distressed him a great deal. The nurses called to tell me his vitals were up. We've been able to stabilize him but you could have killed him."

"I'm sorry. I didn't know he was in such a fragile state."

"That's because I'm the doctor in charge here, not you."

"You are in charge, and I was wrong for going in there without your permission. I'm sorry, especially since my presence harmed him."

"Yes, but—"

"There's no but. Guilty as charged." I paused, bowed my head a little so maybe he'd think I was more remorseful than I was. It looked like he wanted to lean into me some more, yet was hesitating. I wasn't.

"There's something I need to ask you, though."

"I knew it."

"You're a doctor and a cowboy. Of course, you know these things," I said, buttering him up. I could tell he liked it even though he knew it was bullshit. That's the thing about bullshit. Sometimes you can spot it, but even if you do, if it's good bullshit you respect it.

"I hope you know I meant no harm to Cliff. But I'd found out something that would help to solve this whole issue. I just needed to talk to him about it."

"Was it worth it?"

"I hope so. Ask him tomorrow. But let me ask you something. I know his memory's coming back and I know he's also lying about it. How much in either direction I don't know. Do you?"

"He doesn't lie to me."

"Well, you know, it's not smart to lie to the person who's trying to help you. But I wonder if he isn't withholding stuff till he's back on his feet and can figure out what's what."

"That's possible. I wouldn't know."

"Not even a little?"

"People are usually excited when they remember something new and want to share it. He's been less forthcoming so maybe he's holding back or maybe it's just coming back to him slowly. I can't honestly say."

"I'm hoping that what he told me is the truth as he knows it."

"My truth is, I'd better move away from the guacamole."

I stayed with the guacamole. Why leave a good thing before you've had enough of it?

It wasn't long before Michael was by my side. He looked like he'd gotten an extra helping of sun.

"Looks like you logged in some time by the pool," I said.

"Actually, I went out hiking and forgot to put on any suntan lotion because it was foggy in town. I'm paying for it."

"I'm sorry. I know that price can be pretty irritating. Where did you go hiking?"

"I like to drive up in the mountains, find a promising site and take off."

"Sort of blaze your own path."

"I guess. This time of year, you need to keep an eye out for rattlesnakes and mountain lions."

"What mountain lions? Are they up by Painted Cave?"

"You bet."

"That's something that Esalen doesn't have. Although I'm not sure you want to put that in the brochure."

"If there is a brochure."

"What makes you say that?"

"You know. The old story. Money."

"I know you had some concerns about that. You said Cliff was being kind of secretive about it. Did you get a chance to talk with him this week?"

He took a moment, then looked up to the right. It's not an exact science, but there's a lot of anecdotal evidence suggesting that when people look up to the right they're constructing an event; when they look to the left they're remembering it. So while I wouldn't have bet my house on it, I took what Michael said with a grain of salt.

"No, I basically followed the doctor's orders and didn't bring up anything that would upset him."

"Very respectful of you, but I know you're upset."

"Not that upset. I just don't like that he wasn't forthcoming. It makes me uneasy things are happening that exclude me," he said while loading up a chip with the guacamole.

"I get that. I wouldn't like it either. You said he'd told you Margot held the purse strings."

"He said that a while ago, but nothing more since."

"Any theories on why Elizabeth was killed?"

"That's the hot topic today. Everyone's been theorizing. I heard someone it was possible she caught someone trying to steal something, but I'm not sure what's worth stealing. I heard they keep no money in the office."

"There could be some documents there."

"It's possible. No one knows why or has any real information. Maybe she was killed somewhere else and dumped at the offices."

"Like Cliff was dumped at the Courthouse."

"Similar but different. Could be connected, could not.? Lots of theories. No facts."

"If she was killed elsewhere and taken there, it was a statement of sorts, maybe another warning. But who's it directed at?"

"There's the mystery. You're supposed to have a knack for figuring these things out. What do you think?"

"What do you think about what?" asked John. He came up next to Michael, who put his arm around him.

"I'm so sorry about Elizabeth," I said. "My heart goes out to you."

"Thank you. That's kind. What was it you were talking about?"

"We were talking about Elizabeth, but we're happy to talk about something else."

"No, I want to hear what you were saying."

"John," Michael said, "as I told you earlier, I wish there was something I could do to make it better."

"One thing you can do is continue your discussion. Please don't treat me with kid gloves."

"Sure," Michael said. "We were wondering if someone purposefully took Elizabeth's body to your offices, like they maybe took Cliff's to the clerk's office."

"We don't know any details. My mother told the police we're

having a gathering tonight and didn't want to hear the details until tomorrow. It's enough, she said, just dealing with her loss."

"I can understand that."

"Yes, but I don't agree. I want to know what happened, but out of deference to mother we're waiting till tomorrow to talk with the police. It's an interesting question—whether she died there or somewhere else. Right now, all we can do is speculate, which is not that useful, but I can't help it. I don't know why anyone would deliberately kill her or take her to the offices."

"Perhaps she was dropping by and came upon someone." I said.

"I know people are suggesting that, but she hardly ever came to the offices after hours. Although there might have been something there she wanted."

Might have been something there she wanted. I didn't want to be insensitive, but he had said not to treat him with kid gloves.

"What do you mean by 'there might have been something there she wanted'?"

"Nothing really. Sometimes we leave things for each other to pick up."

"Oh, sort of a central drop-off spot."

"Exactly."

"By the way, have you been able to get a hold of Margot? I'm sure she'd want to be here."

"Françoise may have gotten a hold of her, but I'm not sure. Now if you'll excuse me, I need to attend to something."

"Certainly," I said, wondering whether Françoise really had been able to get a hold of her.

After he left I said, "He didn't seem particularly crestfallen about his sister."

"It's a very stiff-upper-lip group. Have you seen Eleanor or Vic? You'd barely know something had happened. They're putting out the let's-not-talk-about-it vibe, and people are keeping things low key."

"To each their own. It doesn't sound overly surprising."

I'd noticed that Michael was no longer paying me his full attention. His eye seemed drawn to a brunette in the corner. Guys subscribe to a friendship code that allows for conversations to be dropped and plans cancelled once a promising prospect appears. This one looked promising.

My own romantic interests had been pretty muted all week. Aside from the seize-the-moment moment in the hotel lobby, neither Rachel nor I had prioritized romance. I envied Michael a little as he made his way across the room, but I had other matters on my mind.

Dr. Novatt came back for another round of guacamole. I couldn't blame him.

"I've got another question for you," I said. "I crossed a line when I went into Cliff's room without your permission. And I was wondering… was I the only one?"

"If people followed doctor's orders we'd have a healthier, happier world." With that and another scoop of the guacamole, he was off.

So maybe someone else had gotten to Cliff. Maybe the person who'd beaten him up had checked in on him and let him know there was more where that had come from. Or maybe I was the only one and the doctor had just shared one of those vague Zen doctor things that means something but isn't particularly useful. One thing I do know is that doctors follow their own orders as often as the rest of us.

CHAPTER SIXTY-FOUR
Fiesta Blowout Heats Up

It was another one of those chamber-of-commerce evenings. Low seventies, a light breeze as the sun made its descent into the ocean. The barbeque was firing, and a couple of rotisseries were cooking what once roamed these lands. Roasting meat met night-blooming jasmine in the air.

While I was taking it all in, Brendon came up alongside me.

"Good evening," he said.

"Oh, Brendon, I'm so sorry about Elizabeth. I know there's nothing I can say or do to make it any better."

"Or any worse."

"That too. Is there anything I can do to be helpful?"

"How about them Dodgers? Can we talk about that?"

"Certainly. It seems you're not alone in that desire."

"The family has decided we'll put up an unflappable appearance tonight and carry on. That said, please let's not talk about the Dodgers."

"I noticed the containment. It seems to be something the family does well. How's that working for you?"

"Very nice, Doctor. Slick of you to slip in one of those therapy questions. Actually, it's working fine. I'm a family man, as you know, so if we zip it up, we zip it up."

"Part of the cost of being in a rut."

"Precisely."

"What would you like to talk about if not the Dodgers?"

"The weather, perhaps."

"I was just thinking it's a lovely night."

"Just another day in paradise."

"Since we've pretty much exhausted our Dodgers and weather talk, can I move on?"

"Depends on what you have in mind."

"Margot. I've been wondering about her. John said maybe Françoise had been able to reach her, but he wasn't sure."

He hesitated, then said, "That would be nice."

"Yes, I'm sure she'd want to be here. I don't know any twins but I bet they have a love/hate thing going on. You've experienced it up close. What have you observed?"

Before I could hear his answer, Vic and Eleanor joined us.

"I'm so sorry for your loss," I said.

"Thank you," they said in a practiced way.

"Brendon," Vic said, "we've been trying to remember the name of that movie you had us see. You know, the mystery with that New York couple."

"*The Thin Man*," Brendon said.

"That's it. We were suggesting it to some people but couldn't remember the name."

"Glad you liked it. I know it's not *The Right Stuff* but thought you'd enjoy it."

"Nora is my kind of woman," Eleanor said.

"Nick ain't my kind of man, but I got a kick out of watching them with their highfalutin city ways."

"They certainly lived a way of life that seems quite distant from here," I said.

"Sadly," said Eleanor.

Eleanor, Vic and Brendon left together. Next up was my newest client, Mr. Parmacelli.

"So, Doctor, you making the rounds?"

"Hi, Mr. Parmacelli. I was just talking with some of the family. What a terrible loss for them all."

"Yes, she was a lovely woman."

"What do you think happened? I know a lot of people have been speculating. Do you have any thoughts you want to share?"

"No. I'll wait to hear what the police say."

"That's smart. It's comforting for people to have more information. In the absence of it, they fill in the blanks."

"Perhaps. I'm a facts person. Until I get those, I don't waste my time guessing."

"I hear you. Did Elizabeth or Margot ever go on any of the Visitadores rides?"

"Men only."

"I thought I heard that women were sometimes involved."

"Only for entertainment purposes. Some of the guys dress up now and then and put on a little show. That's about it."

"I'm guessing you're not one of those guys."

He looked at me in a way that made me want him not to look at me.

"I've got a question for you. You've known Margot and Elizabeth since they were kids. They ever play those tricks twins do? Pretend they're each other?"

"People don't play tricks on me."

Then he left. I was glad to see him go but wasn't sure I'd done anything to build our therapist/client rapport.

The meat was cooked. A buffet line opened and people queued up. Soon Michael was eating with the brunette, Rachel was eating with the Playmate and John. Brendon was with a group of what looked like other rut-dwellers. Alan was nowhere to be seen. I sat by myself and welcomed the opportunity to do some last-minute game planning.

I checked the cassette player in my pocket for the hundredth time to make sure the batteries were working and it was ready to go. I'd opted to go with "For a Dancer." We wouldn't be rockin' tonight.

After dinner, the gathering would start to thin out. I'd tell John that I had something critical to tell him and the rest of the family, and ask him to round them up and meet me in Vic's office. While he was doing that I'd gather Michael, Alan, Rachel, and Mr. Parmacelli.

Vic wasn't used to taking orders from anyone, although he'd liked the movie suggestion, so maybe he'd be open. I had no idea what Mr. Parmacelli would say; I'd need to make him an offer he couldn't refuse. I wasn't looking forward to that therapeutic exchange. All in all, it wasn't my preferred approach, but I couldn't conjure up a better way to get everyone together. I just hoped they'd all show.

My plan was this: once everyone was assembled, I'd tell them we'd know who'd killed Elizabeth by the time we left the room. I hoped that would get them to stay. If not, I'd mention that Mr. Parmacelli could testify to my skills. I hoped he wouldn't bust me but figured that throwing his name out there would garner some extra respect and keep everyone in place, at least until he stormed out or had me beaten up.

Things were a little hazy about what would come next. I'd need to recount some of the events of the past week and ask some questions about what people had or hadn't done. Revelation by revelation, they'd become suspicious of each other. Then—and this was the even hazier part—I'd need to share some of the secrets I'd learned and start exposing people. Exposing secrets is a big thing in the therapy world. Get someone to tell a secret and it won't be long until someone else joins in. Self-disclosure begets self-disclosure is what they say. If I could get this tight-lipped group to open up, maybe someone would leak the truth.

CHAPTER SIXTY-FIVE

The Reveal—Act One

When I saw Lt. Flores I couldn't help but be reminded of the Robert Burns-inspired saying "The best-laid plans of mice and men often go awry." He didn't look like he was there for the festivities. He found Vic, who found John, who found Eleanor, and on it went. One by one, they headed for Vic's office. I told Rachel, Michael, Alan, and Mr. Parmacelli that there was an emergency meeting in Vic's office. When I arrived, the whole group was there, plus a few other people I didn't know.

"I'm very sorry," said Lt. Flores. "This is your time of mourning, but I come with a heavy heart as I need to tell you that we've just found the body of Margot Spalding."

There were gasps, wails, cries and tears. The room took some time to absorb the news. No one was hugging or holding on to anyone. Finally, someone I didn't know said, "Is there any more you can tell us?"

"All I can say is that we found her body up on Painted Cave. She'd been shot and was dead when we found her. When we know more I'll pass that along."

After a few moments of silence Vic said, "Thank you, Lt. Flores."

Stiff upper lip firmly in place he continued, "We owe you and your men a debt of gratitude for the fine work you do."

"It's my job. I'm going to leave now but I wanted to come over and let you know personally."

"That's very thoughtful of you," Vic said.

Flores left. Nobody moved or said anything. Slowly people began to splinter into groups and whisper to one another. Not the ideal moment, but it was the only one I had.

"Excuse me," I said. "This is a horrible tragedy and I know we're all grief-stricken. There's no right or wrong thing to do now as none of us know how to deal with something like this. But before we leave this room, I want to ask for your indulgence." I didn't give the naysayers a chance to get a word in. "As Mr. Parmacelli can attest, I have some skills that, if you give me a few minutes of your time, I will enable us to leave this room knowing who killed Elizabeth and Margot."

That was an attention-grabber. Now they were all locked in.

"You know who did this?" someone asked.

"In a few minutes we all will," I said, ducking the question but putting the emphasis on a shared goal we could all get behind. Well, all but one.

"I want to begin by thanking you all for staying. I know we'd all prefer to be somewhere else. But if we work together we can solve this mystery and get on with our mourning. I happen to know the killer is in the room and I'm hoping they'll step forward and save us all a lot of turmoil."

It was a long shot, but who knew? Maybe they'd opt in.

They didn't.

But everyone stayed.

Either group pressure was taking hold or they were too stunned to move. I wanted to make it impossible for someone to leave without significant suspicion falling upon them.

"I'm going to recount some recent events and ask some of you to share what you know. Sort of a pot-luck thing. We all add something and when we put it together we'll have a meal."

I regretted saying that as soon as it left my mouth. This wasn't exactly your pot-luck crowd. I could feel myself losing them. I needed to move it along. For someone who disdains foreplay, you'd think I'd know when to do less of it.

"A few years ago, Alan—this gentleman over here—and Michael—the man next to him—had a conversation with Cliff, Rachel's father. She's sitting over here," I said, pointing. "Michael and Alan, like Cliff, are therapists and they dreamed about building a healing/learning center in Santa Barbara. Cliff found a property on Painted Cave that he knew would be ideal for their dream. However, they didn't have the money to make the dream come true. Alan, who lives in Tahoe, wasn't as involved in moving the dream forward as were Cliff and Michael—who now lives here as well."

It occurred to me in that moment that I hadn't broken into Michael's house. I didn't have time to dwell on it, as I'd gotten the group's attention and didn't want to lose it, but maybe I'd missed something.

"Fortunately, Cliff met Margot. They got to know each other and fell in love. Margot became interested in helping out financially but started to question whether Cliff loved her or her money. They'd intended to marry and build the place together with his friends, but their marriage plans were on and off. While Cliff was courting Margot and trying to arrange the financing, he cut himself off from Michael and Alan. They'd been partners in the center's conception. But were they still? Michael and Alan didn't know."

I looked over at Michael and Alan, who shrugged.

"While Cliff and Margot's romance was wavering, someone else caught his eye. Elizabeth and Cliff were drawn to each other. Cliff had fallen for Margot for who she was and what she was worth. Maybe in Elizabeth he saw the same wealth but someone more to his liking. Elizabeth, however, told Cliff about a pre-nuptial with

Brendon that would severely financially hurt the one who broke up their marriage. Maybe she could afford to give up her wealth for love, but Cliff couldn't. He needed the money. He'd have preferred money and love, but the center was his true love."

If we'd been in group therapy I'd have asked everyone what they felt/thought about that, and what their true love was, but that wasn't the kind of therapy group I was facilitating tonight.

"My timing might be a bit off on this, and maybe you, John, can help me. Do you remember when Margot supposedly left to go to Europe?"

"It was last week. Friday the twenty-second. Or Thursday."

"Did you see her then? When was the last time you saw her?"

"I saw her on Tuesday or Wednesday for lunch. That's the last time."

"Anyone in the room see her after last Tuesday or Wednesday?"

Silence.

"Okay, well, sadly, it's going to be the police who'll tell us when she died, but I'm pretty sure it was Wednesday the twentieth. And I'm pretty sure I know who did it. Unless someone else wants to confess." I paused. "Last week, Elizabeth and Margot got into a major conflict. They met up at the Painted Cave property to have it out. Before I tell you what happened there, Mr. Parmacelli, can you tell us what they were arguing about?"

"That's a private matter."

"I'm sure it is, but since their family's here and will consent to your telling us, please do so." No one objected, including—to my relief—Mr. Parmacelli.

"The property."

"What about the property?"

"It's complicated."

"That's okay. We're all very interested."

"Margot decided she wasn't going to finance the center. She thought Cliff just wanted her for her money, so she bailed."

"And yet her name is on the property deed."

He shrugged. "I told you, it's complicated."

"Can you tell us how Margot's name ended up on the deed?"

"Maybe it was forged. I don't know."

There were some gasps. People were perking up.

"It was forged?" someone asked.

"Someone went to the clerk's office and filed those documents," I replied. "I don't really know how things work down there, but if someone had their identical twins driver's license for identification, it would be easy to impersonate them."

"What are you saying?" asked Rachel.

Way to go. Coming through with backup.

"I'm saying that Elizabeth signed the property deed and the marriage and business licenses as Margot. And the reason that she did it is because she'd killed Margot."

"What? No!" said Vic. "That can't be."

"I'm sorry but it's true. They got into it up on Painted Cave and it ended up with Margot dead. Elizabeth buried her there."

"This is ghastly," said Eleanor as she folded into a chair.

"I know. It's one horrible thing after another. There's no one in this room who feels good about any of this. Plus, someone else killed Elizabeth and the county clerk, and had Cliff beaten up. One bad thing after another, which hopefully we can put a stop to now. I have some other news to share but, first, I have a few more questions."

It was like being in a classroom where the teacher asks a question and everyone hopes they don't get picked on.

"Rachel, since your dad isn't here, maybe you could answer some questions on his behalf. I know you've only been reunited for a few months so there's a lot you're just learning, but can you remember anything he told you about the finances for the center and Margot's involvement?"

"He didn't tell me anything. I just learned about it all this week."

"Very well. What about Margot? Did he tell you things weren't going well there?"

"Not really. He was honest about it being a marriage of opportunity… that even though she wasn't his true love, the chance to build his dream took precedence."

"Did he tell you about his relationship with Elizabeth?"

"Just that he liked her. He didn't talk much about her family."

"Okay, did he tell you that he found out Margot was going behind his back and buying the property with Mr. Parmacelli?"

"What? No. I thought the property had been owned by some family for years."

"Not anymore. There's a property deed signed by Mr. Parmacelli and Margot."

"That's impossible. You said she was backing out of their relationship."

"Yes, I did. Which is why Margot didn't register the property. Elizabeth did."

"That makes no sense."

"I can see that, but there may be something you're not seeing."

"What's that?" someone asked.

"Elizabeth loved Cliff. She killed her sister because of that—she'd had a lifetime of hating/loving Margot and was locked into a loveless marriage. Then a path opened up for her. Margot bought the property with Mr. Parmacelli a month ago, but didn't register the deed. Maybe she had misgivings. I don't know. But when Elizabeth found out, she killed Margot, impersonated her, and registered the deed because she knew that Cliff would inherit Margot's share through the will. Because she forged that too."

I was out on a limb there; I hadn't actually seen the will. But I was guessing no one else in the room had either. It helped make my point, so why not? It probably was true.

"You're saying," John said, "that Elizabeth laid out this whole plan just so Cliff could get the property?"

"And so she could afford to leave Brendon."

"I get that," said John. "But who killed her?"

"Yes, who killed her, and the clerk, and beat up Cliff? That's what we're about to find out."

CHAPTER SIXTY-SIX

The Reveal—Act Two

PEOPLE LOVE STORIES. When we ask our friends how their week's going, we're going to hear a story. The cop flashes you down for speeding, you're going to tell them a story. Our ancestors huddled around the fires in their caves and told their stories. Both real and imagined.

I had a story to tell, but I'd already told most of what I knew. Now I'd need to fabricate. I'm better at telling the truth than spinning it, but I hadn't come this far to let my limitations stop me. Hurt me, yes. Stop me, not yet.

"The last few weeks have been busy ones at the county clerk's office. Cliff came in with Elizabeth posing as Margot. Michael, Alan, and Rachel dropped by. I've been in a few times. When you file something, they log having received your documents and then file them someplace. But, lo and behold, some of the documents filed recently are in the register but not in their respective filing cabinets. Someone stole them. Any guesses?"

"The clerk," a few voices said, and I agreed.

"She's our most likely suspect. She was the recent beneficiary of ten thousand dollars. And for that, and for her efforts, she was killed. Why? Was it to ensure that she'd never name her benefactor? I'm guessing so."

I was quiet for a moment while the group collectively turned their attention to Mr. Parmacelli, knowing that he had the requisite skills to have handled this matter. I valued my life too much to accuse him of anything directly, but I did feel a need to state the obvious.

"We don't know who killed her. We suspect it was done to keep her quiet. Someone in this room carried out the act or paid another to do the dirty work for them."

Given my proclivity for living, I didn't linger on that point too long. I was also careful not to look in Mr. Parmacelli's direction. They say that looks can kill. I didn't want to join the newly departed.

"How is the clerk's killer connected to Elizabeth and Margot? And what about Cliff? Someone beat him up or had him beaten up. I've checked the hands of everyone in the room except you people over there. How are your hands? Any bloody knuckles? Could we see a show of hands?"

Hands waved. As they did I realized that the pugilist could have used gloves, but I was too far down the road to turn back.

"Thankfully, the person who beat up Cliff isn't here, but their employer is among us. Maybe that hired hand also took care of the clerk, even Elizabeth too. But it's also possible that these are separate events with one perpetrator here and another there. We shall see."

I looked left to right to illustrate the point that the guilty party could be anywhere in the room.

"When I was in eighth grade the boys in our class learned how to box. I faced off against one of my friends. We were clowning around, not really wanting to punch each other. The instructor yelled at us to fight and my friend landed a hard punch to my face. 'Screw you,' I said, and walloped him back. The only real damage was to our friendship. I never felt quite as close to him after that.

"But I digress. My point is that there were limits to how far my friend and I were willing to go. I didn't really want to hurt him, but he'd hurt me a little so I wanted to hurt him back a little harder. I'm guessing that the person who beat Cliff up was told not to kill him. Maybe because the one giving the orders was a friend or family member."

I let that soak in.

"So why beat him up? To teach him a lesson? Who would want to teach him a lesson and what lesson was it exactly?"

I could see some people's wheels turning; others looked dazed. I can do that to people.

"I need to ask you some more questions."

If there were desks, they'd have been slinking behind them.

"Vic, is it okay if I ask you a question?"

"I suppose so."

"Thank you. I was wondering how hands-on you are with the property end of the business. Were you aware of the property on Painted Cave? Did anyone come and talk to you about it? Ask you what you thought it was worth and if you'd help pay for it?"

"John had me go up there and take a look."

"When was that?"

"Some months ago."

"What did you think? Is it a good spot? Could you see a retreat center going up there?"

"I didn't look like a good business deal. There are plenty of spas in Santa Barbara. I didn't see locals driving all the way up the hill to get a massage and a soak. Maybe tourists would come and stay there, but it's too far off the beaten path."

"I can understand that. It's close to the city but not that close. That could work for and against it. Why did John come to you?"

"Margot asked him what he thought since he oversees our properties."

"So, John, how come you went to your father on this? You

must be pretty savvy about real estate. How come you wanted a second opinion?"

"I didn't need Dad to weigh in but Margot was insistent. At first, she wanted the family to buy the property, but I couldn't see the upside. She asked me to get Dad's opinion and felt that if it came from me he'd give it greater consideration."

"What happened when he said no?"

"I told Margot. She seemed okay with it. Said she was souring on the idea."

"What about Elizabeth? Did she speak with you?"

"No, she didn't."

"Thank you. So you and your father considered the property an unwise investment. Why did Mr. Parmacelli see things differently?"

"You'd have to ask him."

I didn't really want to ask him anything, but I needed to know.

"I'm sorry to bother you again, but can you help us understand why you, a sharp business person, saw value where Vic and John didn't?"

"We all see things differently."

"Yes, that's true. But I'm guessing you saw something in this deal that maybe John and Vic didn't."

"What's that?"

"They were looking at the property as a retreat. Maybe you saw it as vineyards. I'm not a vintner but is the temperature up there's pretty much in line with some regions in the Mediterranean?"

"That could be."

"Did Margot or Elizabeth talk with you about that possibility?"

"Not both."

"Who?"

"When Vic said no, Margo came to me. I had some people look at it and agreed to buy it with her. Now I'm not sure if it was Margot or Elizabeth who approached me."

CHAPTER SIXTY-SEVEN

The Reveal—Act Three

I HADN'T MADE much headway with upping the emotional ante so that someone would blurt out more than they'd intended. It was time to turn up the volume.

"We've got a lot of brainpower in the room; let's see if we can put it to good use. Alan, want to tell us who had Cliff beaten up?"

"Not really."

"I know you don't want to tell, and I'm not sure telling will serve you well, but you haven't exactly been forthcoming."

Everyone focused in on him. Truthfully, I wasn't sure if he knew, but you can't go for the low-hanging fruit all the time.

"I really don't know. At first, I thought it was one of Mr. Parmacelli's associates. I knew Cliff was putting pressure on people to help pay for the property and I figured maybe he'd pushed Mr. Parmacelli too hard."

"How could Cliff do that? Mr. Parmacelli isn't the kind of person who's easy to push around."

"Cliff must have known that Margot had asked about the property and not gotten any financial support from her family. He told Elizabeth and they decided to ask Mr. Parmacelli if he'd be interested. Maybe Cliff put some pressure on him to help."

"I hear you say the word 'pressure', but come on. What kind of pressure could Cliff put on Mr. Parmacelli?"

"Cliff told me he had a client tell him things about Mr. Parmacelli that he wouldn't have wanted known. Cliff could have told Mr. Parmacelli he'd keep his mouth shut if he helped out. I could see Cliff getting beaten up for that."

I took a peek at Mr. Parmacelli. His face was red. Sometimes the flush of ire is impossible to hide. I didn't want him boiling over just yet, but it was good to see his temperature rising. I just hoped he wasn't the only one feeling the heat.

"You said that was what you thought at first. That's not what you think now."

"Right."

"What do you now think happened?"

He gave Michael an "I'm-sorry" look and said, "Michael had him beaten up. Michael loves Cliff like a brother, which is why he wouldn't have had him killed. But, Michael, I know you thought Cliff was going to exclude us, and when he wouldn't include you, you resorted to other measures. I don't like saying it, but it's my truth."

"The hell with you!" said Michael. "Yeah, I was pissed at Cliff. I still am. He locked us out and wouldn't talk with us. I knew he'd do something self-serving so, yeah, I also went to John and Vic and Mr. Parmacelli and asked them to help out. And, needless to say, they didn't. I went and talked with Margot, but she wasn't interested anymore. I knew the money was coming from someone. I tried everything I could to get him to not screw us over, but I never had anyone beat him up."

The jury seemed to be split. Some believed him; some didn't. I had my own thoughts but I wasn't ready to show my hand.

"How could you do this?" Rachel yelled at him. "You're his best friend. He told you to trust him."

"You're right. I didn't trust him. I wish I had, but I didn't. I still don't. But I didn't have him beaten up."

The temperature was up in the room. It was time to raise it a little higher.

"Okay, let's leave that for now. Hopefully, Cliff will regain his memory and tell us who attacked him. Let's move to the one question we can answer clearly tonight. Who killed Elizabeth? Eleanor, can you help us with that?"

"Excuse me?"

"I know this is a horrible, horrible day for you and we can't even begin to grasp how this affects you. I apologize for asking you, but I do so in the service of finding out who killed your daughter. Can you tell us anything about the men in their lives? What did they think about each other's choices?"

"We all love Brendon. He's a gentleman. As is Cliff."

"I'm sure we all agree. I know that Elizabeth was involved with Cliff. Was Margot involved with Brendon?"

She looked over at Brendon. He looked away. I couldn't tell if he was looking up to the right or the left, but I had a hunch.

Eleanor wept. Her detached demeanor was gone. The pain had overcome her. I like to believe I'm a sensitive fellow, but as a therapist I've learned that when there's a crack in the veneer you need to open it up.

"I know this is very hard, Eleanor, and all of us here want to support you. Certainly, you have much to cry about. To lose two children—it's unfathomable. And yet your tears are not just for them."

It wasn't easy watching her tears turn to sobbing. Most of the people in the room had spent their lives avoiding dealing with emotions on this level. Most wanted to be somewhere else but were trapped. To leave would be disrespectful, but to stay was exceedingly uncomfortable. I needed to turn the screw.

"Eleanor, did you do something that you need to tell us about?"

People were squirming. I could feel their outrage at my picking on the grieving mother. Yet they knew there was something she wasn't sharing.

"We all want what's best for you and want you to be able to speak your truth. Can you do that?"

"Stop it. Stop it. Stop it!" Brendon cried out. "Can't you see how much she's suffering? Leave her alone."

"Yes," said Vic emphatically. "Leave her alone."

"I want to leave her alone but, Eleanor, do you want me to leave you alone? Do you want us to leave you or do you want to tell us the truth?"

I know she heard me even if she wasn't really listening. I'd said that more to get people to back off. The discomfort in the room was tangible. I knew I wasn't being nice. I knew I was using her. But I didn't know another way.

"Eleanor, let me make this easier for you," I said with no intention of doing so. "I know you're holding a terrible secret. I know it's tearing you apart holding it in and yet it's going to hurt you more to share it. There's no way to make this better than it is. But the truth will set you free. If you tell us what happened there will be relief."

She wasn't taking that last step, though she was on the verge. Her teetering kept everyone hushed in anticipation. I saw some movement out of the corner of my eye. It was time to push her off the edge.

"Rachel, can you tell us what Eleanor can't?"

"What? No, I can't do that. What are you talking about?"

"John, can you?"

"No way."

"Okay, I'm sorry to do this, but I don't feel I have a choice. Eleanor, you're the only one who knows the truth. I know that's why you're not talking. You think that if you don't say anything, no one will ever find out. But that's not correct. If you don't share it, I will. I don't want to. I don't want to destroy your life more than it's already been destroyed, but I will if I have to."

"No you won't," said Brendon, moving toward me.

He took out a gun and pointed it at me.

"Do not say another word, Eleanor. It's all right. You don't have to protect me anymore. I'm going to leave now. None of you will ever see me again. Elizabeth deserved to die. She killed the only woman I've ever loved. I could handle her loving Cliff. I didn't care. She could do what she wanted. But she went too far. I'm sorry it came to this."

With that, he raced out of the room.

Things got a little crazy after that. Everyone was talking. Vic and John rushed over to comfort Eleanor. Michael went and talked to Rachel. Alan stood alone. Mr. Parmacelli came my way. Before he got to me, the door opened and Brendon came back in. He was with two guys who looked like they knew how to beat people up.

They escorted Brendon over to Mr. Parmacelli.

"What do you want to do with him, boss?" one of them asked.

"Go take him out by the barn. I'll come back there and have a talk with him."

Before they got to the door, Vic went over to Brendon.

"You traitor. What the hell did you do?" With that he unloaded a punch to Brendon's gut that folded him in half. "Take him away."

Brendon gave him the finger as they took him away. I assumed that leaving Elizabeth's body in the Spalding offices had been another way to strike back at the family that had imprisoned him in a rut of his choosing.

Mr. Parmacelli stood by his friend to console him. After a couple of minutes, Vic waved me over.

"You're a bastard," he told me. "I don't like what you did here tonight, but I'm grateful. My friend here told me you're okay. But neither of us ever want to see you again."

The feeling was mutual, and I was glad to be getting away unscathed.

But before I left, I needed to talk with Eleanor. She was

surrounded by people but the waters parted as I neared and soon I was face-to-face with her.

"I'm so very sorry for all this," I said.

"You did what you had to do."

"As did you. I know your family's been torn apart and you wanted to protect Brendon. You've lost enough, but I couldn't let him get away with this. He killed Elizabeth because he loved Margot, and Elizabeth killed Margot because she loved him. I know that depth of love doesn't come easily and I'm sure they were worth that devotion."

"Love is a dangerous thing."

"It can be. But I suspect Brendon loved you enough to trust you with his truth, and you honored that love. You're a strong woman. I couldn't understand why you stayed here, but I suppose it was the love you had for your daughters and Brendon that stopped you leaving."

"This is the worst day of my life."

"I can only imagine."

"And yet I feel some relief. I don't know about tomorrow and what it will bring. My life will be hollow in a way it has never been, and yet there may be more love ahead for me."

As I left her I wondered if that love ahead had anything to do with those letters in the closet.

CHAPTER SIXTY-EIGHT

Summing It Up

August 5, 1983

THEY SAY IT's lonely at the top. I wouldn't know about that. I can tell you it's lonely at the bottom. I left the ranch pretty much without saying goodbye to anyone. I took a look at the barn and saw that Brendon wasn't having any quality time with Mr. Parmacelli and his associates. Since he was my client, I'd confided in Mr. Parmacelli that we could be discovering Elizabeth's murderer and suggested that he have some of his associates stand outside Vic's office door. The first person who came out would be someone they'd want to detain.

 I'd told Mr. Parmacelli that since our conversations were confidential he might want to admit he'd taken care of beating Cliff, stealing the records and disposing of Ellen, but he hadn't been totally invested in the therapeutic process. During my sit-down with Lt. Flores I'd hinted enough without breaching any non-disclosure laws and, more importantly, without Mr. Parmacelli knowing I'd fingered him. At least I hoped so.

 Whatever heroic glory I'd hoped would come my way by virtue of my investigative prowess wasn't manifesting. I had to pat my own back for figuring out whodunit. I'd never really understood what a pyrrhic victory was until now, so in that sense I'd learned another lesson.

I turned on the cassette and listened to Jackson Browne sing "For a Dancer." My fanciful idea of playing it hadn't materialized but it seemed appropriate that in the end there was one dance I did alone.

In the morning, I went up to the registration desk to collect my continuing-education certificate. They reminded me I was one unit short and that if I hurried I could catch the last workshop and get the unit.

Wouldn't you know, the workshop was titled "Saying Goodbye," and in the group were Michael, Alan, and Rachel. It seemed fitting to have them there. I didn't pay much attention to what the facilitator was saying as it was kind of the same old thing. Every ending is a beginning. We spend our life saying hello and goodbye. We say hello with hope and goodbye with regret.

The thing about humanistic psychologists is that they encourage you not just to talk the talk, but also to walk it. Lots of therapists do therapy, but they don't all fully participate in it. They don't let themselves experience life to a greater degree. With that in mind, the facilitator wanted us to look everyone in the eye, and say hello and goodbye. We had a minute each.

It was awkward. There were people there I'd never said hello to before and now I was connecting with them in some touchy-feely way that felt real and imposed at the same time. It was both too little time and too much.

Michael and I looked at each other silently.

"You messed up my friendships. We'll clean it up some. But they're forever damaged. Like you and the kid that walloped you."

"I get that. I didn't mean to hurt you. I just wanted to find out what happened to Cliff. I hope you can repair things as I know your relationship is important to you."

"Trust isn't easy to regain once it's lost, but we'll see how things go once Cliff gets out of the hospital. It shocked me to find out he was involved with Elizabeth and didn't tell me. He kept a lot from me. Alan and I have some mending to do. I can't fully comprehend how he could think I'd had Cliff beaten up, but when we talked last night I understood why he did. Still, I didn't like it."

"I'm sorry."

"Yeah. Me too. Goodbye."

Next came Alan.

"Hello."

"Hello."

"I'm sorry I made you finger Michael, but I really thought it was for the best. I know that it's messed things up between you. He's not happy with me, and I suspect you're not as well. I like you both. I didn't want to hurt you. I just wanted the truth to be told."

"It's okay. Michael didn't trust Cliff. He can't get around that and neither can I. And I don't think Cliff will. Yet I still hope that one day we can find a way to build that center."

"Me too. I'd be happy to meet you there and do our continuing-ed."

"We'll see. Goodbye."

Next up was Scarface. "I have to speak with you."

"Yes?"

"I didn't like that you thought I was following you and had bad intentions. I talked with my friend Jacob who told me he did the intimacy workshop with you. He said you talked to him about mischief."

"Yeah. I remember that."

"He told me you were a smart-ass, but that you helped him out by partnering with him."

"I did? I'm glad to hear that."

"Yeah, well you helped me out too. I know the scar gives off bad vibes and I need to find ways to compensate for it. I was mad at you for being leery of me. I still am, but I realize you were just overtly saying what people are covertly thinking. I don't like you, but you helped me too."

"Okay, thanks for telling me."

"Goodbye."

Then came Rachel.

"Hi. How you doing?" I asked.

"I'm okay. I want to thank you. I'm not sure I like you as much as I did, but you found out the truth and that's worth something."

"Sorry you don't like me so much. I spoke with Lt. Flores and he'll probably be able to find who beat up your dad."

"We know who. I'm not so sure we'll ever be able to prove it."

"Yeah. That could be."

"It's okay. Just as long as he gets better."

"I hope so. I was kinda thinking since we're both in LA we could get together sometime."

"What for?"

"Maybe to solve another mystery. Hang out. See another movie."

"Maybe. Right now I'm going to help my dad. Once he hears about all this he's going to be in another world of pain."

"He'll be glad to have you nearby to help him out."

"Goodbye."

And that was it. I got my certificate for continuing my education and learned a lesson in therapy and murder.

Parts of this story are true. Other parts are mostly true, somewhat true and pure fiction. The Association of Humanistic Psychology does exist and used to conduct annual conferences. Aside from that fact, everything else about the conference is fiction. In describing Santa Barbara, I tried to stay as true to the town as possible, though I took some license with the Fiesta celebration and stretched it out a few days. The places I describe were there in 1983. The Spalding ranch and family live only in this book. Some of the characters may resemble people you know; but they exist in this book only, although may appear in another. The Rancheros Visitadores are an actual group of horseback riders about which I know very little; I invented most everything I wrote about them. Mr. Parmacelli is of my imagination. Gary Novatt is an exceptional doctor in Santa Barbara, but I made up everything about him, except he does perform at the rodeo.

If you'd like a peek into what the future holds for David, take a look at what comes after the Acknowledgments.

ACKNOWLEDGMENTS

Most every day, my wife Jill and I walk our dog Lefty and catch up with the various goings-on in our lives. When I began this book, I had an idea that the hero of my story would go to a conference of therapists and trouble would ensue. That was all I had on page one. Each day on our walk, after Jill had finished talking about her day, I'd tell her what was happening in the book. Her debriefs covered many topics, while mine were monopolized by the book and the characters. Jill would make suggestions and give me feedback and encouragement that helped shape the book. When I was done with the first draft, my contributions to our walks expanded.

I also want to thank and apologize to my two closest friends, Stuart and Steve, whose love and support has guided me through my adult life. I have taken qualities and anecdotes from our lives together and spread them among some of the suspects. I have a hunch they might be seeing more of themselves displayed in the future.

Once again Chrissy and the artists at Damonza have been instrumental in the creation of the cover and formatting of the printed versions.

Jake Robertson, the audiobook narrator of my books has discovered the knack for bringing them to life. His considerable talents have enriched the stories.

Finally, if you have enjoyed reading this book it is because my editors, Lulu Swainston and Cally Worden have smoothed things out and made the journey easier for you.

A LESSON IN MYSTERY AND MURDER

DAVID UNGER, PHD

A LESSON IN THERAPY AND MURDER

DAVID UNGER, PHD

PRELUDE

"The best I ever read. That's tough. I have favorites, but it's hard to pick the best."

"I know, but this is how we begin. You gotta put your money down and place your bet. What's the best mystery ever?"

"Let me just check what we're betting on—what is the best mystery book ever, as voted by attendees at this week's conference? Not my personal favorite? Is that right?"

"Right, but you can name your favorite or what you guess the group is going to pick, but whatever you choose you're going to be wrong because I alone know the answer."

"You're so full of it. You alone know the answer. You've seen the future and you know how the three hundred-plus people here are going to vote."

"You got it. Want to bet on it?"

I was hooked. How about you? You want to take the bet?

I was in the registration line at the Mystery Writers of America's annual conference in Las Vegas. It was 1984 and the guy in front of me was telling his buddy he knew which mystery book the group would name best ever.

We could all come up with some contenders. *The Maltese Falcon*, *And Then There Were None*, *The Hound of the Baskervilles*, *The Big Sleep*, *Murder on the Orient Express* … and the list goes on. But to know which one would get the nod is sort of like knowing who's going to win the Oscar. You know the nominees, but you never know how the crowd will be swayed year to year.

I usually don't like know-it-alls, although I can be a bit of one myself. They say in the therapy world you don't like in others what you don't like in yourself. But the guy in the line, with his safari jacket and smug attitude was winning my annoyance all by himself.

I wasn't buying the man's clairvoyant skills, but I know that in a town built around gambling, some people know how to work with the odds to get the results they want.

If you've been to any conferences before with me, you know it's a good bet something untoward is going to happen, and that I'm going to get involved.

CHAPTER ONE

Hocus Focus

Monday, August 6, 1984

I'VE BEEN DOWN this trail before, I said to myself as I packed my car and headed out to Vegas. I don't know if you've been there, but it's all those things you think it is and worse. And not always for the better.

Left to my own devices, I wouldn't have gone to the Mystery Writers of America's annual conference. First, I'd have had to become a member—perhaps not be a bad idea given that I'd written a few Lesson books. Second, it meant spending a week in Las Vegas, which was probably five days too much of something that was already too much. Third, I wasn't sure I wanted to pal around with a bunch of mystery writers. It was bad enough being at a conference with therapists, but at least I spoke their language. I was just learning how to talk mystery, let alone walk it.

But, as fate would have it, I was there in my capacity as a therapist. My client (whose name I've obviously changed) asked me to accompany him. You'd know him by his books. He gets very nervous when he has to speak to large groups, and was due to give a sixty-minute presentation as well as participate in a panel. He wanted me there to help him through. He also had some concerns involving his new girlfriend, who was along for the trip.

I'm a therapist with an office where I see people. I also see them out of that space—in their homes, at family meetings, work gatherings and on plane trips. I even accompanied one to a music festival. I charge by the hour so these extended therapy sessions are costly. I used to charge much less so more people could afford to hire me out, but I've garnered a bit of a reputation and, now as the child of capitalism, I've raised my rates.

Bennett is a very successful mystery writer. He's always got "New York Times Bestseller" stamped on the front of his books. He isn't my mystery writer of choice, but he is on a lot of people's shortlist. Being a shrink, I tend to like the mysteries where the protagonist does some self-reflection and struggles with their humanity. Bennett was more a bang/bank, shoot 'em up, move it along cliffhanger to cliffhanger type of writer. Which is why his books are on the bestseller lists and the ones I like need to be discovered at the bookstore.

The conference was running for seven days, starting Monday evening, August 6. Bennett and I had looked at the schedule and roughed out one for ourselves. I would meet him for an hour or so every morning, then again in the afternoon, as well as any other time he needed. His panel was Wednesday and the presentation on Friday. I'd make myself available to him for both of those full days, even though he wouldn't want me around the whole time.

I looked over the schedule to see if there were any workshops or panels I wanted to attend. There were some authors I wanted to hear speak and a couple of workshops that might help me out with the writing of my books. I penciled them in. From previous experience at conferences, and despite my initial good intentions, the events of the moment tend to limit my attendance. At the last conference I'd gone to, in Santa Barbara, I just managed to squeak in enough workshops to earn my continuing-ed credits.

Since my meter would have been running for a full week,

Bennett and I had settled on a flat fee. Plus, he'd pick up my hotel bill, expenses including food and transportation, but not gambling losses. It was a good deal. I don't particularly like Las Vegas but if I'm going to go it's better to come home a winner.

Of course, going in, that's what everybody thinks.

Made in the USA
Columbia, SC
25 February 2023